A TIME TO PRAY

It was cold in the cloister, with just enough of a breeze to lift her veil. Frevisse pulled at the heavy door to the church, and went into dimness, two nuns close behind her. At first the black shape stretched on the altar steps made only a vague impression, a thicker darkness among the gathering shadows.

Sister Thomasine went forward first. But it was Frevisse who suddenly realized what she was seeing and moved sharply forward as Thomasine knelt, one hand outstretched toward the shape.

"Thomasine!" she said sharply, stopping the young woman's hesitant hand. More quietly, she added, "Come away, Thomasine. Don't touch her."

Sister Thomasine's veiled head came around, her eyes, blurred shapes in her white face and white wimple, wide with bewilderment.

"But I think she's dead," she said.

"Very authentic . . . The essence of a truly historical story is that the people should feel and believe according to their times. Margaret Frazer has accomplished this extraordinarily well."

—ANNE PERRY

Dame Frevisse Medieval Mysteries by Margaret Frazer

THE NOVICE'S TALE
THE SERVANT'S TALE
THE OUTLAW'S TALE
THE BISHOP'S TALE
THE BOY'S TALE
THE MURDERER'S TALE
THE PRIORESS' TALE
THE MAIDEN'S TALE
THE REEVE'S TALE
THE SQUIRE'S TALE
THE CLERK'S TALE
THE BASTARD'S TALE
THE HUNTER'S TALE
THE WIDOW'S TALE
THE SEMPSTER'S TALE
THE TRAITOR'S TALE

Also by Margaret Frazer

A PLAY OF ISAAC
A PLAY OF DUX MORAUD
A PLAY OF KNAVES
A PLAY OF LORDS

THE SERVANT'S TALE

MARGARET FRAZER

BERKLEY PRIME CRIME, NEW YORK

THE BERKLEY PUBLISHING GROUP
Published by the Penguin Group
Penguin Group (USA) Inc.
375 Hudson Street, New York, New York 10014, USA
Penguin Group (Canada), 90 Eglinton Avenue East, Suite 700, Toronto, Ontario M4P 2Y3, Canada
(a division of Pearson Penguin Canada Inc.)
Penguin Books Ltd., 80 Strand, London WC2R 0RL, England
Penguin Group Ireland, 25 St. Stephen's Green, Dublin 2, Ireland (a division of Penguin Books Ltd.)
Penguin Group (Australia), 250 Camberwell Road, Camberwell, Victoria 3124, Australia
(a division of Pearson Australia Group Pty. Ltd.)
Penguin Books India Pvt. Ltd., 11 Community Centre, Panchsheel Park, New Delhi—110 017, India
Penguin Group (NZ), 67 Apollo Drive, Rosedale, North Shore 0632, New Zealand
(a division of Pearson New Zealand Ltd.)
Penguin Books (South Africa) (Pty.) Ltd., 24 Sturdee Avenue, Rosebank, Johannesburg 2196,
South Africa

Penguin Books Ltd., Registered Offices: 80 Strand, London WC2R 0RL, England

THE SERVANT'S TALE

A Berkley Prime Crime Book / published by arrangement with the author

PRINTING HISTORY
Jove edition / August 1993
Berkley Prime Crime mass-market edition / November 1993

For information, address: The Berkley Publishing Group,
a division of Penguin Group (USA) Inc.,
375 Hudson Street, New York, New York 10014.

ISBN: 978-0-425-14389-6

BERKLEY® PRIME CRIME
Berkley Prime Crime Books are published by The Berkley Publishing Group,
a division of Penguin Group (USA) Inc.,
375 Hudson Street, New York, New York 10014.
The name BERKLEY PRIME CRIME and the BERKLEY PRIME CRIME design are trademarks belonging to Penguin Group (USA) Inc.

PRINTED IN THE UNITED STATES OF AMERICA

20 19 18 17 16 15 14 13 12 11

For, be we never so vicious withinne,
We wol been holden wise and clene of synne.

"The Wife of Bath's Tale"

Geoffrey Chauncer

Chapter 1

THE HOUSE SAT on the muddy track beyond the village church, drawn back with its two neighbors from Prior Byfield's single broad street. Like the other village houses, it was framed in heavy, square-cut timbers, roofed with thatch, walled with wattle and daub thinly plastered. The doorsill of its single door sat nearly flush to the ground, with a single slab of stone in front of it against the wear of feet and coming dirt.

Meg's first task every morning since she had come as Barnaby's bride had been to scrub or broom the sill and stone; it hurt now to see them scabbed with mud and realize she was simply too tired to bother. Instead, she stood in the doorway, staring into the inner shadows, waiting for her eyes to grow used to it, glad for just this small respite from doing.

It was Christmastide and cold with a damp, spoiled blackness that sank into the bones. In a few days it would be New Year's, 1434, though some said the year did not begin until March, and some few others that it began with the winter solstice just past. At any rate, it was the tenth year of King Henry VI, not that it really mattered to her. One year and then another, and each worse than the one before, no matter what she did or how hard she tried, so what was the use of trying?

But despair was a sin, Father Henry had said at the harvest sermon. There had been reason enough to talk of despair then, considering how bitterly bad the harvest had been, and the prospect of a hungry winter before them.

Now she stood in her cottage doorway and despite Father Henry, yielded just a little to despair, notwithstanding the gleaming penny hidden in one fist.

She worked at the priory whenever she could, and these past two days while Domina Edith had been ill in bed, Meg had simply stayed, sleeping with the regular servants on a straw pallet on the kitchen floor. It had helped that Barnaby had been gone three days; she had felt safe in trusting Sym and Hewe to see to things at home. They were, after all, sixteen and thirteen and forever telling her how near they were to being men.

But not near enough, it seemed.

Her nose had told her that, even before she could see in the cottage's gloom.

Two days—the longest she had ever spent away at one time since she had been married. Coming past the church she had seen her home with new eyes; seen how its thatch had gone dark with age and rot, and sagged swaybacked on its ridgepole. And the plaster, meant to keep the walls from decaying in the weather, was crumbled away in ragged patches, leaving the daub bare to the rain. The cowshed—not that there were any cattle to keep in it anymore—slumped drunkenly against the far end of the cottage.

Losing the cattle had been the greatest disaster. Barnaby had sold the cow a year ago, and last autumn the ox. He'd been half-drunk each time and gotten the worst of both bargains. Without the ox, he was no longer a member of the village plow team, which meant he could not keep up the daywork he owed the lord in return for the field strips and cottage.

Meg had gone to Father Clement once, after the third of her babies died, grieving over it and Barnaby's drinking. He had told her to pray, for every trial that came to her was by God's will; and if she endured her earthly troubles patiently, she would sooner come through Purgatory's pains to eternal joy in Heaven.

But Father Clement was dead this year past, doubtless

enduring his own pains in Purgatory, while things had gone slowly, steadily worse; and just now, under the gray, heavy sky, faced with her unkept house and shiftless sons, Heaven seemed very far off and despair very near.

But that made it no less a sin and, signing herself in half-felt penitence, Meg went inside.

The cottage's single door led into the cottage's single room. To Meg's right were the animals—the milch goat and the dozen chickens—kept in the cottage for warmth and safety. To her left was the house's larger part, with the stone-circled hearth in the middle of the floor and what she had for furnishings—the bench and two stools, the table, chest, and bed, the few pots and bowls. There should have been some warmth to the hearth, a faint glow of well-banked coals; but it was as dark as all the rest. Meg went and stooped beside it, but not to build a fire. She lifted a rock from the circle, one not marked in any way different from its brothers, and probed in the soft earth beneath it, found a tiny clay pot stopped with a wad of rag, lifted it out, pulled out the rag, and put the penny in. It fell with a chink that showed it was not alone in there, though there were not many to greet it. She replaced the rag, and then the pot and then the rock, pressing the earth around it with her fingers.

Only then did Meg go to the window and slide down the shutter. Daylight made only more clear how much her sons had left undone. Grimly, for anger at the failure of one's children was allowed and good if it led to correcting them, Meg set to what needed doing.

The animals—Nankin and the chickens—first. They needed feeding, and their stinking waste removed. Nankin was dry at present, but spring would come again, and there would be yet another kid for the pot and milk for the summer. Nankin had been faithful at that for a good many years; but she was old and Meg doubted there were going to be many more summers for her. This spring, if the kid were female, it would be time for Nankin to go into the pot.

But what if they had waited too long? What if there were no kid? Meg worried about that as she went from nest to nest, looking for an egg and finding none. The hens laid less often in the winter, and even less when they were not properly fed or kept warm. There had been times when they gave an egg or two a week in the winter, but all this December there had been only three. But what better could be expected?

She should not go to the priory, or else should not stay overnight even when she had the chance. But she must have the money her work brought, little though it was. With one thing and another—Barnaby's quarrelsomeness and his drinking and his selling the ox, scanting what work he was given in its place, letting his holding and his strips in the fields decay—he was out of favor with Lord Lovel's steward. It was almost a surprise that he had been entrusted with the task of finding a cart and horse and getting himself to Oxford to pick up a wine tun and deliver it to Lord Lovel's manor for the Christmas feasting. It would hardly put a patch on how much he owed, but done well and timely it was a start.

Meg would be satisfied if he did the task as ordered and brought back the cart and horse unscathed. They had had to borrow them from Gilbey Dunn, and ungracious he had been about it, though he was their near neighbor and as bound to the lord's service as they were. He was the sort who would be quick to make claim for damages if the horse came home lame or the cart even slightly hurt. Worry over that and worry over whether Barnaby might have found a way to get drunk while he was gone were mixed with her wondering when he would be back.

Had he been gone too long? She knew less than he did about the world beyond the fields and pastures that were Prior Byfield's boundaries, and had no way to judge how long he should be gone or when he should return.

But fretting over Barnaby didn't set the house to rights. By some oversight there was enough water in one of the buckets by the door to give Nankin and the chickens a drink. And deep in the ashes on the hearth she found a tiny spark of live coal to be teased to life with careful blowing and a bit of dried grass, then nursed into a proper fire to set the cold back a little while she went to the village well for water, her two buckets hanging from her neck yoke.

When she came back, she set a pot to boil while she

scrubbed at the dried oatmeal on the table. The table was the one good piece of furniture she had. Its thick, smooth boards sat on sturdy trestle legs that had a finely-detailed pattern of vines and leaves carved into their flat sides. When Sym and then Hewe had been small, she had used to sit on the dirt floor with them, tracing their fingers along the patterns and telling them stories of what a fine house the table must have come from. She had never been in a fine house, but there had been the chair and chalice and embroidered cope in the village church, and the Lovels had once ridden down the village street with hawks on their hands and their clothing gay with gems and embroidery, and Meg's aunt's husband had once spent an evening telling her tales full of crowns and peacocks and bright woven tapestries when she was a little girl. From all of that she had made stories for Sym and Hewe. The other babies, the little girls and the other boy, had not lived long enough for her to tell them stories.

But the table, like the house and herself, had suffered with the years. Despite all she did and however much she nagged, its top was scarred with all the places Barnaby and Sym and Hewe chose to thrust in their knives instead of laying them by their bowls like decent folk. For all that she scoured it, even with sand, there was no way to unmar it. But she scrubbed at it anyway today. It was her stubbornness that had kept her going all her life, and especially these last years as Barnaby went more to drink and the boys began running wild. It was her stubbornness that took her up to St. Frideswide's priory, trying to earn enough money to buy back at least the ox. And maybe—but that was her secret hope; and as if in answer to her unfinished thought, the cottage darkened with someone standing in the doorway, and Meg looked up to see Hewe there, blinking as if surprised.

There had been a baby born after him but it had died and so he was her last chick, her baby, the one she was most careful of. It was a little disconcerting to see, when the light was angled just so along his cheek, the beginning of beard touching it with gold. He was fair-haired, slender, and fine boned, but no longer boyish. His manhood was coming soon;

at thirteen there was not much time left to save him from being no more than his father and brother were.

Meg said harshly, "So you've come at last. And where's your brother? Not working, surely."

Hewe shrugged, careless, and sprawled across the bench. "It's Christmastide, and God set aside twelve days not to work, so what's the to-do, Mam?"

"We're excused only from the labor owed Lord Lovel. Our own work needs doing, and you've been a slacker." She pointed sharply at the goat and chickens at the room's other end.

Hewe sniffed and shrugged again. "It smells good enough to me. You've been too much with the nuns, Mam; it's made you finicky."

"There's muck from two days under their feet and I want it out of here! And so do you, if you've any thought of eating anything before I leave again," she added, forestalling whatever reply he was about to make. "I muck out, or I cook," she continued. "I don't do both, and I won't cook in a house that smells of muck."

"Well, at least can't it be warmer in here? There's almost no fire, and I'm near clemmed."

"There's the last of the wood already on the fire, and you can fetch more if you'd be warmer."

"That's Sym's task, not mine!"

"And where's Sym to do it? Most of the things I do are someone else's task, or ought to be. Get on with you. The mucking first. I want to see it done before I go."

"You're going back again? What so needs doing there you'd leave us to be dark and hungry?"

"It's not what needs doing; it's the ha'penny they pay me for doing it. You know what I want that for."

"Aw, Mam! I've no call in my heart to the priesthood, I've told you that and told you that. Better you stay here and keep us happy. And take what you've saved and buy the steward off Da's neck. That'd be more to the point."

It was a familiar whine. It was what they all said, but Meg knew they were wrong. Years ago she had sent Hewe to Father Clement to learn his letters. At first proud to be singled out, he had tried hard, and learned with an ease that only confirmed her instincts. And it wasn't mere cleverness; though he did it but to plague the priest, he asked Father Clement questions about his Catechism that had left the poor old man groping in confusion. More than that, Hewe could figure such things as how many fourpence in three dozen pennies without resorting to his fingers, while all Meg knew of sums was the old joke that two stewards and an executor made three thieves.

Yes, Hewe would be a priest if she could earn the money to buy his freedom from villeinage. She said sharply, "My money is not for your Da. He makes his own bad luck, does Barnaby, and your brother takes after him. But there's no reason you have to live like a beast, too, if I can buy you clear. Now see to that mucking so I can be on with my own business here."

He made a rude sound under his breath but went to the other end of the cottage. Meg did not care what he said so long as he obeyed. She squatted by the fire to clean the bowls and spoons and then the pot with the water it had been heating. The bowls and spoons she set on the table. The pot she emptied out and filled with clean water and put to boil. She set beside the hearth the sack of oatmeal that would be supper. She would have stirred an egg into the stuff if there had been any, but there was not.

Still, with an edge of pride, she took a little napkin-wrapped bundle from her apron pocket and put it on the table.

Hewe, who could fail to see a piece of work that needed doing even if it was sitting under his nose, looked up from the last of the chicken muck and said, "What's that, then, Mam?"

"A something from the priory. They said I could have it for a Christmas treat, but I brought it home for you. Finish your chores, and wash yourself and I'll show it to you, but you must wait for the oatmeal before you taste it."

For once he washed without complaint. She had often spoken to him of the fine things they ate at the priory, but this was the first time she had actually brought something home.

The low overcast had thinned to westward by the time she

called him to the table. Weak, orange-tinged light slanted through the slatted window to lie in stripes across the cottage floor. It had little warmth but its light was welcome; and as Hewe bent forward to look at the napkin, the sunlight caught and burnished his pale hair to gold. Meg tucked her rough hands under her apron to keep from stroking it, knowing how much he hated any gesture of affection anymore, being too old to want his mother's and too young yet to seek another woman's. "So open it," she said. "It's all for you."

At her word, he pulled the napkin open eagerly, and she laughed aloud to see the wondering wariness on his face as he stared at what was in front of him.

"It's seed cake," she said triumphantly. "You won't find the like of that outside of a lord's hall or a monastery." She watched him sniff it while she held her own breath. He would like it, surely, sweet to the taste; and then she could point out it was the sort of thing he would have in plenty if he but pried himself out of the village and into the priesthood. But as she watched him, the wonder on his face suddenly meant nearly as much to her and she said with fond laughter, "Go on, then. Eat it. Your oatmeal will keep." If he ate it now, she would not have to make him share it with his brother, and that would save a quarrel.

Unexpectedly Hewe looked up at her. He had the cake in his hand, ready to taste, but he held it toward her instead and asked, "Share with you, Mam?"

A warmth that nearly brought her to tears spread up from Meg's breast, that he would think of her in the midst of his pleasure. Surely, surely, he was meant for something better. She shook her head. "I had a bite of one at the priory. They've many of them, and other fine things, things you wouldn't believe, in the kitchen there. That one's all for you. Go on."

He did not offer again. Though his first nibble was tentative, his second was not, and after that he was all too clearly in a fight between prolonging the pleasure and wolfing the sweet richness down all at once.

She went back to stirring the thickening porridge. "That's

the sort of thing the clever priest can get as often as he likes—"

"Leave be, Mam!"

And because she did not want to sour his pleasure, she said quickly, "Aye, I'll let it go." And to distract his frown, "I wonder where your father is."

"Somewhere close to here by now, probably. Or maybe singing his favorite song in the middle of the great hall, if Lord Lovel gave Da a cup of something when he arrived."

She gestured sharply at him to hush, but the other hand slowed its stirring. The thought of Barnaby's drinking set her to worrying all over again. Barnaby drunk was even less able than Barnaby sober to cope with the hazards of travel in such lawless days, and for the first time the thought welled up that Barnaby might have gone so far as to broach the tun of wine before he delivered it. To come into the mercy of an already angry lord was almost past imagining. Maybe he had gotten drunk less dishonestly, and must needs stop to sleep it off under the cart and be freezing to death this minute somewhere along the road.

Which would be worse? she wondered. To have a husband in danger of being hanged by his lord for theft, or to lose him to a natural death?

It was a hard thing to be deprived of a husband before his sons were grown enough to care for his widow, even if she did not much believe anymore that the next fine or beating he would receive might finally bring him to give up drink.

She quickly prayed he was alive, and that by some wonder he had stayed sober.

"Hewe, the oatmeal's nearly done. Run quick and fetch some firewood before you eat."

He rose with a sigh, but stopped at hearing his mother's name being called outside.

"Meg! Meg, are you home? There's bad news! It's Barnaby!"

Meg swung the pot safely off the fire even as her heart lurched in her breast; burnt food was both a disaster and a shame. But Barnaby—what had he done? She hurried to the door, her thin face twisted with apprehension.

Hewe had reached it before her, but he stepped back for her to lift the latch and open the door in time to startle plump Annie Lauder, her hand already raised to knock, her round face red with exertion and excitement.

"Oh, you poor woman! He's been found on the road, sore hurt! They've only just brought him in and I've come to fetch you fast as might be."

Meg looked toward the village road but saw no knot of villagers coming with Barnaby among them. "Where?" she asked, wringing her hands in her apron. "Where is he?"

"The priory," Annie said, still gasping. "'Twas travelers found him and didn't know him, and so took him to St. Frideswide's. And that's maybe best; Dame Claire's trying to save him."

Meg's mind swam in an abundance of information: the priory, Dame Claire, Barnaby, the travelers. Her legs went weak, and she leaned against the door frame, trying to grasp it all. But she managed to whisper, "Is he going to die?"

Hewe forestalled Annie's reply. "Was it robbers? Did they steal the wine? Or the horse? Is the cart all right?"

"The cart went over on him, they said," Annie replied. "That's all I know." She saw Meg's knees buckle, and took a strong grip on Meg's other arm. "You better sit down. I'll fetch your cloak."

"The cart!" Meg moaned, sinking to the stone step. "And the wine! If the wine's spilled, his lord will hang him sure!"

"Only if he lives," Annie said, throwing the cloak around her shoulders. "Now come on."

Chapter 2

THE TWELVE DAYS between Christmas and Epiphany were the dark time of the year. Holidays and the cold kept folk at their own hearths, and casual travelers were few. St. Frideswide's, even with its two guesthalls, was too removed from main roads and lacking in the wealth and luxuries that might have drawn nobility to its hospitality in the holy days.

So Dame Frevisse, the priory's hosteler, responsible for its guesthalls and guests, was expecting no one as the afternoon drew on toward nightfall and Vespers. But, as duty required, everything was kept in readiness and she was walking through the guesthalls to be sure of it.

A small boy tumbled through the doorway of the lesser guesthall, nearly into her skirts. He recovered himself and bowed deeply before bursting out, "There's a man hurt! We found him on the road and they're bringing him here!"

He was a handsome little boy, perhaps all of eight years old, in need of a thorough scrubbing and more excited with his news than dismayed. Frevisse did not know him; he certainly did not belong to the priory, and his speech, his bow, and the cut of his worn clothing showed he was no villager. But she had no time to think on it.

"Where is the man? What happened to him?" she asked. And added in the same breath to a servant near at hand, "Go out and tell them to bring him in here."

"We found him under a cart," the boy explained. "It was overturned, in a ditch. Bassett says it looks like the horse dragged it, with him under it. He's all bloody, and they're being careful of him as they can. They're just behind me."

He pointed, and Frevisse nodded the servant on his way, then gestured to one of the women. "Bring out one of the pallets. Set it here where the light is good. And blankets. And someone go for Dame Claire." Dame Claire was the priory's infirmarian and saw to the hurts and sicknesses of nuns, guests, and villagers.

Well trained, the servants were laying out the straw mattress and blankets as voices warning, "Watch it, then" and "Be careful of the leg" and "Mind the door," announced the hurt man's arrival. Unlike the better guesthall across the courtyard, there were no steps here to climb.

Frevisse reached the outer door in time to hold it open for two men, a tall boy, and a woman, all in the heavy, drab cloaks of winter travelers. They eased past her, each holding the corner of a long, thick yellow cloth with the unconscious body of the hurt man slung in it, being careful of him despite his obvious weight.

Briskly she said, "Over here beside the fire. Who is he?"

"That we don't know, my lady. He's a stranger to us and hasn't roused since we found him," a stout older man gasped, the effort clearly telling on him.

"We'll take care of him from here," Frevisse said. "God's blessing on you for your kindness in bringing him. Here, put him down here."

An ironic look passed between the younger man and the tall boy, but she had no time to wonder about it as Dame Claire hurried in. A small woman, the infirmarian was dwarfed by her box of medicines and a bundle of bandages, but she moved briskly, their weight familiar to her. Behind her, more slowly, came young Sister Amicia, carefully balancing a steaming basin of water. Dame Claire stepped around the gathered knot of people and took charge.

The infirmarian eyed the injured man sympathetically and said in her surprisingly deep voice, "Build up the fire here. Make it large. We want to take the cold out of his wounds, and keep it out.'' She bent closely over him, peering at his slack-jawed face, then lifted aside the cloak that had been tossed over him. There was a sharp intake of breath among the onlookers at the sight of his torn and bloodied clothes and body.

''I'll need more water. And more cloths. Now,'' Dame Claire said crisply.

Two of the servants hurried away. The others stayed, some staring outright, others taking flinching looks at the man's hurts. Even Frevisse, who had a stronger stomach than most, cringed inwardly as she assessed his damage. Clearly he had been dragged under his cart. His right hand was the worst, mangled almost past looking like a hand. There was an awkward crookedness in his left shoulder; and his breathing was ragged, his face beneath its dried-blood mask deathly pale.

One of the servants crossed herself. ''It's old Barnaby from the village. Looks like he's done for himself this time.''

''He's one of ours?'' Frevisse asked. She didn't recognize him, but she had little to do with the village villeins, even those who did belong to the priory.

''He's one of Lord Lovel's.'' Annie Lauder, the broad-boned priory's laundress, was usually to hand if something interesting were happening in St. Frideswide's. ''I know him.''

''Does he have any family?''

''Wife and two sons, and this will finish the ruin of them and his holding, that's sure.'' Annie's voice held the assurance of someone who had often said it would happen.

''What he's surely made is a ruin of himself.'' Dame Claire was cutting away the strips of bloody cloth with a slim knife. Now, seeing more of his hurts, she said, ''Mercy, his ribs! Someone had best fetch his wife.''

''I'll go,'' Annie Lauder said. ''I know their cottage.'' With a bustle of importance and elbows, she pushed her way out from among the cluster of people and was gone.

''Who's building up my fire?'' Dame Claire demanded, not looking up.

Frevisse, knowing the man was now entirely Dame

Claire's responsibility and that her own duty was simply to serve her, said, "Jak's here with more wood." Frevisse gestured the man forward. "Sister Amicia, if you're going to be sick, go outside to do it. And so long as you're going, fetch more bandages." Frevisse had no sympathy with Sister Amicia's stomach; since the young nun had been eagerly taking in every word and detail, Frevisse judged that her queasiness was more choice than necessity.

The travelers who had brought the man stood clustered near the other hearth at the hall's far end, where a priory servant was building a fire for them. As Frevisse approached, the stout older man stepped forward from the others and bowed much as the boy had done.

Frevisse bent her head to him slightly. "We'll have a fire and food for you very shortly. The day is drawing on, too late for traveling much farther, and I hope you'll accept St. Frideswide's hospitality, both on your own behalf and as thanks for your goodness—"

She paused, aware of a wordless exchange among the group. Their leader was well past being young, his hair grayed and his face seamed with age and laughter and many years of wayfaring, as used to the open air as to walls and roof. He carried his large frame with upright dignity, and now to the question she had not yet fully asked, he pulled off his hood and bowed again, a low, dramatic one.

"Your offer is welcomed, my lady, and most happily accepted. A generous fire and good shelter in good company is a blessing from the Lord these cruel midwinter nights."

His rich voice flowed like satin, and Frevisse felt a spasm of dismay. "You," she said, almost accusingly, "are not simply travelers."

"No, good lady. We're players, on our way from one place to another. Thomas Bassett is my name and this is my company. And though you've offered to us your hospitality, we'll go on our way if you say the word."

He knew, far better than she did, how unwelcome his kind could be. Wayfaring players were travelers of no fixed place or lord, belonging nowhere, always strangers and met always with suspicion, too often well founded, since folk dependent on the tossed coins of other people frequently turned to thievery to augment their income.

Frevisse's hesitation was barely momentary before she said, "You have done a man a service that may save his life. I have offered St. Frideswide's hospitality to you and, as you say, midwinter nights are cruel. It would be ungrateful and unchristian of me to take back my offer. I pray you, be at ease and take what comfort we can give this night."

She felt tension flow out of the little band at her words. They had been braced to be sent on their way, and were greatly thankful for being allowed to stay. She doubted they would give trouble for whatever little while they were there.

"You have a cart and horse that need seeing to?" she asked.

"Tisbe our horse follows to heel like a dog and should be waiting in your courtyard now, and our cart behind her. There's only the four of us. And Piers, of course."

At mention of his name, as if on cue—and Frevisse suspected it was—the small boy she'd seen before stepped away from the woman who had been lightly holding his shoulders, and bowed very neatly. She bent her head to him in solemn return. His sweet-faced charm had probably wooed goodly pence from doting women on more than a few occasions, Frevisse thought, and hid her own amusement behind an unsmiling face.

The flaxen-haired player whom Frevisse had taken for a tall boy said, "I'll see to Tisbe and the cart and bring in what we need for tonight." Now, as soon as he spoke and she looked directly at him, she realized he was fully twenty years old or more, not a boy at all despite his slender, lean-hipped build and smooth face. Since his hair was so pale, his beard did not show unless it was looked for.

"Young Joliffe," said Thomas Bassett by way of introduction, "who plays our women's roles."

Meeting the young man's bold, assessing gaze, Frevisse was ready to believe that playing the woman was a skill in him, not a trait, and suspected that he probably wooed more than pence from women when he set his mind to it. With some asperity, she said, "But you will play the gentleman here, I trust."

Joliffe made her an elegant bow. "In such an holy place as this, humbled by your kindness, surely."

Frevisse forebore saying that she had sincere doubts about his humility, and was spared any reply at all by a raw, strangled screech behind her, as if a cat had been tossed into the fire. She swung around. The clot of people still around Dame Claire and the man Barnaby had pulled back somewhat, making room for the newly arrived woman. She was small, no more than thin flesh sunk down onto small bones, tanned and aged with years of weather and work. Frevisse had noticed her around the priory these few months past, but from her poverty had thought her a widow. Now she stood huddled and aghast, her hands pressed over her mouth and her eyes huge with fear and horror as she stared down at the hurt man. Her husband.

Dame Claire had had him moved onto the straw-filled mattress, and been cutting away what was left of his clothing to assess his injuries. Except for a cloth draped modestly over his loins, there was nothing to hide his body's ruin.

Unable to take her eyes from him, rocking back and forth, the woman began to keen, "Oh, God. Oh, God, oh, God, oh, God. He'll never work again, he'll never work again. Look at him. Look at him."

A whey-faced boy, trying very hard not to look at the man, stood beside her. Awkwardly he put an arm around her and said, "Mam. Mam, it's going to be all right. He'll heal fine, you'll see." But he did not believe it any more than she did.

On Meg's other side Annie Lauder made no pretense of her curiosity. "Will he live at all? He looks like to die, if you're asking me."

"There's no one asked you," said Dame Claire firmly. "So near as I can tell, there's nothing broken inwardly beyond my reach, nothing here that will surely kill him, if I can keep sickness out of his hurts."

"His hand," Meg moaned. "Holy Mary, Mother of God, look at his hand. It'll never heal. Look at it."

Dame Claire ignored her. "What I want is someone here to

help me set his shoulder back in place. It's only twisted from its socket, not broken."

"That I can do." The third man among the players stepped forward. "I've seen it done a few times, and helped at it myself. But we'll need some strength beyond our own to hold him down."

He was a handsome man, not tall but boldly proportioned, with thick black hair and a self-assured swagger. Dame Claire eyed him dispassionately, judging his usefulness, and said, "Here, then. Best do it while he's still unconscious. Someone take the woman away. And the boy. This will not be pleasant to see."

Chapter 3

THE PLAYER HAD not boasted. Frevisse had seen joints reset before and knew it took as much strength as skill to put a shoulder back into its socket. The sinews that allowed a man to swing a scythe all morning or wrestle a plow along a furrow were equally able to resist the effort to slide bones back into their place. Insensible though he was, Barnaby groaned while two of the priory men held him down and the player pulled and twisted with seeming brutality at his arm, until at last there was the unmistakable snap of arm bone into shoulder joint.

The men stood back, grinning at one another in shared triumph, and Barnaby subsided into low moaning.

"My thanks to you," Dame Claire said. "Your name, that I may properly thank God who sent you to us when we were in need of you?"

The black-haired man bowed to her. "Ellis, my lady," he said.

He returned to the others, still smiling.

Dame Claire said to the gathered gawkers, "You can go back to your duties or your rest, except you and you and . . ." Her gaze fell on Sister Amicia the same moment that Frevisse's did.

Sister Amicia had come to St. Frideswide's because, after dowering her four older sisters, her father's purse had run thin, and he had chosen to save the remainder and increase his reward in the hereafter by offering his last daughter to St. Frideswide's as a nun. A good daughter, she had done as bidden and taken the veil six years ago. But more than vows and veil were needed to make a nun of her. She was mostly obedient and devout at her prayers; but despite the Rule, she was given to ribbons and other pretty things her sisters brought when they came visiting, and just now she was regarding Ellis's retreating back with far too much awareness that he was a tall, well-built, not unhandsome man.

". . . Sister Amicia. I think you can go back to the cloister now, Sister, and see what we left undone in the infirmary," Dame Claire finished, matching Frevisse's own thought.

Frevisse, as ready as Dame Claire to see to work, said, "Annie, take that yellow cloth and set it to soak so you can scrub it clean come morning. We can do that much more for the folk who saved him. The rest of you, about your business. See there's enough wood for both these fires, and bedding brought for our other guests. And someone tell his wife she can come back now. I'd best ask Dame Alys what food can be spared from the kitchen for our guests. Sister Amicia, come."

Sister Amicia, all lowered eyes and humility, murmured, "Yes, Dame," and followed Frevisse out the door.

The players' horse and cart were waiting in the courtyard. The horse, a mare, was a raw-boned creature with a malformed forehoof, but no thinner than to be expected of a hard-worked animal that only rarely saw grain. Young Joliffe had already unloaded a few things from the cart and was now standing at the mare's head, gentling her nose in his cupped hand and murmuring in her ear. Frevisse told Sister Amicia to go on and turned aside to speak to him.

He let loose of the horse as she came up to him, and made a bow that was as humble as Bassett's had been theatrical. But when he straightened, his gaze was critical, and Frevisse felt again the uneasy awareness that he was far older than he looked.

"My thanks along with Master Bassett's for letting us stay,

my lady,'' he said. His gratitude seemed genuine, neither forced nor false. But his speech was bold for someone so dependent on the whims of the stranger.

Frevisse kept her opinion to herself for now, and said, ''It would have been poor courtesy to put you back on the road after the kindness you did. Stabling for your horse is back out through the gate to the outer yard and to your left. Someone there will show you where to put your cart.''

Joliffe began to lead Tisbe forward and around, saying casually, ''Kindness is a rare commodity, true enough. It would have been a shame to pass up so plain a chance to give it where it was so sorely needed. And here, you see, we're receiving it back again.''

''You've been on the road long?''

Ensuring that the back of the cart would miss the wall as he turned, Joliffe answered, ''Do you mean me, or all of us together?''

''I mean, how long has it been since your group had a roof for the night?''

''We've managed a roof all but the last two nights. We spent—hup, Tisbe, come around now—we spent Christmas Day at Fen Harcourt manor, and we're meaning to be in Oxford for New Year's and stay through Twelfth Night. Master Bassett knows an innkeeper there.''

''So you're not in need of anything but a night's rest from us?''

Joliffe brought Tisbe to a stop and turned his full attention to Frevisse. ''Why such concern?'' he demanded. ''We're none of your people, that you should be particularly caring. You've done your duty in giving us shelter and promise of fire and food.''

Meeting his look, Frevisse answered as boldly as he asked, ''I know how hard the road can be in winter, and you've a child and a woman with you.''

He had the grace to look almost abashed, but before he could respond, the cloister bell began to ring, calling to Vespers. Frevisse inclined her head, turning away as she said, ''Pray pardon me. I'll come again before Compline to see how all is going.''

The Vespers service went its strong, graceful way, declaring the day's richness and hoping the blessings it had brought were unending. *"Et exsultavit spiritus meus in Deo, salutari meo."* My spirit has found joy in God, who is my Savior, because He has looked graciously upon the lowliness of His handmaid.

But its flow and beauty were severely marred in St. Frideswide's by a general croak-throated snuffling among the nuns.

The illness had begun before Christmas among the servants, had spread to the nuns, and had not yet run its course, though Dame Claire—busy with poultices and herb brews—assured them it would. The worst of Frevisse's own sore throat was gone, but she still made steady use of her handkerchief and lacked her usual energy. Like most of the others, she had to be careful of her singing, that it did not turn to sudden croaking; and like them, she often failed.

And today, unfortunately, Dame Claire was still with the injured man so that her deep, rich voice, almost fully recovered from her own rheum, was not there to carry the others. Without it, the strongest singer was Sister Thomasine, whose thin, bright soprano rose now over everyone else's broken efforts.

Despite her apparent frailty, Sister Thomasine had flourished in the year and a little more since she had joyfully taken her final vows. Her holiness was as accepted a matter in the priory as the seven daily services, and Frevisse had heard it being whispered among the nuns that it was her holiness and the answering grace of God that kept her alone from succumbing to the present pest of sneezing and wheezing.

About that, Frevisse worked very hard to have no opinion, for if she had allowed herself one, it might have been that Sister Thomasine was kept free of disease to test Frevisse's patience.

After Vespers most of the nuns had their period of rest and reflection before supper. But today Frevisse, feeling her duties to the priory's guests were unfinished, returned to the guesthall. There she found the players had gathered around the farther hearth and were settled in with their belongings around them. The woman among them was stirring a pot set close to the flames, her thin features flattered almost into beauty by the shifting orange light. The boy Piers was curled up near her, asleep on someone's cloak, even more sweet-faced asleep than when he was awake. The three men were sitting across from them in close talk that dissolved frequently into laughter. Ellis tossed the small pieces of the stick he had been breaking between his hands into the fire with a casual, relaxed gesture.

There was no ease in the gathering beside the other hearth. Only Dame Claire, the hurt man, Meg and her son, and an older boy were left. Another son, Frevisse thought. That was good; even if her husband died, poor Meg would still have her sons, and the older boy looked old enough to inherit. Lord Lovel's steward was a fair-minded man; if they could keep up their duties and rents they would keep the holding even if Barnaby died.

She went to stand where she knew Dame Claire would be aware of her, not intruding, willing to wait until there was pause for the infirmarian to tell her if there was anything she could do. The man's hurts had been cleaned and the worst of them bandaged, including the gash along his head. Closely covered in blankets, with his shoulder in place, he did not look so hopeless a matter as he had at first. He was still unconscious, or asleep, his head rolled to one side and his mouth slacked open, though he was breathing with such heavy effort through his nose that it was probably broken, too.

Dame Claire, with great care, was picking up his injured hand. Barnaby moved his head toward her, but his eyes did not open until, tentatively, she moved his forefinger. Then he made a wordless cry and opened his eyes wide. They were glazed and bloodshot and seemed to see nothing. She let go of his finger and he subsided to silence, his eyes closing again.

"Please don't do that!" whispered Meg hoarsely. "It's no good. His hand's no good and never will be anymore."

The first horror was gone from her now, if not the shock. She was sunk down on the floor on her husband's other side, one hand clenched into a fist and pressed between her meager breasts, her other hand holding tightly to her younger son's arm as he sat leaning against her. Her strained, haunted eyes stared at the ruin of her husband's hand as Dame Claire gently put it down, and she did not seem to notice her older son, hunched down on his heels behind her, reaching out to rest a hand on her shoulder.

As often is with brothers, the two boys were not much alike. The younger had his mother's small bones, the fair skin and blond hair she might have had when she was young, though she was years past showing either of them now. The older boy was more like his father, tall and big in bone, with coarse dark hair, his boy's face already beginning to flesh out in what would be heavy-jowled manhood. A manhood that was going to come on him sooner than it should have even if his father lived.

"Now, Mam," he said, "let her be. Maybe she can mend it."

"Nothing can mend him, Sym. Hush you," Meg said without emotion, not looking around at him.

Dame Claire touched the first two fingers of the swollen hand laid on Barnaby's stomach. "By some wonder," she said, "these bones right here seem to be the only ones broken, but they're broken right back to his wrist, and they're not bones I can set, being so small and many jointed. All I can do is wrap his hand close to its proper shape, and pray it mends so he can use it."

"He's going to live?" asked the younger boy.

"I don't know. If he's taken hurt inside, if there's something broken where I can't tell it, or he's bleeding where it doesn't show . . ." She drew a deep breath and said more firmly, looking at Meg, "We just won't know for a while and a while yet. If he lasts the night and recovers his wits, then there's hope. Do you mean to stay here or would you rather go home? Dame Frevisse or I will watch by him all night if you would rather go home and rest."

"We'll watch by him," Meg said without hesitation. "He's ours and we'll keep the watch. Better there's faces he knows when he awakes. Or when he goes,'' she added in a lowered voice, her gaze returning to his face.

''I'll see to their bedding,'' said Frevisse. ''Tell me what I should watch for, then go to your supper and Compline. I'll manage here.''

''You haven't eaten, either,'' Dame Claire said. ''I'll bring your supper along with what he's going to need to cover the pain when he wakens.''

Meg stood up. ''I can fetch the lady's supper, by your leave,'' she said. ''I work in the kitchen and know my way.''

''*That's* where I know you from,'' Dame Claire said. ''You brought the posset I wanted for Domina Edith when her cold was so bad two days ago.''

''And I fixed it myself,'' Meg said a little eagerly.

''It was excellent and served her well. Yes, bring Dame Frevisse's supper. I'll see to the medicine.''

Chapter 4

MEG MADE A low curtsey, glanced at the boys in silent warning to stay where they were and not make noise or mischief, then hurried away. She left the guesthall for the cold darkness of the courtyard, crossed it quickly, and let herself into the cloister by the nuns' gate. It was not the way she usually came in but the corridor beyond it was familiar, and she turned toward the main kitchen and the need to brave Dame Alys's temper.

But Dame Alys was gone to dine with the other nuns in the refectory. There were only the lay workers in the kitchen, and in return for the chance to pour out their questions about what had happened and how her husband was, they filled a bowl with bread pudding and cheese, and pressed it and a mug and pitcher of hot spiced cider into her arms while they talked.

The kitchen was warm and bright with fire and lamplight. They were among the things Meg treasured from her hours at the priory: fires in the kitchens and the warming room; and another in the prioress's parlor and even in her bedroom, so she could be warm when she undressed for bed at night, a luxury Meg had never dreamed of before she saw it here in its reality. And lamps and candles lighted when the days were merely overcast so the gloom was pushed away into the corners instead of brooding down on everything. That and how clean all was kept, with stone floors that were scrubbed when the weather was warm, and swept every day no matter what; and nothing left to spoil the wholesomeness of the air, not rushes, nor food more than a few days old, nor animals. Why, the nuns would have been scandalized at the thought of sleeping in the same room with chickens and goats!

It was like dragging herself away from some corner of Heaven to go out again, leaving the warmth and friendly gossip behind her, to the chill night of the courtyard and then the lesser comfort of the old guesthall. Dame Claire was gone but the other nun—Dame Frevisse, she was, a brusque person to be in charge of the priory's main charity, the minding of its guests—had built up the fire. By its light she could see Hewe and Sym sitting beside their father, their two faces dissimilar even in expression, Sym brooding and Hewe looking lost in prayer. She smiled at them when they looked up at her coming but she went directly to Dame Frevisse and held out what she had brought.

"This is more than I need, surely," Dame Frevisse said.

Meg flung desperately through her mind to find an apology, but the nun only continued, as if it hardly mattered, "So let me take a little of this and a little of the cider. The rest of it divide among you. You'll need something if you mean to watch all night. I'll set the pitcher by the fire to keep it warm."

Meg hardly knew what to say, but Dame Frevisse did not wait for a reply, only went to speak with the band of players.

Meg took the food and drink to the fire. The bread pudding was full of raisins and sugar, treats she had not managed for years. Even the bread was mostly wheat, not bran, and the whitest she had ever eaten. The boys crowded eagerly, and she was glad to share, but she kept a close eye on them, and stopped them far short of it all being finished. "We'll save some for later in the night. If your father wakes, the cider will help warm him," she said, and for once even Sym did not protest.

As she straightened from setting the pitcher back beside the fire, a cold draft swept the hall from the opening and shutting outer door, and Father Henry, the priory's priest, hurried out of the shadows toward them. He was cloaked and ruddy faced as if he had been awhile in the cold, and the tumble of curls around his tonsure was in more disarray than ever. Meg and the boys made courtesies to him, though Meg had to nudge them as a reminder. Father Henry gave them all a nod but his worried gaze had already turned to Barnaby. "I was gone to Hamlin's croft to baptize the baby before she died. I've only just come back and heard. Am I needed, Dame Frevisse?"

Dame Frevisse came toward them. "According to Dame Claire, he's badly hurt but seems holding steady. He's not regained his wits, but if he does, and his wounds don't fester, he may live. He surely needs your prayers, but as for last rites, I think his wife should say."

She and Father Henry both looked at Meg, distressing her with this unexpected responsibility, though the priest's voice was kind as he asked, "What do you think? Should he have the sacrament now while we're sure of him?"

Meg pressed her lips together and stared at the floor, trying to think. It always disconcerted her when someone important noticed her; Father Henry's attention was as bad as being asked questions by the steward. She would not have been so disconcerted had it been old Father Clement, the village priest, and a common person like herself. But he had died last year and no one had yet been put in his place—for shame! But that was not Father Henry's fault. Now he was waiting for her answer and words did not come quickly to her.

Dame Claire seemed to think Barnaby had a chance of living, but it might be better to be safe and let him have last rites. But there were always pence to be paid when the sacraments were needed. If Barnaby died unshriven, the cost might be his soul, as his sins were many and mortal. On the other hand, pennies were very few and likely to be fewer with Barnaby dead or even just unable to work.

And if he died, there would be other costs, their best beast being claimed by the lord as heriot; and then the gersum, a fine Sym must pay to enter into his father's holding, and the cost of a wake for Barnaby, and then the Mass penny for his funeral and the price of his shroud, and the opening of his grave. All that to come out of the little she had managed to save. Or none of it if Barnaby lived. But Father Henry had offered to pray for him anyway, and surely God would not ignore the prayers of a priory priest. So as he was maybe going to live—

"Better he be awake for it," she said. "Better he knows about it."

"My prayers for him then," Father Henry said. "Send someone for me anytime in the night you want me. My house is between the inner courtyard wall and the church."

He moved to leave, but Meg said with a sudden thought and rare daring, "Father, could you take Hewe, my younger here—" She pushed him a little forward, her hand on his resisting back. "And show him somewhere good he could pray for his Da?"

"Mam—" Hewe began.

Meg cut off his protest. "Father Clement taught him his letters and said he might, with work, become a priest. That's my fondest hope, to see my Hewe a priest someday. If you could talk to him, teach him some of your prayers?"

She did not know where her daring came from, to ask so bold a favor. But if Hewe got a look inside a priory priest's house, he'd see how different it could be from a villager's daily grubbing. For his sake she could be bold. For his sake—and Sym's—she had nerved herself to ask for work at the priory, so they would have a little more between them and the disaster Barnaby was making of their lives.

She kept her hand hard against Hewe's back, warning him not to speak against her request.

And, thanks be, not seeming offended at all, Father Henry said, "Assuredly. And he's named Hewe? After our own St. Hugh of Lincoln, surely." Meg nodded eagerly, not sure at all; Hewe had been her father's name. But Father Henry went on happily, "In his travels St. Hugh was forever seeking out boys with the hope of priesthood in them, and helping them. So should a priest say no to a boy named Hewe? The church is cold this time of year but there's a prie-dieu in my chamber, and a fire. We can pray there for your father."

Hewe cast a look of resentment at Meg, as he had spent the past year since Father Clement died happily forgetting all the old priest had taught him. But then he looked at his unconscious father, kept his mouth shut and went, albeit scuff footed and head down, with Father Henry.

Meg nodded after Hewe, not caring how he felt about it, knowing what was best for him. The need to do things, to manage somehow, was bringing her out of shock. Making the decision about the last rites had set her mind moving again, and now she said to Sym, "There's still the horse and cart we don't know about. You'd best ask those folk who brought him in where this happened and how bad the cart is. The horse must have broken loose or those folk would have brought it in when they brought Barnaby. It's probably gone back to Gilbey Dunn but we'll rest easier if we know it has. Take you back to the village and ask. If the horse at least, pray God, is in good case, that's one thing less we have to worry on. If it isn't, we'll never have the end of it from Gilbey."

Sym grimaced, acknowledging the threat of that. Relations with Gilbey had once been so good there had been talk of his daughter, his only child, marrying Sym. But the girl and her mother had died of a fever the spring before last and that had been the end of that.

Sym rose and stood staring at the players. He was not as given to talk as Hewe was, but far more given to work than his father. It hurt Meg to see him coarsening under the load he was carrying, trying to do a man's work already. The worst of it was, he was finding his escape the way his father had, at the alehouse. She watched him stride away toward the folk at the hall's other end, then called belatedly after him, "Mind to thank them for what they did."

Dame Frevisse went to put another log on the fire, and stayed there. Meg, left to her own thoughts, looked down at Barnaby again, watching him breathe, listening to the broken sound of it, and worrying. Gilbey Dunn had only agreed to Barnaby using his cart and horse because the steward had made him, and let him off a day of spring field work in exchange. That was always the way of it: somebody else gaining because of Barnaby's losses.

Gazing at his slack face, unable to find anything of the brawny, pleasant youth her parents had arranged for her to marry, Meg shook her head to herself. ''Barnaby not-so-bright,'' she whispered. ''Have you done for yourself at last, this time?''

No matter what Dame Claire said, his hand was crippled past healing. And what if he were so crippled inside that even if he lived, he'd need her care of him all the rest of his life? Then she would have to give up her desperately needed place at the priory. And there would be the broken cart to repair, and money for the horse if it were injured or stolen. And how would she find the silver to make Hewe a priest? If only St. Hugh were still alive, with his blessed practice of taking promising boys and seeing to their education! She had not even the price of a candle to offer the saint for his help. Nothing but her prayers, which she was already saying. For Hewe, for Barnaby, for the horse to be all right, for the cart to be only a little broken.

By the low waver of firelight she went on looking at her husband's face, praying, waiting for whatever change might come, and hardly noticed when Dame Frevisse gently laid a blanket around her shoulders.

Chapter 5

THE WINTER'S BLACK cold had set in about St. Catherine's Day, snowless and bleak under overcast skies until by then, at December's end, all the world's chill gray seemed settled into the nuns' very bones as thoroughly as the rheum was into their chests and their general mood into petty quarrelsomeness.

Frevisse, huddled down into the several woolen and linen layers of her habit, was finding them poor comfort against that cold as she waited at the warming-room door for her sister nuns scurrying hunch shouldered and shivering along the cloister to join her for the morning chapter meeting. Their faces as they came were as red nosed and bleak as she knew her own to be. Morning Mass was finished and it was time for the daily chapter meeting, when the nuns gathered to discuss their priory's business and grievances.

St. Frideswide's was small enough, and poor enough, not to have a separate chapter house for these meetings. Instead, chapter was held in the same rectangular room in the cloister that served as warming room in winter and summer gathering place for the nuns' late-afternoon hour of recreation when the weather was too rainy for walking in the garden. It had one of the priory's few fireplaces, and this bitter winter Domina Edith had given permission for its daily use.

Frevisse opened the door to its warmth as the nuns reached

her. They bustled through, hasty and out of step. Well behind them, coming at her own age-slowed pace, was Domina Edith, in company with Father Henry and Sister Juliana, this month's chaplain, each holding her by a brittle elbow.

The prioress was old and had been ill. Frevisse knew there could be no hurrying her and went on waiting patiently until, looking up, Domina Edith gave her an acknowledging and dismissive nod. Frevisse gratefully stepped back into the room, closing the door to keep in what warmth there was from the high-burning fire on the hearth.

The other nuns were already gathered there, warming their hands and—by a stealthy lifting of black skirts—their shins, instead of taking their places on the eleven stools set in a double curve in front of the prioress's chair facing the hearth.

Frevisse slipped in among them gladly until the sound of a hand on the door latch brought them all quickly around to go stand before their stools where they were supposed to be. She had noticed that the hand that never otherwise fumbled often fumbled with that latch on chill winter mornings, just long enough to give them all a chance to take their places.

Father Henry came in, Domina Edith still leaning on his arm, Sister Juliana behind them. He brought her to her chair and seated her.

There was something more than the usual deep respect in the nuns' curtsies as he did so. This was Domina Edith's first attendance at chapter in almost two weeks, a longer absence than ever before in all her more than thirty years in office. The rheum that was only a severe nuisance to the others had settled into her lungs and nearly killed her. Dame Claire had fought against it with all her skill in herbs and pungent plasters, aromatic steams, and strengthening brews, and had won. So now Domina Edith was come back to sit in her accustomed place, more pale and thin than she had been at winter's beginning, wrapped in a warm furred robe, but her eyes reflecting her keen pleasure in returning to them.

Frevisse's pleasure was equally keen. During her illness, Domina Edith's place had been taken by Dame Alys, as was her right and duty as cellarer. But Dame Alys even at her best was ill-tempered, and was presently much worse, aggravated out of her limited patience by her own coughing, blowing, and spitting.

So in the few moments while the nuns seated themselves in a rustle of veils and skirts at Domina Edith's gesture, Frevisse watched her prioress with relieved affection, then followed her gaze as it went past them to Sister Thomasine sitting in her chosen place as youngest and most determinedly humble of the nuns, at the far end of the stone bench built out from the lower courses of the wall, most distant from the fire.

The shrinking humility that had been Sister Thomasine's promise of worthiness when she was a novice had eased after she was safely and forever the spouse of Christ; but now and again Domina Edith saw need to remind her that humility and comfort were not mutually exclusive. She crooked a finger at the girl now. Obediently Sister Thomasine rose and came to curtsy low in front of her. Leaning forward to spare her voice, Domina Edith said, "You've not yet caught this winter sickness, have you?"

"No, Domina," Sister Thomasine whispered.

"And it was your voice almost alone that carried us through the services this morning, was it not?"

Sister Thomasine dared not lie, even in humility. "Yes, Domina."

"Then you will sit in the place designated for you, there on your stool, near the warmth, that you may continue in health to raise your voice in praise to God so long as He allows."

Sister Thomasine curtsied again, even more deeply, whispered, "Yes, Domina," and went to her stool, head bowed.

Irk twitched at Frevisse; so much insistent modesty wore at her nerves.

"Now," murmured Domina Edith. *"In nomine Patris, et Filii, et Spiritus Sancti. Amen."*

Crossing themselves along with her, her nuns all bowed their heads for the prayer to the Holy Spirit for guidance and blessing in this meeting. Then Father Henry read the chapter of St. Benedict's Rule designated for the day, first in his stumbling Latin and then again in English. The Rule was short, only seventy-three chapters, and most chapters only a paragraph or two in length, so that with reading one chapter a day, it was heard in its entirety three times a year. Chapter 72, to be read on April 30, August 30, and this day, December 30, dwelt on the "good zeal" that nuns should have. "'Thus they should anticipate one another in honor,'" read Father Henry, "'most patiently endure one another's infirmities, whether of body or of character; vie in paying obedience one to another—no one following what he considers useful for himself, but rather what benefits another. . . .'"

At the end he did not offer his usual commentary. He was almost over his rheum but his deepening complexion as he read showed that the need to cough was still with him, and at the last he settled for blessing them quickly with hand and soundless lips before going out. When he was gone, Domina Edith looked at her nuns, noted that Sister Emma's hand was up in request to speak, and nodded to her.

Sister Emma stood up and Frevisse settled herself resignedly. Sister Emma was sure of her voice's charm; she always went the longer way around to what she meant to say, and even today, rough with her cold, she was plainly going to be no different than usual.

"We're all—" Sister Emma cast a glance at Sister Thomasine sitting serenely without a handkerchief. "—almost all—of us most grievously suffering together with our aches and rheums. But rather than lessening our duty to be concerned and careful for one another, our mutual trial but increases the need for consideration. Time and again these past days I've passed in the cloister walk where someone has failed to tread out their sputum on the pavement. The treading out of sputum is a thing St. Benedict himself mentioned in our Rule, and so it seems surely a matter that needs speaking to now, that we may live in decency and good respect with one another. After all, 'The wicked shall be cut off from the earth, and the transgressors rooted out of it.'"

Only one proverb and fewer than three times the number of words necessary to make her point, Frevisse thought; Sister Emma's cold must be troubling her sorely indeed to make her so brief.

With all solemnity Domina Edith agreed on the necessity

of good manners among themselves no matter how grievous their bodily discomforts were, and pronounced that good manners should prevail. Sputum should be promptly trod out by the spitter as provided for in the Rule. "And aught else?" she asked.

And inevitably there was. This was the time when accusations and confessions of faults were to be made and discipline and penance given. There came the usual mentions of small rudenesses needing pardon, and confessions of minor lapses troubling consciences, interspersed with coughing and sneezing. Quietly, giving no space for little matters to spread into great ones by too much talking, Domina Edith judged and settled while Frevisse, her back near the fire, sank into a warm lethargy. All too soon she would have to bestir herself back to duties in the cold world, so for just now she was enjoying being able to be still and warm while the chapter meeting ran its way.

The meeting shifted to reports on matters at the priory in general.

Dame Alys stood up, snorted, hacked, and said, "The pig we've fattened for the villeins' penny ale this Christmastide was slaughtered yesterday and dressed out at near to fifty pounds, more than we'd thought it'd be. Though whether there'll be cider enough is another matter. Dame Frevisse has seen fit to be giving it to people in the guesthall without asking my leave or need in the matter and if that goes on, I don't know where we'll be."

Frevisse, roused from her comfort, cast quickly through her mind and realized Dame Alys was talking about yesterday when Meg had brought her some cider from the kitchen. She could make some sort of defense of that, but on the whole it was better that Dame Alys's displeasure should fall on her rather than on Meg's overburdened head.

Domina Edith asked, "Have you answer for that, Dame Frevisse?"

Frevisse rose. "No, my lady."

Domina Edith sighed and said, "We must observe the rules set down for all our good, especially for the kitchen since food is scarce this winter and costly, not even to be given to guests without Dame Alys being asked first and her permission given. In penance you shall go without your portion of cider at supper these next three days and apologize to Dame Alys for failing in courtesy to her.''

Somewhat stiffly, Frevisse said, ''I beg your pardon for my failure, Dame Alys.''

Dame Alys, blowing her nose, nodded ungraceful acceptance and said to the room at large, ''If there's to be spiced cider for the villeins' wassailing in the orchard on Twelfth Night, we must mend our ways. Even so there may not be enough to see us through to Lent.'' She raised meaningful eyebrows at Frevisse.

Dame Perpetua, as always, expressed her regret that such frivolity as wassailing continued to be encouraged by the priory among the villeins. No matter how old the custom, it seemed to have little to do with holy days from any Christian view she had read. Domina Edith, as always, agreed with her without providing for reform, and asked for the rest of her obedientiaries to report.

One after another, they said *omnia bene,* all was well, except Dame Claire who was concerned that her supply of horehound for sore throats might not be sufficient for the winter.

At the last it was Frevisse's turn since her office of hosteler was least among the obedientiaries. Very briefly she reported that there were no people in the new guesthall and nine people in the old: Lord Lovel's villein, Barnaby Shene, who was seriously hurt, his wife and two sons tending to him, and five travelers, including a sick child.

''He awoke in the night with a sore throat and has a cough and fever this morning. They will be staying until he is well enough to travel, by your leave, Domina.''

Domina Edith nodded her approval and looked at her nuns. ''Is there aught else that must be said now?'' she asked. After quick glances among themselves, they all shook their heads. She smiled. ''Then let me only remind you that no matter how ill or well we are feeling—or sounding—we must remember before all else that what matters more than our feelings are our prayers and singing in the daily services, especially at this holy time of year. It is our souls' grace and God's worship we are supposed to be accomplishing. It is our inward being, not our outward seeming, that matters most to God. Remember that, rather than dwell on our imperfections."

She was more pale than when she had come in, her aged skin pulled thin over her face's bones, her body sunk deeply into her cloak. Frevisse knew that Dame Claire was poised to go to her the moment she dismissed them to their day's work.

But a discreet knock at the door turned all their heads toward it, and Domina Edith said, "Enter." Her voice had no strength behind it and she gestured to Dame Alys to call again.

At Dame Alys's booming croak, the lay woman who was supposed to keep watch at the outer door into the cloister put her head in to say, "It's Roger Naylor, my lady, craving word with you as soon as might be."

A stir of curiosity passed among the nuns. Naylor was the priory's steward, in charge of their properties and the other worldly matters necessary to sustain St. Frideswide's spiritual life. Occasionally, as his duties necessitated, he came into the cloister to confer with Domina Edith. Now, at her nod, he entered the room.

He was a dour-faced man whom Frevisse had come to know a little since her hosteling had begun to take her out of the cloister more. She was not sure she liked him but knew that his long, lined, rarely smiling face fronted a mind not only keen to St. Frideswide's best advantage but mostly fair in pursuing it.

He came now the length of the room to kneel on one knee before Domina Edith, who left him there as she said in her soft voice, "There must be more than usually grievous trouble, Master Naylor, that you presume to come here. What is it?"

"Not so much trouble yet, my lady, as trouble to come if it's not dealt with now. Do you know who bides in your guesthall this while?"

Domina Edith frowned, both at his words and the general stir among her nuns. "Yes, we know who bides in our guesthall. A man hurt maybe to his death though he yet lives, and his family tending to him, and five travelers who are staying on because of a sick child among them."

"It's not plain travelers they are, though they're surely minded to keep you thinking they are. But I heard two of the men talking in the stable. They're players. For all they'd have us think they're honest folk, that's all they are and nothing better."

Domina Edith said, "You may rise, Master Naylor," and looked with mild questioning at Frevisse. "Did you know this, Dame?"

"That they were players? I knew. They never sought to hide it from me, Domina."

"But you never said so!" Sister Fiacre's shocked voice broke in, as unexpected as it was seldom heard. She had always been given to nerves and flutterings, mostly expressed in hand wringings or, if very sorely distressed, in tears. These months past an illness had been draining her to the point where much was forgiven her. Now she so far forgot herself to exclaim, "If you knew what they were, you should have said, Dame Frevisse!"

Frevisse retorted crisply, "I've not made it custom to tell more than how many guests we have and why they're here. Chapter meetings aren't for gossip."

"But traveling players!" Dame Alys croaked. "They're not decent. Not fit to be inside our honest walls, for certain."

She glared at Roger Naylor for confirmation. Frevisse was amused to see him torn between agreeing with Dame Alys and disliking her support. As cellarer, Dame Alys had the right to interfere in his office, and often did.

Gazing somewhere over Domina Edith's left shoulder, he only said, "I'd like to know whether their boy is truly ailing, or shamming so they can linger long enough to choose what to steal."

"Dame Frevisse?" Domina Edith's neutral tone gave Frevisse both permission to answer that and a warning to keep watch on her ready tongue.

"The boy is truly ill, with a cough, inflamed throat, and

fever. If he stays warm and quiet, he should better quickly, but the raw weather would be dangerous for him now.''

''And you're sure he's not shamming?'' Naylor insisted.

Dame Claire stood up. At Domina Edith's nod she said with the assurance of authority, ''I saw him this morning. There is no doubt of his illness.''

''And beyond that,'' Frevisse said, unable to restrain herself, ''you do wrong to suspect folk who've done a service to a hurt man and no harm that we know of.''

''They're lordless men,'' Naylor replied. ''Answerable to no one and belonging nowhere. Their sort are never to be trusted.''

''Some players have a patron who answers for them,'' Domina Edith said with a questioning look at Frevisse.

Frevisse shook her head. ''They've mentioned no one to me.''

''And surely they would have if they belonged to someone,'' Dame Alys put in.

Sister Fiacre rose to her feet with unusual fierceness. ''And even that's no surety. My lord father was patron to some, but when my brother inherited the lordship he turned them off because he found they were misusing our name to base ends. All such are of a kind and none of them honest!''

So long a speech left her breathless. As much in need as in embarrassment, she pressed her sleeve over her mouth and, coughing, sat down.

''That's no more fair a thing to say than that all stewards are thieves because some are,'' Frevisse retorted, meaning it a jibe as much at Naylor as she did at Sister Fiacre. ''All we know of these folk is that they did an honest service to a hurt man and have asked for the shelter the Rule binds us to give them and are kept here by a sick child. It's unjust to assume they are other than they've shown themselves to be.''

''By the time they show what they are, it will be too late,'' Naylor responded. ''Give them a medicine for the child and maybe an extra blanket and send them on their way.''

They had both forgotten Domina Edith and were speaking directly at each other. Frevisse said, more sharply than she intended, "Better we be wronged by them than that we wrong them without cause."

"They're gadelings."

"Lordless, yes, but not without a living. They were employed at Fen Harcourt over Christmas, and have work in Oxford when they reach there."

Domina Edith raised her hand. "Enough."

Naylor closed his mouth over what he was about to say. Frevisse, startled to realize how heated she had become, bowed her head, tucked her hands into her sleeves and subsided. Dame Alys trumpeted into her handkerchief, letting her red-faced glare take the place of words, while Sister Fiacre wrung her hands silently.

"It is not our place to judge these people," Domina Edith said. "There is no harm in keeping some small watch on them, which you may set if you so wish, Master Naylor, so long as it is done without offense to them. But we have offered them shelter and are bound by the Rule to give it so long as it is fit and they do us no wrong. Indeed, they may do us a good. This is a season when the Holy Church bids us make merry. Do you think it possible, Dame Frevisse, that they would perform for us? A play suitable to the place and season tomorrow or the next day maybe, if they stay so long?"

"Oh, yes, please!" Sister Amicia exclaimed with a glad clap of her hands. Then she covered her mouth in shock at her breach of manners.

"Three paternosters on your knees before the altar, Sister Amicia, before this evening's Compline," Domina Edith said without even looking at her. Sister Amicia's flares of frivolous enthusiasm were familiar to all of them. "Dame Frevisse?"

"Yes," Frevisse said. "I think they would willingly do that. I'll ask them and then tell you what they say."

"Do so. And that, I think, ends this morning's business." Domina Edith raised an unsteady hand in a gesture that included all of them. "Go with God's blessing on you and your duties through the day."

Chapter 6

In the cloister walk, Frevisse was overtaken by Naylor. He was not a tall man, hardly her own height, but he carried himself to the fullness of it, meeting her eyes as she turned in surprise to look at him. "Dame, you were eloquent on behalf of these players. Why are you so willing that they stay?"

Frevisse arched her eyebrows in deliberate surprise. He knew as well as she did that the Rule forbade casual talk in the cloister. But as he had never been a casual man, if he was wanting to talk to her, he had a purpose, and she twitched her head toward the cloister door into the courtyard to show that she would speak with him outside. As they walked on, he persisted. "Men who roam the roads lordless and landless—players, beggars, jongleurs, any of that sort—are knaves at best, and more likely plain rogues. Why be so willing to risk this lot here for longer than it takes to turn them out of doors, Dame?"

Frevisse walked faster, reaching her hand for the cloister door, but Naylor moved more quickly and was ahead of her in time to open it. Frevisse bowed her head partly in thanks, but more to hide her face from him for the moment it took to go past him. She had been half-ready for his question or something like it, but not for the surge of remembrance that came with it.

But by the time he had shut the door and turned to her, she

had both her expression and answer ready. "I wasn't bred to the nunnery, Master Naylor. My parents were of the world. And very worldly. I've learned better than to believe something simply because it's said. Nor am I so ignorant that I think a man can be condemned out of hand for being one thing instead of another. Not even for being lordless and landless. If I condemn a man because he's a player, knowing no more of him than the tales told of players, then judging by the tales I've heard of stewards, I can as readily condemn a man for being one of those."

Roger Naylor's eyes narrowed. Stewards were stock figures of corruption and mercilessness in too many stories for him to miss her point. He looked as if he would say something, but stopped himself and instead turned on his heel and strode silently away. Frevisse looked after his eloquently rigid back, her satisfaction at routing him stronger than any regret she should have had for her forward speaking. And she felt warmer than she had for hours.

"That was a shrewd hit for so gentle a nun," someone said mockingly.

Startled, Frevisse turned to see Joliffe sitting on the step at the foot of the well on the courtyard's near side. Wrapped in a cloak gray as the shadows, his hair pale as the well's stone wall, he was easily unseen so long as he did not move or speak.

"And that's an odd place for someone to be resting," Frevisse responded. At this hour of a winter's morning, the well was still in shadow under its hawthorn tree; the rime of frost around its rim and step betrayed how cold a place it was to sit.

Joliffe rose to his feet and came toward her. "Or it's not. Depending on one thing and another. Did I hear the word 'player' in your talk? I take it your steward has been complaining of our existence."

"Of your existence here, assuredly. He'd probably not mind in the least if you existed somewhere else."

"So we're to go?" He asked it lightly enough, as if it did not matter to him if they had to pack and leave within the hour. But Frevisse had long since learned the use of reading a person's stance and face as much as their voice. And she saw that though Joliffe had learned to live with being forever sent on his way, he had not learned to like it. "No. You're to stay as long as need be for Piers's sake, and be welcome."

The almost imperceptible stiffness went out of him, and he asked, disconcertingly, "And I may take it that you championed us? That you persuaded your prioress to this over Master Naylor's protests and were eloquent on our behalf?"

With what she meant to be asperity, Frevisse said, "Eloquent enough, it seems."

Joliffe's smile etched laughter lines into his face with all the roguery that Naylor suspected his kind of having. "Then St. Genesius's blessing on you, lady, for your kindness and your golden tongue."

Despite herself, Frevisse warmed to his amusement. Matching his tone, she said, "I suspect St. Genesius has quite enough to do in tending to you without considering me. I'll be satisfied with St. Frideswide's blessings, thank you. But it will be Dame Claire you'll be needing if you go on sitting out in the cold this way. Haven't you better sense than that?"

Joliffe gave her a small, respectful bow. "Alas, that's a matter oft debated. But surely you must know quite well how tedious it is to live too closed in with people for hours into days into weeks on end? No matter one's mutual interests, the tedium does grow." Frevisse lifted her chin at his presumption. But Joliffe grinned at her, friendly and knowing together, and despite herself her mouth tweaked toward an answering smile. As often, truth lay in a jest; she understood exactly what he meant, especially being so newly come from chapter meeting. But Joliffe did not press the advantage of her tacit admission. Instead he said, no more seriously, "I should warn you, though, that Ellis is in a black mood. Piers being ill has waked the father in him and made him perilous to live with. Or at least direly unpleasant."

Suppressing an urge toward another smile, Frevisse said, "I doubt Piers's peril is very great. Kept warm and quiet, he should mend. I didn't realize he was Ellis's son." She glanced toward the courtyard gateway where a man dressed like a noble's servant was riding in.

Joliffe followed her look but went on with his banter. "He maybe is and maybe isn't. Ellis is happy to think so. But he's maybe Bassett's. Or maybe mine. Rose won't say, bless her for a clever wench." He sighed and placed a dramatic hand more or less over his heart. "We'd have a happier time of it if Ellis were only like me, all dismal, my heart in tatters at a small boy's peril, but my temper ever soft and flowing as a silken ribbon."

"But now and again Ellis takes his possibility of fatherhood too seriously?"

"It comes from too much sobriety. If it goes on too long, he begins to have temper and fancies."

"He's given to drink?" She hoped not. If he were, the players' stay might be less easy than she had hoped.

"Not of ale or wine. It's emotions he craves. A few days without performing and his unused feelings build up in him, turning him tense and very . . . tedious."

Frevisse turned that thought over in her mind. Unused emotions, held in too long, were a common enough trouble in a nunnery. She might even admit that her own tolerance for tedium was thinner than it ought to be; and a volatile man could indeed be burdensome to those around him. "Then mayhap I've a solution for you. Our lady prioress is wondering if you would perform for us." She caught a glint of impure mischief in Joliffe's eyes and added, "Something suitable to the season and the place, you understand."

Joliffe's expression changed to show surprise that she could imagine he would ever think anything else. "My lady, your prioress honors us by her request. Surely we have something proper to this time and place."

She glanced over to see that a servant was taking care of the new visitor. Frevisse judged that he was probably someone's messenger seeking brief respite from the cold. Any of the guesthall servants could see to him; he did not need to concern her.

Joliffe had begun to walk toward the guesthall. Frevisse fell into step beside him, her own long stride matching his as she said, with due consideration, "If there's chance that Piers is yours, you set to the business very young." She gave Joliffe a slantwise look to match his own at her and added, with an eyebrow raised in caustic questioning, "Or are you perhaps trying to shock me?"

Joliffe laughed out loud delightedly, delightfully, and paused to flourish her a bow. "You are a very Solomon!" More soberly he added, "It's Rose's way of keeping us together. She shares his fatherhood among us, and because none of us wants to lose his claim on him, our band stays together. And has stayed together so long now that we've grown into something better than the usual ragtag miscellany of road folk banded together for a season or a year or two."

The servant who had been talking to the newcomer crossed the yard to intercept them. He bowed and said, "If it please you, my lady, there is a man with a letter for you."

Frevisse looked over to see that the messenger was waiting while another servant led his horse away toward the stable. Now that she looked closer, something about him was familiar. For a moment she hesitated, then went toward him, and he responded by eagerly coming to meet her. He bowed low to her and as he straightened, she exclaimed, "Hobden! It is you, then?"

"Aye, lady. It's me." He grinned all across his broad face. "And I was thinking it was you. Even all dressed like that, you're still you and no mistaking. When were you last on a horse, is my question?"

"A good long while, I promise you. But I've not forgotten. I could still give you a race if we came to it."

"There's no doubting that. You had a way in the saddle that lasts longer than lessons."

"Is May well? And your girls?"

"May is well, thank you for asking. And the girls have made me a grandfather thrice over now."

"Have I been gone that long?" Hobden's daughters had only begun to look at boys when she had left her uncle's keeping to enter St. Frideswide's. "Yes," she added before he could answer. "I suppose I have."

"Long and long, lady," Hobden agreed.

He was, indeed, now that she looked at him, far older in his face than he had been when he was one of her uncle's main stable hands. And so must she be, too, she thought, though lack of mirrors in St. Frideswide's spared her too detailed knowledge of the fact.

"But that's the way of things." He was cheerful enough

about it. "If you don't grow older, it's because you're dead, and I'm not ready for that yet."

"And my uncle. How does he?" she asked eagerly, and then belatedly, "And my lady aunt?" Aunt Matilda was her mother's sister, and Thomas Chaucer her uncle only by marriage, but it was with him she had been closest while growing up in their household. Their friendship, begun when she came at age eleven, had lasted the years despite how rarely they saw each other anymore.

"Well, lady. Both of them very well. And here"—Hobden drew a packet from his belt pouch—"is a letter from him for you."

Frevisse took it with delight, recognizing both her uncle's clear script and his seal. "Hobden, much thanks. Will you be here a while, that I'll have time to write an answer?"

"Surely. Master Chaucer gave me leave for that if you wished. And I'd rather sit by a good fire than travel the road this bitter day."

"Then let me see you to the guesthall and assure the servants you're to have their special care."

She took him to the greater guesthall and gave him into the keeping of one of the kitchen servants there with orders that he was to be made comfortable and well fed. She looked at the letter, but thought she would like a leisurely time over it, and instead of opening it, tucked it up her sleeve.

As she went down the steps and turned toward the lesser guesthall, she realized her pleasure in seeing old Hobden had been much like her pleasure in bantering with Joliffe; and that was odd, because she had known Hobden for years of her life, and Joliffe hardly a few hours, and yet felt the same fellowship with him.

Actually, it was not just with Joliffe, it was with all of the players. She liked them, she trusted them, they brightened her day with their presence. Why?

Because of the way they were with one another. That was what made her like and trust them beyond the ordinary. They were bound to one another not only by the needs of their work, but by a strong tie of caring deliberately made and kept by Rose around her son. Frevisse knew full well how strong a tie that could be, and what a shield against the troubles of the road, no matter how unblessed its basis was.

Raised voices startled her as she entered the other guesthall. Her first thought was that the man Barnaby had roused and was complaining loudly. But as she thought it, she saw that Meg, sitting beside her husband's body, was looking not at him but, dry-eyed and tense, down the hall toward her sons in close and obviously angry talk with Bassett, Ellis, and Joliffe. Or rather, Sym was talking, shoving himself into Bassett's face while Hewe, like a fair shadow, was poised behind him, clearly ready for whatever was going to happen. Frevisse started toward them, but before she reached them, Ellis said something that brought Sym around to face him, his voice rising for Frevisse to hear. "And I say my father was never so drunk in his life he couldn't keep a cart on the road!"

With insultingly deep indifference, Ellis said, "Then yesterday he was drunker than he's ever been before. When he drove past us, he'd beaten that nag into a mockery of a gallop and was standing up in the cart waving his goad and singing—" He turned to Bassett. "What was he singing, Thomas?"

Bassett for answer began in a mellow baritone, "I have a noble cock, whose crowing starts my day, he makes me rise up early—my prayers for to say!"

Joliffe, grinning, joined in harmony, "I have a noble cock, his eye is set in amber; and every night he perches—in my lady's chamber!"

Ellis was opening his mouth to join them when Bassett caught sight of Frevisse and cut him and Joliffe both off with a sharp, embarrassed gesture. "And that's the truth of it, lad," he said more courteously. "It was no surprise to us, only a grief, when we found him smashed up a while after that."

"So you're saying. But there was no one else than you to see it, was there? I say it's more likely you forced him off the road and into that crash, for a chance to dip into his pockets!"

"Boy, a glance would've told a simpleton there was nothing about the man, or his cart, worth taking," said Joliffe. Before Sym could respond, Frevisse moved between the two sides and said, keeping her tone level, "They've already told us this. What's brought you to questioning it now?"

Jerked out of his anger's stride, Sym fumbled for the humility expected toward his betters, his eyes shifting hotly between her and the players. He finally burst out resentfully, "I asked the use of their mare. I've need of her to fetch in what's left of Gilbey Dunn's cart but they think her too good for the likes of me to use."

"And so you're trying to make other trouble," Frevisse said coldly. "Saying things for which there's neither proof nor likelihood. Better you put your passion into praying for your father than accusing the men who helped him."

"Helped him into the ditch, most likely!" Sym burst out.

"Helped him to here rather than leaving him to die in the ditch where he'd put himself," Frevisse snapped back. Sym was far beyond his bounds in speaking back at her and she cut off whatever else he meant to say. "Enough! They are the priory's guests and this is no place for quarreling."

Sym glared at her, his hands twitching halfway toward fists while he fought for control, until finally he dropped his eyes away and shoved his hands behind his back.

To smooth the matter, Bassett said, "Tisbe is as tired as the rest of us. And our own need of her is too great to be chancing her to a stranger's hands, no matter what reason. There must be horses in your village you can borrow."

Sullen and unconvinced, Sym avoided looking at Frevisse but swung his look from one to the other of the players, wanting to hit someone and knowing he could not. "Pah!" he exclaimed. "Maybe I don't want to use your nag after all, you and it being no more than plain dirt off the road!" Unable to unleash his temper into action, he jerked away from them, nearly blundered into Hewe as he swung away, and took his revenge by swinging at him. But Hewe was clearly used to that and ducked the blow easily, backing toward their mother who still sat beside Barnaby, her anguish plain on her face. Sym, seeing Meg, ducked his head again, away from her, and lumbered into a heavy, swift walk, to go slamming out the door. Hewe stood where he was, unsure what to do until his mother, not meeting anyone else's gaze, gestured for him to come to her and, when he had, pulled him down beside her to go on with the vigil over his father.

Bassett, holding Ellis from following Sym by a hard hold on his arm, said, "Dame Frevisse, I pray you, witness we've done nothing to warrant his anger at us."

Frevisse nodded. "I doubt his tempers last long. He's not likely to bother you with it again, but I'll warn the servants to be mindful of him. Meanwhile I bring you a request from our lady prioress."

Bassett immediately swept his deepest bow. "My lady, it will be our chiefest joy to serve you and your mistress."

"She asks if you will perform for us—"

"Something sweet, meek, and gentle as the lady nuns themselves," said Joliffe in a sweet, meek, gentle voice.

Frevisse glanced at him sharply. After her set-to with Sym, she was in small mood for trifling from anyone. "Something suited to the season and our worship," she amended, giving her voice the same edge she had used on Sym. "Perhaps a miracle or mystery play?"

"Surely, my lady," said Bassett. "We have several such ready to hand. You can look through our book to see which might best please you. Or let the lady prioress do so. It's here to hand. Piers, fetch me that chest there, the little one—" He pointed toward their stacked belongings beyond the circle of the hearth and Piers began obediently to crawl out from his covers near the fire.

"Piers, stay," Ellis ordered, stopping the child with a gesture even more quickly than Rose putting out a protesting hand to him. "You stay warm and covered like you've been told. I'll fetch it."

As he went, Rose's look thanked him and his own look dared Bassett to argue, but Bassett was uninterested, so long as the shabby collection of bound sheets came to him. Instead he began to ask Frevisse where in the nunnery the play could best be held and how many folk would be coming to it. The two of them settled into a satisfying talk of details and possibilities that ended in deciding the church would do best, and that probably they would perform *The Magi* the day after tomorrow, or the day after that if Piers took that long to better, so that he could give his voice to the angelic choir.

Chapter 7

Frevisse found a quiet corner in the cloister that the sun had warmed a little, and the wind couldn't reach. She pulled the thick paper from her sleeve and unfolded it. Her uncle's distinctive italic warmed her further just seeing it. For a moment she was transported home—with the Chaucers she had found the only permanent dwelling place of her life before she came to St. Frideswide's—the house new-built when she came to it, bright outside with unmellowed Cotswold stone, bright inside with many large windows. She smiled, remembering how proud her uncle had been to greet visitors in his magnificent hall.

She opened the letter and began to read. Thomas Chaucer had not inherited his father's gift for soaring imagery, but he was lucid and fluent, with more than a hint of his father's sense of the ridiculous.

To my dear and right well beloved niece Dame Frevisse at St. Frideswide's Priory: I greet you as heartily as I am able and so does your aunt Matilda, who begs me greet you in her name.

This winter proving severe, and my age beginning to weigh on me, I am staying at home this Christmastide. We, for a wonder, have no guests, and so are more than amply provisioned, all matters considered. Therefore I write to ask if you have any secret desire for some treat more than St. Frideswide's can provide. Sugared almonds, perhaps, or three oranges to eat and share with Dame Claire and Domina Edith?

The King has been much busied with Parliament and his council at Westminster, and is gone to Bury St. Edmunds for the holy days. There has been much to-doing now that Bedford is come from France to settle matters between Gloucester and Beaufort yet again, and I am happily out of it for the present. I would quote Ecclesiastes at you, but you already know my choice of verse.

I have required my messenger to wait upon your reply, so stand not upon lengthy ceremony, but make your request and put it into his hand. He will receive it gladly, and perhaps repeat gossip of things hereabouts, which I command you to take with a grain of salt. May the blessings of this holy season fill your heart with joy.

Frevisse smiled over the letter, reread it twice, then tucked it back into her sleeve. She would share it with Domina Edith later, as it was against the Rule to have a letter whose contents were unknown to the prioress. She did indeed have a special request, and would write it down in brief and send it posting down the road to her uncle.

Meg had hardly slept last night and not at all today. Now, in late afternoon, aching with her exhaustion, she went on sitting hunched beside Barnaby's unconscious body, watching his slack face and listening to the unchanging pattern of his noisy breathing while her weary mind went endlessly over all her fears and possibilities.

Even if Barnaby lived, he could not work. And if he could not work then he had no right to hold the house and land that were their living. It might be that the steward would advise Lord Lovel to allow Sym to take up his father's rights and duties. That way they could keep the little they had left. He had the right of inheritance, and that was not easily set by, so there was some hope.

But Sym was only sixteen. Or maybe seventeen; the years

blurred into one another anymore. He was well grown and strong but not a man yet. And he had already quarreled twice, with his father's help, with the steward. And even if he did take up Barnaby's place, there would still be Barnaby, and the little she had saved so far would go to pay for his accident if nothing else. Only it had not been an accident, and that would cost them more. He had been drunk and singing; the players had seen him and even known the very song, one of the only two he knew. Everyone in the village had heard him lurching home drunk and bawling the words often enough to believe their story.

At least Sym had found Gilbey's old horse as it wandered grazing on the village green in the dark last night. "Too stupid to go home," he had said. "Or too smart, if Gilbey Dunn is as stingy with its fodder as everything else. The old boy's not hurt, any rod, except some scrapes on his knees and hocks that don't go deep enough to matter. Gilbey's got nothing to open his mouth about."

But Gilbey would open his mouth, and loudly, because though Meg hated to say it about anyone, let alone a neighbor, he was a mean and calculating man. Besides, the horse was maybe not so sound as Sym was saying; he had his father's way of wishing a thing to be so and then believing it was. And she suspected that what was left of the harness would take a deal of mending, if it could be mended at all, let alone that there was no salvaging the cart.

It had been the players saying that that had set him into a temper at them. He had asked to borrow their horse, it being easier for him to ask from strangers than from folk who knew him well. But the dark-haired one had refused him, saying, "That thing won't run on wheels again. Better you take another cart to bring the kindling home," and Sym had lost his temper. It was always easy to set Sym in a temper, and easier when there was work to do that he did not want to bother with.

Hewe was not so hard to deal with. He had a temper, right enough, but it went to sulks more than to fury. He was lying beside her now, curled into the blankets on one of the guesthall's thin straw mattresses, his head on her thigh. With the fondness she rarely had chance to show, Meg stroked gently at his golden fair hair, then let her hand rest again on his shoulder while she went on watching Barnaby. She was still worried for Hewe. He was not thick flesh and muscle like Barnaby and Sym, he needed tending more than they did. She had made him rest and be warm again instead of going for the cart with Sym; and was nursing a small hope that maybe last night had changed him. He had come back quiet, as if thoughtful, from his time with Father Henry.

Father Henry lived cleanly, easily. He had a servant to take care of him in his own little house, which probably had a fireplace, they being so common at the priory. Hewe had to have seen the difference; he had to have finally understood what she had been telling him all these years. That he did not have to be as mired into the village as his father and brother were. That he could live better if he would only try.

It was different for Sym. In the right way of things he would have the croft and its fields and duties and rights after his father died. God in his wisdom had made Sym strong like his father, suited for his work. And Sym, unlike Barnaby, would maybe take strong hold once it was his, and put it right. If he had the chance.

Meg's hands clenched. Barnaby had brought them to this. He had always claimed that he made his own luck. Had claimed it loudly, swaggering, through those days when her parents had been after her to marry him. She had often, when it was far too late, wondered why she had. Except she had grown tired of her mother's nagging and her father's hard hand across her head, and been excited by Barnaby's demands.

But now she was mostly past almost anything except a final longing to save something out of all of it. To save Hewe from being no more than his father and brother were.

But what if that wanting was somehow against God's will? No, how could it be, since she was trying to give him to God, not keep him for herself, no matter how dear he was to her? Surely if she could bring him to the priesthood . . .

Hewe moved sharply, sat up to look more closely at his father, and then whispered, "He's waking up."

Meg turned back from the far wandering of her thoughts to peer at Barnaby's face, and saw that Hewe was right. There was the beginning of awareness there, a flickering of eyelids and muscles that had been lax all these hours past.

Meg clamped her hand around Hewe's wrist, not noticing how her strength made him wince, and whispered, "Go find someone to go for Dame Claire. Find someone now."

Hewe scrambled out of the blankets and went. Meg leaned nearer to Barnaby. His breathing had changed, strengthened and become uneven. With a soft moaning murmur he opened his eyes. Unfocused, he blinked vacantly, then seemed to realize that the ceiling was unfamiliar. He frowned, and shifted his eyes without moving his head, until he found Meg bending toward him. His mouth moved slightly, soundlessly. His lips were cracked with dryness; Meg reached for the clean cloth in a bowl of water that Dame Claire had left, telling her how to use it. Carefully, she squeezed the cloth past dripping, then held it to Barnaby's lips and squeezed again, gentling the water into his mouth.

He licked his lips and wanted more. She gave it and finally he managed to say hoarsely, "I'm hurt."

Meg nodded.

"Bad?" he asked.

Meg hesitated, then nodded again. "Your ribs are broken and your hand, too, and we don't know what else maybe is. Best you lie still. Dame Claire will come. She's been tending you."

Barnaby closed his eyes and moaned, "I'm hurt horrible. I'm hurting. . . ." He opened his eyes wide, fear shining in them. "I want the priest. You fetch the priest, woman."

"He'll come," Meg said. "We'll send for him, too."

Feeling someone at her back, she looked up over her shoulder to see the woman who traveled with the players and the fair-haired youth who had helped mock Sym standing close behind her. Uncertain, vaguely alarmed, Meg stood up to face them but before she had found anything to say, the woman said kindly, "Do you need help? Is there anything we can do?"

Meg glanced from them to Barnaby. His eyes were shut

again, his breathing uneven with his pain. "He's hurting. My boy's gone for someone for Dame Claire, but he's wanting the priest now."

The woman glanced at the fair-haired youth who said, "I'll go for him," and left.

Meg wanted the woman to go, too, but she stayed, circling to Barnaby's other side and sitting down on her heels to look closely at him, not as if intruding but to see if there was anything more she should do. Unsure how she should be toward the woman who was, after all, a lordless wanderer without place and without claim to anything but charity and contempt, Meg said nothing. She was less than Meg; less than anyone in the village; less than any servant in the priory. But disconcertingly she did not seem to know it. Slender in her simply cut brown gown that was long past being new and yet was graceful on her, she held herself more like a lord's lady than someone less than a peasant. And it was hard to guess her age. Not young, Meg thought; the woman's brown hair, worn in a single braid wrapped crownlike around her head, was touched with gray and her face had too many years of knowing to be mistaken for a girl's. But neither was it worn, lined, and hardened the way all village women's faces were. She did not look the way she should and, uneasy, Meg sat down by Barnaby again, covering her unease by taking his unhurt hand. It was chill to her touch. He did not stir, and she said, "He's cold."

"He should be kept warm." The woman rose and without asking leave took the blankets from Hewe's mattress and spread them over Barnaby.

Meg moved quickly to help and when the woman stood back, went on fussing the blankets closer under Barnaby's chin and smoothing them over his shoulders, to show that it was her place to tend him, not the other woman's.

After a few moments the woman said, "I think he's unconscious again."

"Or sleeping," Meg said defensively.

"Or sleeping," the woman agreed. She paused, then said, "My name is Rose."

Meg eyed her uncertainly. "I'm Meg."

"The two boys with you, they're your sons?"

Meg realized the woman was trying to be friendly. Willing to be distracted, she said a little more easily, "Our sons. Sym and Hewe."

"Sym is the older one?"

Meg stiffened, remembering his quarrel with her men, and nodded.

Rose did not seem to notice her stiffening, just said, "He'll make a well-grown man. There's strength in him."

Pleased to have someone notice one of the good things about Sym, Meg nodded. "He's like his father."

"And the other boy is a handsome one."

Meg warmed to the woman. "And bright," she said. "He knows his letters." It helped to say it aloud, made it more real.

"It's good to have two sons. They can be a help to each other as well as to you."

The idea of Sym and Hewe a help to each other held Meg silent for a disconcerted moment. But she knew her duty to a conversation and said, "You have a son, too."

The warmth of Rose's answering smile betrayed how deeply that fact mattered to her. "Piers," she said.

"Is he feeling better?" Meg asked.

"Yes, thank you. His fever is still high but he's resting quietly and keeping warm and Dame Claire says it shouldn't worsen."

At the mention of Dame Claire, Meg's head twitched around toward the door, wondering how long it would be before help came. Rose asked, "Do you work here at the priory?"

Meg did not want to think about her work at the priory and how near she might be to losing it. "Sometimes," she said. "You and the others are all players?"

"Not me," Rose said with soft laughter. "I do the tumbling that brings the crowd to us and help to hold them afterwards long enough for us to gather their pence in payment for our shows."

"Tumbling?" Meg said. Tumbling was what children did on a summer day down a grassy slope.

"Like this." Rose stood up with swift grace, her arms raised over her head, then, as if it were a natural thing, bent backwards, doubling over the wrong way for any body to go. Too quickly for Meg to quite understand what she was seeing, Rose's hands touched down behind her, and with a twist in the air she was over and upright.

"God grant mercy!" Meg breathed, crossing herself for protection against such strangeness.

Rose smiled. "It's something I learned when I was little." She turned sideways to give herself more room, tripped forward to land on her hands as she flung her feet up and over herself and back to the floor, bringing her upright with a little bounce. "See?"

Meg put a protective hand on Barnaby's chest and waved the other at her to stop. It looked like something demons would do to mock God's proper ways. "No more," she begged.

"Indeed, no more," said Dame Frevisse from the doorway.

Chapter 8

FREVISSE STEPPED ASIDE to allow Father Henry and Dame Claire to go past her into the hall. In the moment of entering she had been startled to see Rose's forward flip, then had to smother her reaction of amusement on seeing Meg's fright; it was Meg's ignorance, not stupidity, that made her so easily frightened. Besides, what they were here for was not amusing.

Oblivious, Father Henry went past her, making the sign of the cross and saying, "*Pax hic domui.*" Peace to this place.

Frevisse and Dame Claire, following him side by side, responded, "*Et omnibus habitantibus in ea.*" And to all who live in it.

Rose and Meg together answered, "Amen." Meg, on her feet now, bowing her head and making a hasty little curtsey in respect for the priest, cast Rose a startled glance as if surprised to hear an amen from someone like her. Rose, not noticing, made her own graceful curtsey to the priest and withdrew down the hall to her own fire.

Barnaby opened his pain-filled eyes. Hope and fear together slid over his beard-stubbled face as he saw the priest standing over him, and he rasped, "Father, your blessing. I hurt like to die. I want God's help."

"It's here," Father Henry said reassuringly. Draped around his neck and hanging almost to his knees was a black silk band embroidered with crosses, flowers, and bunches of grapes in shades of penitential purple; and he carried with careful hands the gilt box embossed with sacred symbols that held the Host. He went to stand at Barnaby's feet. Frevisse picked a wisp of straw from the hearth and took a bit of fire to light the candles she and Dame Claire carried and then joined him as he began the sacrament meant to assure the soul's safety after death. His inaccurate Latin was reassuringly loud, and Frevisse saw both Barnaby's and Meg's faces ease as he made his way through Psalm 31.

As he finished, she and Dame Claire set down the candles on either side of Barnaby's head, and Father Henry stooped so Barnaby could kiss the crucifix he held out to him. Meg began to sob quietly. Dame Claire put a hand on her shoulder.

"*Dominus vobiscum,*" intoned Father Henry, opening his book of ritual.

"*Et cum spiritu tuo,*" Frevisse and Dame Claire replied together, Meg following a half moment after them.

Father Henry began to pray. Barnaby moaned "Amen" whenever the priest paused or hesitated, and since Father Henry's Latin reading was only somewhat better than his remembered Latin, the amens were frequent and often inappropriate. It was unsettling to Father Henry but at last he got to the end, when he said his own amen, and gestured for the three women to withdraw while he heard Barnaby's confession.

Away from the fire's small spread of warmth, the December cold slid under clothing and lay like ice along shin and forearm. Meg began to shiver violently, as much from shock as cold. Dame Claire gave the box of medicines she had been carrying to Frevisse and wrapped an arm around Meg, drawing her close for comfort and what warmth they could share. "We could go to the fire," she offered. But Meg shook her head, and Dame Claire did not press her. As rigorous as she could be toward complaining patients or servants slow to obey, Dame Claire's deepest trait was kindness.

Unsurprisingly, Barnaby's confession took a long while. When he had finished, Father Henry spoke the words of absolution, and began the ritual annointing of eyelids, ears, nostrils, lips, hands, feet, asking the Lord to forgive any evil done with each member. Frevisse watched Meg rather than the priest, saw how she forgot her body's cold in wonder at the magic, as a man known to be sinful was cleansed of all blame and made over fresh, worthy to share eternal bliss with God. There were fresh tears on Meg's cheeks. She stepped out of Dame Claire's embrace without hesitating when Father Henry beckoned and there was something like enthusiasm in her voice when they said a paternoster together.

The priest ended the rite by giving Barnaby the viaticum—food for the journey—a thin wafer of consecrated bread that ought to have melted on the tongue, though Barnaby made an eye-bulging struggle of getting it down. When he was finished, Father Henry gathered up the articles of his sacred work and blessed them all.

When he was gone, Dame Claire took his place, to tend to Barnaby's body now that his soul was seen to. Dame Frevisse stayed in case her help was needed, doubting how much use Meg might be if her husband became desperate with pain. But Barnaby bore the infirmarian's handling with set-jawed patience. He grunted with pain as she felt along his bruised side and chest, and went white around the mouth when she handled his hand, but he held back from groaning or cursing.

When Dame Claire had finished and Barnaby was lying limp and closed-eyed, she mixed a strong sleeping powder into the wine she had brought. Meg sidled close to Frevisse and whispered, "What the priest did—Barnaby's all blessed now, his sins all forgiven and gone? He's sure of Heaven?"

"As sure as any man can be," Frevisse assured her. "And until he sins again."

Meg's cheeks darkened with a faint blush and her eyes dropped. "There's blessing indeed," she murmured.

Dame Claire stood up from pouring the medicine into Barnaby's willing mouth. "You'll soon be feeling very little of the pain and then you'll fall to sleep," she told him. "Sleep is best for you now. I'll have some broth sent from the kitchen for you against your wakening." She turned to Meg. "Keep him warm. If he's still awake when the broth comes, feed him only a little at a time. I doubt there'll be trouble keeping him quiet."

She moved away to put her things back in their box. Meg went almost timidly to kneel beside her husband, wiping the last of her tears away, and said, "You're all blessed, Barnaby. The lady said so. Better even than when you were born. All your sins are gone."

His eyes closed, his face gray, Barnaby said, "I'm still hurting. She said it would stop soon but I'm still hurting."

"She said it would take a while, Barnaby. Just a little while."

He grunted without moving and asked, "I don't remember what happened. Was I fighting again? Was that it?"

Hesitantly Meg said, "You crashed Gilbey Dunn's cart into a ditch and wrecked it. Some travelers found you and brought you here."

Barnaby made a small moan. He opened his eyes and looked vaguely at the ceiling. "Where am I?"

"The priory, remember? St. Frideswide's. They brought you here and the nuns are letting you stay until you're well enough to be moved."

He grunted that he understood and shut his eyes again.

With great softness and, Frevisse suspected, some courage, Meg leaned nearer to him and asked, "Do you remember what happened that made you crash? Do you remember that?"

At first Frevisse thought he was not going to answer, that Dame Claire's sleeping draught was working more quickly than usual. But he finally said, "I was coming home. From Lord Lovel's . . ."

His voice trailed off but his breathing told that he was still conscious. Meg waited but when he did not go on, she asked "Did you deliver the wine?"

Barnaby grunted, drew a tentatively deep breath, and probably found it did not hurt. Dame Claire's potion had begun to work against the pain, and with a little more sense he said, "Just like I was told, and never spilled a drop from Oxford to his lordship's hall. Never a stave sprung nor a drop spilled." He grimaced—or maybe he meant it for a smile around the pain—and opened his eyes to Meg's anxious face. "They had wine at the manor, though. Not pot-brewed ale but real wine, like I'd never had before, a great bowl of it in the hall, for Christmas and all. I sang for them, Lord Lovel and his lady. . . ."

"Not that song," Meg said, flushing with anxiety and shame.

Rough humor tugged at the corners of Barnaby's mouth. "Nay, not that one. The other one. About King Henry that was, God keep him, and his Agincourt battle. . . ."

His voice caught as he fought an urge to cough.

Meg touched his shoulder. "Don't talk."

"Nay," he said. "It's working, the medicine. There's not so much hurting. And before I forget—" He fumbled his unhurt hand under the blankets, groping for something at his waist that was not there.

Frevisse had stayed near, knowing someone should watch until he was safely into sleep. Now she said, "Here," guessing, and reached toward the ragged pile of his belongings they had stripped from his body but not bothered with since. "Your pouch?" she asked, surprised by its weight as she held it out.

Barnaby waved it toward his wife. "For you," he croaked. "Said I'd bring you something. See?"

There was a small-boy triumph in his voice and glimmering twitch of a smile on his pain-grayed face. But with more wariness than pleasure, Meg took the pouch and pulled its drawstrings open, felt inside, and cautiously drew out what had weighed so much.

In the hall's shadowed light, the roundness that Meg held in her hand glowed as richly as a sunset. But a sunset could never be held in anyone's hands, and Frevisse watched Meg's wariness turn to wonder. Plainly she had never seen such a thing, and with a delicate grace that surprised Frevisse, she bent her head and smelled of it, then looked at Barnaby with wonder still in her face and asked, "What is it?"

"A norange," Barnaby said, proud of his knowledge. "There was a whole big bowl of them, big as the bowl of wine, nearly, there on Lord Lovel's high table, right in front of him and his lady. Christmas Day the hall was open to all the servants and guests or chance travelers. And food? Food like you never saw and more than comes my way from one start of winter to the next. And drink.'' The drug was working in him now, or he had forgotten his hurt in the excitement of his tale.

''Good wine, with spices in it, and hardly a let to anyone taking a taste. The steward saw me reach out a hand and nodded and smiled, like I was a proper guest. I'll travel the breadth of England if that steward should ask me, and never a grumble about the going. I had a taste and another, and that's when I sang my song, the one that's fit for noble folk. And they liked it, Meg! They liked it and Lady Lovel herself said it was worth something and tossed me the norange and I saved it for you. Brought it home for you for a Christmas fairing. You've never had the like, now have you?''

Meg, the orange still cupped in her hands and held close to her breast, smiled a slow, spreading smile so clear and whole with pleasure that she looked years younger, and Frevisse for the first time wondered what age she really was.

''Barnaby light, Barnaby bright,'' she crooned softly. ''Longest day and the shortest night.'' The old rhyme for St. Barnabas's Day that came near midsummer; a rhyme with a special meaning, Frevisse guessed, because a smile as whole as Meg's own pulled at the deep-weathered lines of Barnaby's face.

He nodded and said, ''It's to eat. I saw them doing that with them. Eating noranges.''

Meg looked doubtfully at the orange's thick, tough skin and then at him.

''Like this,'' Frevisse offered, holding out her hand. There had sometimes been oranges in her uncle's household, and she knew how they could be peeled to reach the sweetness.

Hesitantly Meg handed over her treasure, but cried out when Frevisse dug a fingernail in at its crest, and jerked as if to snatch it away. She barely stopped herself, and clutched her hands together, her face raw with distress.

Frevisse looked at her with surprise. ''You have to peel it. The peel comes off and then you eat what's inside.''

Meg shook her head mutely, her mouth closed tightly over any spoken protest but her hands betraying how much she wanted the orange back in her keeping. Understanding, Frevisse held it out to her.

Meg took it back, clasping it with both hands to her breast again.

"It won't keep long," Frevisse warned. "Not like an apple."

"Nothing keeps long," Meg answered. "But for a little while?"

That was a plea and Frevisse answered it gently with a nod. "For a little while. A week or two. And if you save the peel and dry it, it keeps its scent a long while after."

Meg did not answer but bent her head to smell the sweetness again.

Barnaby quieted as evening came on. In fact, Dame Claire, seeing to him after Compline, had been pleased. "He's strong. His body seems to have steadied from the shock. I'll be best able to tell tomorrow, but his chances are better with every hour." She nodded toward one of the servants. "Eda knows where I sleep if you need me in the night." Meg, hunched against falling asleep, glanced at the woman and nodded. Frevisse had thought a strong dose of Dame Claire's potion for Meg, and a long sleep afterwards, would have been a good thing, but it was not possible and they had gone back to the cloister and bed and their own sleep.

But now she was awake. The night was sunken into the cold, dead time between Matins and dawn; the dormitory was long since settled out of the restlessness that always came after midnight prayers. There had been the expected coughing, snuffling, smothered sneezing, and finally silence except for the sounds of sleep. But Frevisse was still uncomfortably awake, propped up as best she could manage with her thin pillow.

She knew her wakefulness was partly because of her own cold's misery, but there was something else, too, and the prayers and meditations that usually soothed her and kept her company when these wakeful hours came on her had neither done that nor helped her find why she was uneasy. The stark fact was that she was awake. She was awake and something was wrong and she did not know what or where the trouble was.

She had tried feeling it in the dormitory's silence, listening for anything that should not be there; but everything was as it always was, from Dame Alys's erratic snoring farther along the aisle to the gurgle of water through the necessarium. Nor could she remember anything left undone that could be troubling her. The only thing uneasy and wrong seemed to be her own mind and now, deliberately, Frevisse let it loose. Stopped trying to search out the trouble and let her thoughts drift in the night's deep cold and darkness. If nothing else they might finally drift her back to sleep.

She found she was thinking of Meg's orange.

Disconcerted, Frevisse circled the thought. Meg's orange. She had held it only briefly but could still feel it. Could remember its smell and her knowing of how sweet it was inside. The pleasure of it in her hand.

Oranges.

Oranges on a tree. Where you could reach up and pick them if you were tall enough.

She had been too short, too young. It had been her father who had lifted her up gloriously high so she could pick her very own. She could still feel his strong hands around her ribs, hear his laughter, see his blue eyes in his tanned face smiling up at her when she held out the orange to show him before he put her down.

That was in Spain.

She had forgotten Spain.

Well, not actually forgotten it. If anyone had asked, she would have said she had been there, yes. There was even a cast-lead seashell in the chest at the foot of her bed to show that she had been to the great pilgrimage church at Compostela.

She did not remember her visit as a pilgrim; she remembered Compostela with a small child's memories. Inside the church it had been sweating hot and crowded, and so reeking with incense that she had started to sneeze and could not stop and finally her parents had had to take her outside into the blazing sunlight where she had gone on sneezing until all three of them were helpless with laughter.

She had forgotten that sunshine. And the laughter.

And riding in the basket.

How had she forgotten that? The days' journeyings had been so long that she could not walk with the others, but had ridden in a basket strapped on the side of an ambling donkey. Shaded by a wide-brimmed straw hat and lulled to dreaming and sometimes sleep by the donkey's rocking gait along hours and hours of dusty roads to . . . where? To where there had been oranges for her father to pick for her.

She had gone on no journeyings for a long while now. And that, yes, that was what she wanted, more than an orange. Perhaps, come the spring, she could ask leave to go on pilgrimage.

To where?

The possibilities, like memories, rose up in her mind.

Canterbury, with its flint wall and the tall glories of its cathedral's nave. Walsingham, waiting green and quiet at the end of miles of gentle riding. St. Denis and the exciting bustle of Paris. Compostela again, to be visited with true understanding of the grace it could bestow, sitting beyond the mountains and near the orange groves . . .

Reality slid between Frevisse and her dreaming. No nun from St. Frideswide's would ever go so far as Compostela. Or even St. Denis. Oxford, maybe, to St. Frideswide's tomb; that might be possible. Or Canterbury, if Domina Edith felt that St. Thomas had granted a particularly desperate prayer. But Frevisse had no desperate prayer—except that she wanted . . . wanted . . .

Unworded discontent pulled at her while she fought to leave the thought unfinished. She wanted . . . Sleep, she said firmly to herself. A good, deep sleep and no rheum left in her head when she awakened.

"Dame Frevisse?"

Frevisse realized her thoughts had taken her further away than she had known; the soft voice and the chink of the rings as the curtain closing her cubicle was pushed aside startled her into sitting up abruptly. She had heard no one moving, and whispered a little sharply, "Who's there?"

"It's Eda, my lady. About the man Barnaby. He's dying, seems like. I've told Dame Claire and she said to ask if you would come."

Why, Frevisse peevishly wondered, did people always choose to die in the middle of the night? But she immediately pushed the idea away. It was not her place to question; it was her place to serve those who came to the priory, whether to travel on or to die there. And if she told herself that often enough, maybe she would come to remember it first instead of second.

"I will come at once," she said, matching Eda's humble tone.

Chapter 9

FREVISSE SHIVERED AND wrapped her arms more tightly around herself. There was nothing she could do to help Barnaby, and the hall was as cold as the night was black beyond the dimly lit windows, or even the corners of the hall beyond the reach of the small lamp Dame Claire had set beside the body while she checked it.

The servant Eda, anxious not to be idle, lifted the lamp in an attempt to give Dame Claire a better light, but was shivering so hard that Dame Claire bid her with an impatient gesture to put it down again. Obeying, she moved beyond Barnaby's corpse to put both arms around Meg, and both of them stood shivering and looking everywhere but at Dame Claire. Frevisse wished she had thought to step down from her own dignity of office to comfort Meg. Now, instead, she was left to shiver alone.

Dame Claire sighed with a weariness that had nothing to do with waking before dawn. "It was something torn inside of him, maybe. Or something broken that I didn't find. The foam at the corner of his mouth says it was likely a hurt to his lungs." She drew one of the blankets over Barnaby's face.

Meg moaned and turned her face into Eda's shoulder.

Taking another of the blankets, Dame Claire rose, went to put it around Meg's shoulders, and asked, "What happened at the last? When did you realize he was dying?"

"I didn't," Meg whispered without raising her head. "He was sleeping. I went to sleep, and woke to see he was so still. . . ."

"He never struggled or stirred or . . . ?" Dame Claire pressed.

"No." Meg shook her head.

"But there must have been something. What woke you? Did he make a noise?"

Frevisse put out a hand to stop her. She knew how boldly Dame Claire fought against anyone's dying, and how sternly she sought for reasons when she lost; but this was neither time nor place to make Barnaby's widow more wretched than she was. "Eda," Frevisse said, "take her with you. Let her sleep next to you. It isn't good for her to be alone for the rest of the night."

"Surely, my lady. That's no trouble at all. Come now, we'll find you a place." Eda moved to lead Meg away.

But Meg held back, gesturing at Barnaby's body. "I can't leave him. He has to be watched over. He can't be left alone. Can't we take him to the church?"

"In the morning," Frevisse said. "We'll find someone to take him back to the village church in the morning. And someone will watch by him tonight, but it doesn't have to be you. Go with Eda."

Meg let Eda lead her away then, shuffling her feet as if she lacked the strength to lift them.

When they were gone, Dame Claire asked, "Where are her sons? Why was she watching alone?"

"She sent them home, to see to things. She probably thought there was no danger of this; he seemed better."

"I thought he was," Dame Claire said regretfully. "I truly thought he was. If I hadn't, I would have set someone to watch with her. She was probably sleeping, so exhausted she never heard his dying. Poor woman."

"Poor indeed. The funeral will probably take what few pence she's managed to gather working here, and then there'll be heriot and gersum to Lord Lovel for the older boy to take up the holding."

"The gersum can't be high, their holding is so small," said Claire.

"Still, she'll not have a penny to bless herself with after they do all that, plus pay damages for the cart and maybe the horse and whatever else. The family will be in debt at best and perhaps beggared. The older boy is an ill-tempered, disobedient fool, not likely to do his work even if he gets the holding. He'll be no comfort to Meg, or much use. And the other one is not made for hard work."

"That may change," said Claire. "He's young."

Behind them came the sound of footsteps, and they turned toward the dark shape looming toward them, featureless with the low glow of the players' fire behind him until he was near enough to their own light for his face to show.

But Frevisse had already recognized Ellis by his height and broad shoulders. "Is he dead?" asked the man.

"Yes."

"A pity. Rose is asking if you'll come look at Piers." His request was halfhearted; a woman's fussing over a child's minor illness was deeply discounted in the fact of a man's dying.

But Claire said, "Assuredly." From what she knew of fevers, it was likely to have worsened in the night. Or seemed to; every ache seemed worse in the night, and worse again when it was a child. Small wonder the man dared to ask despite Barnaby's death. She bent to gather up her box and the lamp.

"I'll stay here," Frevisse said. "We said someone would keep watch by him."

Dame Claire paused to look at her. "Are you sure? We can find a servant to do it."

Frevisse shook her head. "I won't sleep again tonight. Go on."

Ellis nodded at the blanket-covered shape that had been Barnaby. "We never heard a sound, not till Meg woke us with her crying."

Frevisse said, "He must have gone quietly, in his sleep."

"A mercy he'd been shriven."

"A mercy indeed," Dame Claire agreed. "Come. Let's see to your little boy."

They went away toward the other fire. Frevisse knelt down beside Barnaby's body and composed herself for prayer and meditation. At least something so distinct as death gave her a focus for her thoughts. There was a soul to be prayed for, and that she knew how to do.

But despite her efforts, her mind would not hold to the practiced words. A recitation of familiar prayers could sometimes take her through the cold and dark emotions of the moment into the harmonies of the seven crystal spheres that were around the world and led by steps of grace into the light and joy surrounding the throne of God in Heaven.

She had learned when she was fairly young that she could do that on occasion—leave the world in mind at least, for a greater, deeper, higher plane. Among her reasons for choosing to become a nun had been her desire to join more freely, more frequently with that high place.

Sister Thomasine could do it with a thought, Frevisse suspected. For Sister Thomasine it was part of her nature; for Frevisse it was a studied effort, which seemed hardly fair. Frevisse shook off that mean thought; petty jealousy would only weigh her spirit down, keep it from the freedom she wanted for it. Deliberately, she turned her thought away from the mundane and began again to reach out of herself toward God.

"*Requiem aeternam dona ei, Domine. Et lux perpetua luceat ei.*" Eternal rest grant unto him, O Lord. And light eternal shine upon him. "*Kyrie, eleison. Christe, eleison. Kyrie, eleison.*" Lord, have mercy. Christ, have mercy. Lord, have mercy.

The release did not come. Her thoughts, meant to go upward, outward, insistently flitted sideways, back to worldly things. To the indignation of Dame Alys in chapter. To the rude questioning of her performance of her duties by Roger Naylor. To Sym's defiance, and Joliffe's laughter. To the hall's cold, now that the fire was dying.

Her undiscipline annoyed her more than her earthbound

prayers for the repose of the soul of the dead man under the blanket right in front of her.

She found herself straining to overhear the hushed talking from the players' end of the hall, and listening to the passage of Dame Claire behind her. She shivered in the icy draft of the opening and closing outer door, discovered she had lost where she had been in her recitation of Psalm 129, and started over with more impatience than reverence.

Which was worse than not praying at all.

Frevisse stopped, and for a while simply knelt there, allowing herself to be aware of the darkness and the cold and the quiet voices at the other fire. Then, less firmly, she set herself to praying again, not trying to use it as a way to anywhere but making her mind see each word as she said it, in simple progression toward her goal.

An unknown while later she felt an icy draft up her back. Someone was coming in, with a rush of night air that fluttered the ends of her veil and pushed her gown against her back.

Her concentration broken, she turned to see who it was. Ellis, she thought, and then was sure as he was briefly silhouetted against the players' fire, handing a small goblet to Rose. Medicine for the boy. With a sound of annoyance at him, and at herself, Frevisse tried to turn her mind back to praying yet again.

But now she was aware again that under the folded blanket was a hard stone floor, and that her nose wanted blowing, and that her fingers ached with cold.

Exasperated, she slipped sideways to sit on the blanket; and after a few moments stood up. She was doing no one any good just sitting there. It was going to take a good deal of praying to free Barnaby's soul from Purgatory, mere sympathy wasn't going to do it. On the other hand, with a sentence as long as his probably was, putting off the prayers for a few hours would make small difference. Frevisse made the sign of the cross over his body. If prayers were failing her—or she was failing them—and all she could do was keep watch, that could be done as well near the players' well-burning fire as here beside the near-gone embers that were all that was left of this one.

The players were all awake. Rose was sitting beside Piers, holding him up with an arm behind his shoulders while gently making him drink from the goblet Ellis had brought. The boy's face was flushed a dry, harsh red, showing that his fever had not yet broken. His mother was holding him firmly against his own restlessness, insisting that he drink while the three men sat on the far side of the fire, pretending they were not watching while talking among themselves as Frevisse came near enough to hear.

"We'll have to find the money somewhere," Joliffe was saying. "Tisbe's been shoeless on that near fore since we left Fen Harcourt. She'll go lame if she has to go on that way."

"If the nuns pay us for the play—" Ellis began.

Bassett rumbled, "No. What we do for them is in return for their courtesy to us, and to Piers."

"I wonder why they've been so kind to us?" said Joliffe. He looked around toward the darkness where Frevisse was. "Who's there?"

Frevisse had not tried to hide her coming, and she came forward now into the light. The men would have risen to their feet but she gestured them to stay seated and said with a smile that included them all, "I've been keeping cold watch over there and wonder if I might share your fire a while."

"Surely, my lady," Bassett said, holding out his hand to the only empty stool among them.

Frevisse hesitated, looking toward Rose. The woman nodded for her to be seated.

"Piers is quieter when I'm by," she said.

Piers, laid down again on his pillow, rolled his head restlessly, his fevered eyes half-shut. They were all watching him, as if their gathered attention would be enough to help him.

After a while Ellis asked, "Is the medicine working?"

Rose waited, then said softly, "He's going to sleep. The way the lady said he should."

They went on waiting until it was quite clear that Piers was soundly asleep. Rose touched his forehead and said, "I think he may be a little cooler." Ellis sighed, his shoulders relaxing. Joliffe unknotted his fingers as if surprised to find them wound around each other so tightly. Bassett straightened his shoulders and set his hands on his spread knees. But no one moved to go back to their pallets, and no one spoke.

It was not quite a comfortable silence. Frevisse felt their awareness of her, felt maybe she should go but did not know how to do it gracefully, and to end the silence nodded toward Piers and said, "He's a likely looking boy, and clever, from what I've seen of him. How old is he?"

"Nine years, come Candlemas Eve," Rose answered, not taking her eyes from her son's face.

The silence came again. Frevisse was about to suggest that she leave to let them go back to their sleeping when Bassett said, "A pity about the villein. Too bad hurt to live, I take it?"

Frevisse answered, "A tear in his lungs, Dame Claire thinks. Nothing that could be helped and we only hoped he was going to be all right after all because we didn't know of it. It's going to be hard for his widow," she added, to keep the conversation from fading out again. "With all the dues owed the lord now and her sons not full grown."

Bassett nodded. "Holding the land, you're held by the land."

Joliffe, more serious than Frevisse had ever heard him, said, "'And now I wax old, sick, sorry, and cold; as muck upon mold, I wither away.'"

Ellis poked moodily at the unburned end of a log with his foot, shoving it further into the flames. "That's us as much as them, though they never see it that way."

The mood was darkening. Against it, Frevisse said to Joliffe, "What you quoted, it's from the Noah play, isn't it? From Wakefield?"

The gleam returned to Joliffe's eyes. He grinned and asked, "How can a cloistered nun be knowing of such worldly things as the Wakefield plays?"

"You can hardly call *The Play of Noah* a worldly thing," Frevisse returned.

"I don't recall the Church tells that Noah's wife has to be hauled bodily into the Ark, and then clouts him alongside of his head when she's there."

"'Welcome, wife, into this boat,'" Frevisse quoted. "And then she hits him. No, I don't recall that from the Bible."

"Ah!" Ellis pointed an accusing finger. "That's from the Chester plays. You've mixed your sources, scholar!"

"Only after one of you did!" Frevisse returned. They all laughed, a friendly exchange that swept away any last constraints.

"A well-traveled lady," Bassett said with interest. "Unless you've somehow come by copies of the plays?"

"No copy but mine own memory, I fear," Frevisse answered.

"And how did you come by that, pray tell?" Joliffe asked.

"I wasn't born a cloistered nun. There was a time when St. Christopher was of more use to me than St. Simon Stylites." Frevisse had meant to say it blithely, to match Joliffe's tone, and was a little disconcerted to hear a sad edge to her voice.

"So what brought you into the cloister after all?" Joliffe asked.

"There are less fleas here than in other places I could name." A flippant answer because a serious one did not seem appropriate.

They laughed again, and Bassett said, "You must have stayed in some of the same inns we have."

"There was one inn," Ellis offered, "where the guests were crowded so many to a bed that the fleas had perforce to sleep on the floor."

"And since that wasn't comfortable for them, they stayed awake all night, biting us," Joliffe added. He had pulled an apple from a bag beside his stool and cut a slice from it. He held the piece out to Frevisse. "But such talk can't be seemly for a nun, however well traveled."

"Perhaps the lady came to a nunnery to escape the roads," suggested Bassett. "The English roads are a shame to a Christian country."

"The worst road I ever traveled," Frevisse said, suddenly remembering, "was in Yorkshire, I think. Or thereabouts. It had been raining. . . ."

"It's weather more than the inns giving sorrow to us who travel," said Ellis.

But Frevisse was not to be turned from her reminiscence. "It was raining enough that the road was puddled from one side to the other in places, and ahead of us as we came riding along was a larger puddle than most. It had a large hump in the middle of it, like an island, and a man squatted down on the edge, looking all discouraged. Only when we reached him did we realize the hump in the puddle was his horse. They'd fallen into a hole so deep the horse could not stand but must swim to exhaustion, and the edges were so slippery it could not climb out, and there we found them, disconsolate rider and drowned horse."

"Brickmakers," Bassett said. "Digging their clay out of the high road." Frevisse nodded. "Was your road maybe in Lincolnshire? That's where it's bad right now, with Lord Cromwell set to have his place all made of bricks."

"And nobody able to make complaint because who around there is going to gainsay Lord Cromwell." Ellis said.

"Nobody between there and the royal court," Bassett said. "And probably nobody even there."

"'When even gold will rust, what then will iron do?'" Joliffe sighed. "Ah, for the good old days when law was law and men obeyed it."

"From what I've heard of times back even to Adam and Eve, there was many a man who dared disobey the law," Bassett said comfortably. "So sing all you like, I won't play fiddle to that tune."

Joliffe made a rude gesture at him, which Bassett would not dignify with any notice.

Ellis said, "Has it been so long since you were a traveler, my lady? Could you still tell London ale if you tasted it?"

"There was a time I could tell it from the ale of King Arthur's Inn near Bristol, if both were fresh. But now I think the ale we make right here is very suitable to me."

"Bristol is outside our circuit so I wouldn't be knowing about King Arthur's ale," Bassett said, "but I mind me there's an inn near Nottingham. . . ."

And they were away. Inns, abbeys, priories, towns. Time might change some things—there was some talk before they agreed that what Frevisse remembered as The Archer between Northampton and Stony Stratford was now The Green Man, though the food was still the best in the county, even though the fat man who owned it when Frevisse was there had to be the father of the fat man who owned it now—but it seemed traveling the old roads did not change that much, or travelers' stories.

Good days' travel to remember—"So warm and the road so easy, I fell asleep walking behind the cart and bumped my nose into it when it stopped," Rose said.

"And wouldn't speak to us the rest of the day because we all laughed at her," said Joliffe, laughing all over again.

"Hush, you'll wake Piers," said Rose, stifling her own laughter.

They dropped their voices but went on talking, of other roads, other inns, other towns.

"We'd have been no wetter under a tree than in that barn."

"And there wouldn't have been the rats."

"That manor's owner is so mean he grudges you the use of the dust you walk on as you pass his gate."

"I remember the time we took a shortcut through a field of wheat, and the hayward caught us, and fined us our hoods for trespassing—"

Rose joined in the least, and her comments were brief, but Frevisse noticed she listened closely all the while and smiled the deep and private smile of someone happy where she was, though her hand never left her son's chest, resting there lightly, as if counting his breaths. The rest of them were deep into comparing palmers they had met—the good, the bad, the improbable—when Rose said quietly, "I think his fever has broken."

She immediately had all the men's attention. Frevisse was only barely ahead of Bassett in reaching to feel the boy's forehead. It was damp to her touch, his hair dark along the edge with sweat and little beads of moisture on his upper lip. "Yes," she agreed. "It's broken. God be thanked."

And suddenly Rose, who had been sitting erect the while, slumped, pale with the exhaustion she had been holding at bay for her boy's sake. Before even Frevisse understood, Ellis was beside her, an arm around her shoulders, saying, "There, now. Are you satisfied? We'll have you sick next and you don't want us trying to care for you, that's sure. Come lie down and leave the watching to us. You'll hear if he rouses. Come."

Rose gave way to him without protest, let him half lift her to her feet and take her to the straw mattress and blankets that were her bed. He gentled her down into their comfort and covered her. Frevisse thought she was asleep before he had finished.

Frevisse was suddenly tired herself. How long had they been sitting here talking?

As if in answer, the cloister bell began to ring, distant but clear. It was time to welcome the dawn with the prayers of Prime. The corpse by the dead hearth on the other end of the room had chilled alone, with no one to watch, no one to pray.

"I have to go," she said.

"We thank you for your company. It made our watching easier," Bassett said.

Frevisse rose, tucking her hands into her sleeves. She would not admit to these people her sin of neglect. "God's blessing on you. I'll return later."

As she crossed the room, the outer door opened. By the gray dawn light that came in with the cold draft, she recognized young Hewe. Telling him his father was dead was a task she had not anticipated, but there was no avoiding it now. She went toward him as he closed the door, and reached him before he had moved toward his father's body.

He bent his head to her respectfully as she came but then craned his neck to see around her, asking, "Where's my mam? Isn't she here? Where's Da gone?"

Frevisse started to tell him but he realized what he was seeing before she had the words out.

"Da?" he asked. His voice was doubtful but as Frevisse took his hand, she knew he knew.

"He's dead," she said gently. "Quietly, in his sleep, a few hours ago."

Hewe went on staring at the blanket-covered body. "Where's Mam?"

"I sent her to have some sleep. I'm glad you're here. I have to go to Prime. You stay here with him until I can come back, or your mother does."

Hewe nodded.

"And pray by him. You know your prayers?"

Hewe nodded again. Tears were beginning to swell in his eyes, and he turned his head away so she wouldn't see them fall. Frevisse patted his shoulder by way of comfort, and left.

Chapter 10

FOR MEG THE day was a thick movement through gray unreality. She knew the things that needed to be done before the wake that night and did them or saw to other people doing them with an efficiency in which her mind and feelings took very little part. At the very start she had sent Hewe to the village to tell his brother and ask some of the men for help in taking Barnaby's body home. She had known the word would spread then without her needing to say more, and she was ready as she and Hewe and Sym came with the slow procession of Barnaby's body to her house for the women waiting to help her with the rest. She had helped often enough at other deaths—her parents' and her children's and her neighbors'—to know she would not be left alone to the work of washing and readying Barnaby's body.

Her only hesitation had been over what would be his shroud, and then decided the older blanket would be enough. Ada Bychurch sewed up its two holes willingly, and then they wrapped him in it before laying him out on the bed for his last rest at home before he would go to his grave. They left his face uncovered and set the customary little bowl of salt on his chest.

The women helped her clean the house. They would have insisted that she simply sit and let them do it, but knew that time to sit and think was not the best thing for her just now.

She took the task of scrubbing and scouring the table; food and drink would have to be set out on it for the wake, and it must not be a disgrace to her neighbors' kindness.

Besides that, there was sympathy to be received, and the telling over to everyone who asked about the accident and Barnaby's hurts and how quiet his dying had been.

"And there's a mercy," more than one woman said, nodding knowledgeably.

The food came, as she had known it would. There was never much to spare at this time of year and after the autumn's bad harvest there was less than usual, but it came. A few withered apples. Two half loaves of bread. Some small cheeses. A pan of roasted turnips. Little by little the gifts came, until at the last there was enough.

While the daylight lasted the men had been busy digging the grave. The winter's cold had been set in the ground for so long that there was trouble breaking the frozen soil; and when that was done, down to below the frost line, the men were among the bones of earlier burials that had to be picked out and saved for putting in the half-derelict shed that served as the churchyard's charnel house. It was warming work but hard, and Sym came in from it cursing his sore shoulders and the cold, then saw the gathering of women around the fire, and went to sulk and rub Nankin on her hard head.

The men followed soon after, and settled themselves around Sym, talking of death dues to the lord and the poor harvest and of how old Austin had drunk himself to a stupor night before last and never made it home, and it was lucky he'd not frozen to death in the ditch.

"He was burrowed so deep into the leaves there, his boy Thad nearly didn't find him even by daylight come the next morning."

"It was his snores told me where he was," Thad grunted. "Nearly cost me my back to haul him home, he was still so thick with ale."

There was laughter at that. Thad, being the smith, was as well muscled as a man could be. The women shushed at the men, reminding them why they were there, and talk lapsed to murmuring again. Sometimes one woman or another would come take a turn at sitting beside Meg on the bench, to pat her hand and murmur well-worn, familiar words; but there were no tears, not from Meg or anyone else. Then four or five men addressed the others about Barnaby in words as kind as they were lying, for the sake of the widow.

And finally it was over. First one woman and then another came to say a final comfort to Meg, collected her man, and went to stand a respectful moment beside the bed before leaving. The smoky light of the rush candles set at head and foot of the bed jerked and flared to the opening and closing of the cottage door. Meg watched as the twitch of light and shadow across Barnaby's face made his dull features seem to move. It was disquieting to see, as if somehow he had begun to breathe again. When the last guest had gone she rose stiffly from the bench and went to blow out the candles, leaving nothing but the low firelight, which did not reach his face.

Tomorrow she would have the bed to herself, but tonight it was Barnaby's, and for an unsettled moment she did not know where she was going to sleep. But then Hewe moved close to her, the blankets rolled under his arm, took hold of her shoulder, and said with uncertain gentleness, "Come on, Mam. It's late and tomorrow will be as hard. Come on up to the loft with us."

She nearly said no, that she would sleep on the floor beside the fire. But it would be warmer in the loft, there in the straw, and her boys nearby.

"Yes," she said. "Yes."

The sky was a lowering dark gray. A teethed wind rattled the bare twigs of the ash tree overhanging the churchyard wall near the open grave as Barnaby was carried in his wooden coffin around the churchyard by six of the men. The bell's flat tolling sounded like a tired housewife banging on a pot bottom as the funeral circled its way properly sunwise from the gateway to the new grave. Father Henry, shivering and hasty, began the words proper to the lowering of the coffin.

All of this was for the comfort of those left behind to earth's gray pains and cold, but Meg was not comforted at all, only so tired that she had made Sym walk beside her from the cottage so she could lean on his arm. He had liked that, it made a show of his new place as head of the family. But she also made Hewe walk on her other side, and held his hand all the way.

So far as Meg knew, Hewe had not cried since his first tears beside his father's body, but she was sure he was grieving. He had burrowed against her shoulder in his sleep last night and stayed near her all day today, quiet and seeming deep in thought. He was seeing the way the world went, she thought. His father's dying might be the good thing needed to make him see his way toward the priesthood after all, without her having to fight him on it anymore.

She was distracted from her thought by Sym's sudden tensing. She looked up at him to see that he was staring away from the grave and Father Henry toward the far edge of the little group of mourners. Meg looked, too, and saw their neighbor Gilbey Dunn standing there no differently from the rest, his hood in his hands, his head bare and bowed respectfully.

"Turd-hearted cur!" Sym snarled under his breath.

He made as if to move toward him but Meg's fingers clamped onto his arm. "You stand fast!" she hissed. "This is your father's funeral, not a brawl!"

"Showing his face here! After the trouble he was to Da, and all!"

Sym jerked to pull free of her but Meg's strength was desperate. Heads were beginning to lift to look at them and she said with all the viciousness she could manage, "You stand and you be quiet! Let the sin of it fall on him and don't go bringing more on yourself! Stand still! Think of your father, not of Gilbey Dunn!"

Sym fell silent, but Meg felt how tense his arm stayed and knew he kept glancing across to Gilbey instead of heeding what Father Henry had to say.

Afterward was the funeral feast in the cottage. There was a little more to eat than there had been last night: Domina Edith had sent down a meat pasty from the priory, and Bess from the alehouse brought a bucket of her latest brewing to warm the gathering. With Barnaby safely under ground, the talk became more cheerful.

But it came to an end soon enough and as they made their farewells and went away, Meg found she was as glad of their going as she suspected they were. She did not even mind Sym and Hewe going away with some of their friends. "For only a little," Hewe said anxiously, but Meg only nodded at him, letting him go without complaint or bidding them come back soon.

Then there was no one else. Meg looked around the cottage, a little bemused to find there was nothing that needed doing. There was even leftover food enough that she would not have to bother with cooking supper. Nothing at all to do except rest.

She lowered herself onto one of the stools. Elbows propped on the table, she leaned her forehead into her hands and shut her eyes. It being winter and the steward elsewhere about his business with Lord Lovel's properties, it might be weeks before they would know whether Sym was going to be allowed his inheritance. Meg guessed that he would be; the faults had all been his father's and no matter what she saw in Sym, he had done his share in the village tithing and in the fields since he was twelve years old. He was well grown for his years. With her to help, and Hewe—

Meg shook her head to herself. There was no going away from the fact that Hewe was going to have to do a man's share of the work from now on, no matter that he was too young for it. She was not going to give up her work at St. Frideswide's. There had to be those pence to buy Hewe free and into the priesthood. He and Sym would both have to see that and help her do it. Hewe as a priest would then be able to help them in turn. Money for new cloth, maybe, to make a good woolen dress or cloak. A pair of boots for Sym. Another ox.

But first there was the broken cart. The only hope Meg saw of paying Gilbey Dunn for it was by persuading him to take its worth in work from one or both of the boys. And that would be hard, persuading not only Gilbey but Sym and Hewe, too. Sym especially would mightily resent it, no matter what sense it made. Why did he have to be so much like his father, so blind to what was necessary? Why was even Hewe so stubborn in such needless ways?

A confident clearing of a throat made her look up to find Gilbey Dunn standing in her doorway, as if summoned by her musing. He had had the decency not to come to the funeral feast; probably he had seen Sym's face in the churchyard. But Sym was gone and here he was, a stocky figure bulking large in her doorway. He was scarcely taller than she was but solidly built and looking larger in his russet tunic, his bald head gleaming a little in the outdoor light, but the cottage's shut-windowed gloom hiding whatever expression was on his blunt face.

Meg was angry that he had opened the door without first knocking, as if he had some right to be there. She said, "They've all gone. The feasting and funeral are done and you've no business here just now. We'll pay you for the cart but I ask you for a day's grace before we deal with it."

As if that were an invitation, he came in, shutting the door against the cold but saying, "Why are you sitting here in the dark? Haven't you even a candle to light? You might at least build up the fire."

"The spare candles went for last night's wake. Sym's gone for more firewood and I'm well enough till he comes back. What is it you're wanting, Gilbey?" He wouldn't be there if he did not want something; his complaining was meant to make her feel small so he could get the better of her. Though his wife had been her friend and they had hoped Sym would marry his girl, Meg had never liked Gilbey.

He sat down across the table from her. "You're in deep trouble, my girl."

Meg frowned, misliking his familiar tone. "You needn't have come out of your way to tell me that. And there's ways out of our trouble, so you needn't be troubling yourself over it, thank you."

"'Tis not out of my way at all but very much in my way," he said. "That's why I'm here."

Meg straightened and for the first time looked directly at

him. He wasn't there to talk about the cart, but something more serious.

"Go away, Gilbey Dunn. For pity's sake if nothing else. I've griefs enough to deal with. I don't need arguing today."

"It's to end the arguing I've come. And a bettering for both of us in the bargain."

Meg's tired brain could not see what he was aiming at. "There's no use in talking to me about the lands. I'd not part with them if I could. They're Sym's."

"That's as may be, and there may be more said on that before it's done, but no, 'tis you who must answer what I've come to ask, Meg."

"And what would that be?"

"That you marry me."

Meg stared at him.

Gilbey leaned across the table toward her. "Think on it, Meg. You'd not have to live in this half barn anymore. Think on my house and how you'd live there. I'd keep on the woman I've hired. She'd help you see to the place. You'd not need to wear yourself so close to the bone as you do now."

Meg kept on staring, wondering just how befuddled her wits had gone. He could not be saying what she thought she heard.

Gilbey put a hand out toward her, but she pulled her own back. His voice warm with persuasion, he went on, "Look you, it would serve us both well. Better than maybe you've thought. How can you hope to keep up, all alone, with what you couldn't even with Barnaby alive?"

"My sons . . ."

Gilbey dismissed that possibility with a wave of his hand. "You know them better than that. Even if Sym is let to take the holding—and that's not certain, mind you. Bailiff and steward both know things about him and have their own mind on the matter—it's still like as not that he'll lose it all anyway, even faster than his father would have. Marry me and there'll be someone to see to you and your land both."

"The lands aren't mine," Meg insisted.

"There's nothing says a widow can't inherit her husband's

property. A strong word from me to the steward would do it. He'd be willing."

His certainty about that made Meg suspect that Gilbey had asked him a long while ago. She rose to Sym's defense. "It goes to the eldest son if there's one. That's where it goes."

"And Sym will lose it. You have to know him well enough to see that, even with a mother's eye. Both your boys will be the better for a firm hand directing them the way Barnaby never could. I'll swear to find them both good marriages if you're wanting that.

"Hewe—" Meg began feebly.

"I'll help him to the priesthood if that's what you're wanting. Your marrying me would make things come right for you, and both the boys as well."

"What are you doing, talking of marriage?" Sym snarled from the doorway. "She's barely a widow and sure not for the likes of you!" He shoved the door back hard enough to crash it against the wall and strode toward the table. "Take your scheming, miserly self out of here, Gilbey Dunn, away from my mother and out of my house!"

Gilbey rose to his feet, not apparently offended or frightened. "Your house? I think not, boy. You're not of age. Even if the steward gives you seisin of it and your land, someone will have the keeping of it—and of you, God help them—these few years more. Maybe your mother. Maybe someone else. But not you yet. And from the smell of ale on you, the day you take it for your own will be the worst day for the holding since your father took it."

"Better that than your having it!"

"It Meg marries me, then you can have the house at least. Let that satisfy you for the while, boy. Let your mother come live where the animals are kept in the barn instead of the kitchen!"

"She'd rather live with animals than you!"

"Sym!" Meg rose to her feet between them. She did not want the quarrel to freshen, not when they were so in debt to Gilbey, not until that was settled and the quarrel could be faced on open grounds, not the hidden ones of debts unpaid, or unpayable. And not with Sym just drunk enough to not think what he was saying. Gilbey had the kind of temper that simmered long and deep.

But Sym was past heeding. "My mother's not marrying anyone. And never you, no matter what! Rather we all starve here than take a thing from you! Don't go trying to lay your hands on anything of ours or you'll find I'm man enough to put you where you ought to be!"

"Sym!" Meg came around the table to grab his arm and shake it. "Sym, you mind your tongue! There's no need for words like that! You stop it!" Still holding on to him, she said to Gilbey, "You'd best go. It's too soon for me to be hearing things like you've been saying. Best you go."

Gilbey nodded, his gaze on Sym speculative. "Aye," he agreed, moving toward the door, keeping wide of Sym's reach though he was the boy's match and better. "I'm going. But you think on what I've said. You're a clever girl, Meg, and you can see the possibilities in our joining."

"There's devilment in it, that's what there is!" Sym shouted at his back and the closing door. He turned his temper on his mother. "What are you thinking of to listen to him like that? And Da not cold in his grave yet!"

"Barnaby's cold enough," Meg said. "It's a winter grave." She sighed. "Sym, there was no need to say those things. Listening does no harm. We need to know what's in his mind. It doesn't hurt to listen."

"But you're not thinking of doing it!" It was no question, only a flat demand, and he sounded like his father as he made it.

As she had learned to do with Barnaby, Meg only looked back at him flatly, until he twitched his eyes away. Then she said, "I'm tired. You go help Hewe find some wood or there'll be no fire by morning. I'm going to bed."

Not even much caring if he obeyed her, she left him standing there and went to crawl under the ragged covers of her cold bed in its corner.

Chapter 11

MEG SLEPT HEAVILY. She awoke once in the dark to hear the tick of sleet against the wall and eastward shutters, but slept again, and next woke to know by the slant of pale light through the crack around the window and under the door that the morning was well along and the day sunny.

It was the thought of sunshine more than anything that drew her from bed. There was a full fire on the hearth and evidence by way of dirty dishes that both Sym and Hewe had managed to feed themselves. She went to stand close to the warmth, taking a bread crust from the table to chew. The coarse weave of her gown shook out its own wrinkles and except for needing to pad her shoes with fresh straw against the cold ground before she put them on, she was ready for the day. She checked the chickens and found they had been fed, too, and the floor under their roost cleaned. That would be Hewe's doing, because Sym scorned to have anything to do with "the clacking things," saying that was women's business—though he ate the eggs readily enough when they could be had. And the goat was gone, probably staked out to graze what winter grass there was behind the house. Maybe Sym had done that, Meg thought.

She gave a silent prayer of thanks for so much help from her boys—or from Hewe, if that was the case—and picked up her cloak. They had told her at the priory that there was no need for her to come back the day after her husband's burying, but with the holiday there was always extra kitchen work to hand. She would be needed, and the priory was a better place to be than here.

There was no trace of last night's sleet. Thin, unwarm sunlight gave brightness to the frozen road and village, but Meg hardly bothered noticing. There was the field path that cut from her end of the village along the hedgerows to come out on the road near the priory gate. That was her usual way to the priory, but as she crossed the road toward it, she glanced leftward toward the village green beyond the church. This time of year there were rarely gatherings of any size outdoors, but from what she could see a goodly portion of the village was clustered on the green. The church hid whatever they were looking at, and with plain curiosity and a little fear Meg turned that way.

But there was nothing fearful. The travelers from the priory had set up some sort of wooden framework on the green, a little taller than a tall man, twice as wide as it was high, and hung with thick red curtains that showed their fading and patching in the sunlight. The villagers were gathered in front of it, and the older man among the travelers was standing before the curtains saying in a powerful, clear voice, ". . . so by your lady prioress's leave we give to you this day the play of *The Statue of St. Nicholas,* that it may please you good folk of Prior Byfield."

He swept as elegant a bow as Meg had ever seen and disappeared around the end of the framework, behind the curtain. Meg had seen players once; some had come to the village when she was a girl. They had been funny, she remembered. And they had wanted money at the end of their performing. So would these, she supposed, and would not have stopped to watch except that she saw Hewe near one edge of the crowd and after a moment's hesitation went to join him.

He gave her a brief look and smile but returned his attention to the curtain as a man came from behind it. This one wore a high-collared, scarlet robe that swept to his feet and was patterned all over with gold-painted crosses and lambs. He carried a fancy curve-topped staff in one hand and wore a tall mitred hat to show he was a bishop, and his face was all immobile with solemnity, his eyes gazing off somewhere above everybody's head as if to Heaven. The crowd murmured with admiration.

Ignoring them, he stepped up on a low box waiting in front of the curtain and struck a pose, his free hand raised in blessing, and froze there. Immediately a lady came from behind the curtain, willowy and fair, her long blue dress trailing on the grass behind her. She was carrying a small chest. Coming roundabout with stately, light-footed grace to the waiting man, she knelt and set the chest on the ground in front of him, then clasped her hands together as if in prayer, raised her eyes to him imploringly and said in an affected, high voice, "O Nicholas, I must a journey make. Guard thou my wealth for Jesu's sake. No other may I trust but thee. Help me as thou did the virgins three. Thou wilt ever my favor earn, if my wealth is here when I return."

The man did not move or answer but the lady seemed satisfied. She rose and turned away toward the curtain, gracefully swirling her gown. Meg, seeing her face plainly for the first time, realized with a start that the lady was the pale-haired young man called Joliffe. She leaned to comment on that to Hewe, but as the "lady" went away behind one end of the curtain, another player appeared promptly at its other end. Dark-browed and skulking, wrapped in a black cloak, he peered around him and apparently saw no one, though the nearest of the crowd was hardly ten paces from him and some were already calling out warnings to the lady to come back. Chuckling wickedly, he slunk toward the motionless man, peered around again and snatched up the chest.

"No, no," Meg complained under her breath. "Why doesn't St. Nicholas see him and stop him? The lady told him to watch her treasure."

Hewe, without taking his eyes from the players, leaned near to her ear and whispered, "He's a statue of St. Nicholas, that's why. He can't move. All he can do is stand there. Isn't he grand? Doesn't he hold still as a statue grandly?"

The thief, clutching the chest, slunk out of sight, back the way he had come. As he went around the curtain, Rose appeared at its other end, wearing a saffron yellow gown that fit closely down to her hips and then flared into full skirts embroidered with green around the hem. Without pause she did three backward flips across the front of the curtains, made a quick, clever curtsey to the crowd, and went the way the thief had gone.

The "lady" reappeared, wearing a traveler's cloak. She came toward the statue, saw the chest was gone, looked around for it frantically, then threw up her hands in dismay and cried out, "O heavy, cruel chance! My treasures are fled! Now I must live in want and dread. Money and goods I entrusted to you, but like all mankind, you have failed me, too. To you I gave prayers and all my trust. Revenge I'll take, as I surely must." She reached under the near edge of the curtain and drew out a short riding whip. "I shall beat you, day and night, until my treasures are back in my sight."

The women cheered and the men booed as she pretended to beat the statue about the back and shoulders. But Meg quickly saw that none of the blows actually hit the statue, and the men began to laugh and the women to jeer. But St. Nicholas never flinched and the lady finally threw down the whip with a sobbing cry and fell to her knees, her face buried in her hands, her shoulders shaking with grief. As she did, the thief reappeared at the far end of the curtain, still clutching the chest. He looked around, seemed to see no one, came further into the open and set the chest on the ground. Opening it, he began to gloat over its contents. Meg craned her neck but could not see what it held, and then was distracted as St. Nicholas, who had been so motionless all this while, stirred. With an awful majesty, he lowered his upraised hand until it was pointing at the thief and in a deep and angry voice he said, "Wretched man, you're not unseen." The thief straightened with a huge start; the crowd laughed. St. Nicholas went on, "Your crime is not unknown. For you my back has beaten been. Bring back these stolen things whose loss has caused such sorrow—" The lady gave a loud, trembling sob. "—or surely on a gibbet high will you be hanged tomorrow."

The thief had turned a terrified gaze on the saint while he spoke, and gradually sank horrified and penitent under the threatening words and voice. Now, in scrambling haste, he grabbed up the chest, sprang to his feet, and hurriedly came to set it down between the crying lady and St. Nicholas who, after a slow, approving, lordly nod, returned to his former statue pose. The thief scurried out of sight and the lady, after a few more fading sobs, raised her head to see the chest set on the ground in front of her. She cried out in delight, "Here is my treasure come again! Joy of my heart, where have you been? Excellent saint, guardian of all, what was lost is here in full. My thanks to you will never dull."

The saint's head inclined to her and he said in the same solemn voice he had used to the thief, "Pray not to me, good sister, but rather only to God. He made the heavens, he made the earth, and by his power is this restored. Leave off your love of worldly ways and turn your love to God."

As he spoke the lady had fallen back in wondering astonishment. When he finished, she stood up, clasped her hands, and exclaimed joyfully, "Here will be no hesitation. This message is a visitation. I will give these goods to all the poor, and serve sweet Jesu evermore. With his blessing I will no more sin, and a treasure in Heaven I will win."

Behind the curtain someone began to play a glad carol on a recorder. The lady reached up to St. Nicholas, who took her hand to step down from his box. Together they turned to face the crowd, and the thief came from behind the curtain to join them, grinning, as Rose came from behind the other side, playing the recorder. The three men bowed to the villagers' ragged but cheerful applause, and Meg realized the play was done. Rose changed to another merry tune, and the saint, the lady, and the thief spread out among the crowd, the former thief holding out his cap, the saint and lady the front of their gowns to collect whatever coins might come their way. Most folk merely drew back, shaking their heads and holding up empty hands, but some dug into pouches for coins. A little glitter of halfpennies gathered in cap and skirts. Not many—coin was scarce in the village—but some; and Constance, who lived in the nearest cottage, hurried inside and hurried back with a good-sized half loaf. She gave it to the saint, who thanked her with so elegant a kiss on the hand that she giggled. Jenet of the forge, liking the look of that, hasted off to bring back an end of bacon. She offered it to the thief and was given a gallant kiss of her own.

The players were taking whatever was offered cheerfully, though Meg noticed the saint tended to find out the older women; the thief seemed mostly to go among the girls, collecting kisses when he could not have a coin; and Joliffe, still playing the lady, teased the men into giving their coins. Gilbey Dunn, boisterously laughing at "her" flirting, tossed a whole penny in his lap and clapped Joliffe on the shoulder in such high good humor it nearly knocked him down.

"Ho, Gilbey," Thad the smith called out. "Is it her fair face or tiny feet you're liking?"

Gilbey's grin broadened. "Mind your tongue or your face won't be so fair, either, my lad," he answered.

There was general laughter for that, because Thad was years past being a lad and his face was as gnarled and knotted as an old hedge stump.

Meanwhile Ellis had made his way to pretty Tibby, the alewife's daughter, and gave her another kiss, not on the hand, and willingly received.

Meg had not seen Sym until then; but now he was there, coming from somewhere to stand behind the girl, a little too closely, a little too possessively. The flush of red up his face at the player's boldness was darker than Tibby's pleased, laughing blush, and Meg with a sudden pang knew, from the way he looked more than ever like his father, what he was meaning to do next. She called out, "Don't, Sym!" but it was already too late.

Reaching over Tibby's shoulder, he gave Ellis a hard shove and said, "There's enough of that. Go kiss your own 'lady' and leave mine alone."

That brought laughter from the villagers around them, and someone called out for Joliffe to come kiss "yon handsome thief." Tibby, used to village ways, stepped quickly out from between Sym and Ellis, leaving them facing each other. Ellis, without taking his gaze from Sym, held his cap out sidewise.

Joliffe, suddenly there, took it and faded backwards in one easy motion, his arm linked through Tibby's to draw her with him further out of reach.

Ellis, left in a suddenly opened space among the villagers, made no threatening move, only said in a peaceable voice, "I was only admiring a fair face, not seeking to take her away. No harm in that."

"There's maybe harm and maybe not," Sym said sullenly, with a slur to his voice that told Meg he had already been to the alehouse this morning. "What about the harm to my father, thief? How much harm did you do him?"

"No harm at all except to lift him out of a frozen ditch and take him to help."

"But who put him in that ditch, hey? What do you know about that, that you're not telling? Who put him there in the first place? That's what I'm asking."

"I'd guess he got there the same way you've come here," Ellis replied coolly. "By way of an alehouse and a few too many emptied cups."

Hewe pulled against Meg's fingers digging into shoulders. She let him go and pushed past him toward Sym. If she could get her hands on him, distract him—

She was too late. Stung and out of words, Sym lunged at Ellis. The player stepped back from him without apparent haste or fear, and abruptly Sym was sitting on the ground, looking astonished.

Meg stopped, cowed by fright, not understanding what had happened, only that it was uncanny. But the villagers were laughing, especially the men and even Hewe. It had all come too suddenly, and now before Sym could rise, the player saint had his hand on Ellis's shoulder, drawing him away. Joliffe was already well out of it, to the side of the crowd with Tibby, whispering something in her ear that was making her smile and flirt her eyes at him, not heeding Ellis, or Sym, anymore at all. Rose had gathered up the box and chest and was going behind the curtain. It was over, except for the laughter.

But Sym gave a gutteral grunt and began to scamble to his feet, clearly intent on continuing the fight. Meg pushed her way between the useless village men and flung herself at him, meaning to shove him down again if she could. "Stop it!" she exclaimed. "You'll not be brawling like a lout with their kind! And on the green in front of everyone. Stop it!"

Sym pushed back at her, too deep in his anger to care. "They're thieves!" he yelled. "Thieves and murderers! Da'd be alive except for them and you're going to let them go their ways, them and their indecent woman and their bastard brat, leaving Da dead in his grave!"

Meg clutched his arm and was dragged around as he tried to shove past her. It was Rose's white, rigid face she saw first, standing beside the curtains beyond the crowd. And then she saw Ellis, wrenched free from Thomas Bassett, coming for Sym with murder in his furious eyes.

Chapter 12

THOMAS BASSETT MOVED more quickly than seemed possible for one his age and weight. Bursting from among the villagers, he shouldered in front of Ellis, pushed him back one-handed and thundered in St. Nicholas's rich voice, "That's enough! Back off, the two of you! Ellis, there's the frame to take down and Piers waiting back at the nunnery for us. Come on."

Meg, still clinging to Sym, with Hewe now hanging on his other arm, saw the fury drain out of Ellis. His face and then his fists slacked. Keeping an eye on Sym, he drew back, then turned away, snapping at Joliffe to come help. And now some of the village men elbowed in around Sym, clapping him on the back and jibing at him friendliwise, trying to draw him off, too. Sym resisted more than Ellis had, shrugging their hands away and swearing, but Meg knew the fighting anger was gone out of him, and let him go. He was drunk enough not to be sure where his quarrel was gone, and they would have it out of his mind altogether in a minute.

But lurching against Hamon's and Peter's pulling on him, he blundered face to face with Gilbey Dunn who held his ground and said, grinning, "Homeward bound, Sym? Making an early day of it?"

Sym knew an old quarrel when it came his way. He jerked loose from his two friends. "You'd be knowing about early days, wouldn't you? And late nights, sneaking out and sneaking in, looking to grab what isn't yours and nipping to the steward every chance you find to tell him how much better our holding would be in your foul-fingered keeping. And now Da's gone, you're nipping after his widow, thinking that's a warmer way to have it. Only you'll not be getting it that way either. You'll be dead first, Gilbey Dunn. Mark me on it! Cold in a grave like Da before you lay hands on anything of his!"

"Sym!" Meg cried in anguished warning. Everyone's attention was swung to Sym and Gilbey, and clearly Gilbey's temper was come up now to match Sym's. His face was dark with it, his eyes gone small and hard, his mouth tight. But all he said was, "You've a bad mouth on you when it's wet with ale. Hamon, Peter, take him home or somewhere else until his head's clear."

Peter, a burly-shouldered youth a little quicker in his wits than Hamon, understood. As if it were all a joke, he said, "Hoy, Sym, there's no sport here. Let's be off."

Sym looked around at him, distracted. Peter swung an arm around his shoulders. "Come on, then," he said heartily. "Let's see what's about at my place." He leaned his head near to Sym's. "There was a bit of honeycomb left the last I looked. How's that sound? Hamon, can you lay hands on some bread?"

Hamon, not much stronger-headed than Sym, blinked and brightened. "Cor, I can that, Peter. Why didn't you say about the honeycomb before?" He hurried off.

To Meg's relief, Sym gave way to Peter's friendly pulling on him. "You hurry!" he yelled after Hamon, and lurched away, leaning on Peter's shoulder. Hewe hesitated, glancing at his mother, then trailed after them. Everyone else, now that the entertainment was fully over, began to drift away.

But Gilbey Dunn stayed a moment longer and said to Meg, low voiced, "He's going to give you trouble, no matter what you do. Think on what I offered. You'll be in safekeeping then, and have someone to keep an eye on him. He needs a man's hand."

"He doesn't like you."

"He'll not be liking anyone that tries to steer him right.

He's Barnaby's own son in making bad choices and you can see it as well as I can."

"You shouldn't be talking so of Barnaby, now he's dead."

Gilbey shrugged. "I wasn't saying ill, only what's true. You know it is as well as I do. You'll never be able to manage Sym and all on your own. And you know I'll deal fair by you. There's none ever been able to say that I don't deal fair."

But Sym had just been saying exactly that; and Barnaby had said it often enough these past months while fighting to hold his own against Gilbey's efforts to have Barnaby's share of field strips and manor rights for himself. But Sym had been talking out of too much ale, and Barnaby out of the ills he had mostly brought on himself. Meg did not know where the truth lay so she kept quiet, looking at the ground between them until Gilbey said with a shrug, "You think on it, Meg," and went away.

Meg stayed, looking at the dead, stiff grass in front of her feet and trying to think. Gilbey might be right about her marrying him. It would surely make things easier. And it did not much matter that she did not like him. But Sym would hate it. No matter how it might work out for the best, he would never make peace with it. Meg was sure of that, and sure that Gilbey knew it, too. But maybe it did not matter to him. Not the way it had to matter to her.

She was abruptly aware that she was cold and that the little she had had to eat was gone and she was hungry again and she had to go to work or there would be no money today. It would have been good to sit down by someone's hearth and talk. But she had somewhere along her way lost the women who had been her friends. The other village women seemed to resent her trying so hard to make things better. They nodded and spoke when she met them, but there was none of them she talked to, and none who came to talk to her.

Her way had taken her without thinking back past the church, across the graveyard toward the field path that ran behind the hedges to St. Frideswide's. She paused at Barnaby's grave. Its dark earth was heaped in clods frozen too solid for the shovels' breaking. Come spring and the rains, they would soften and slump down into a proper mound, and grow grass, and next year a hollow would mark the place instead of raw, broken earth. Meg tried to think of a prayer but nothing came. Barnaby had made confession and been shriven and given last rites. Then he had slept, and died, and no man's soul could have gone to Abraham's bosom more pure and cleansed than that. He was surely there now, in brightness and warmth, with angel choruses singing and the sight of the wicked tormented in Hell far below to entertain him. And someday, with God's help, she and her boys would join him there, as pure and cleansed of sin as he had been.

Meg sank into that thought of being always warm and never hungry in place of her cold and hunger here and now; then started as she realized she was wasting time, and hurried on toward the priory.

Frevisse had come to see how matters went in the guest-hall. With so few guests, and only the older hall occupied these holy days, her duties were few and easily done. She first made sure the servants were not slacking their few duties and then went to see how Piers did, left to himself while the rest of the players were at the village.

He was curled in a nest of blankets, obediently staying down, watching the small fire dance in the hearth. Hearing her coming, he twisted around to see, and showed his disappointment that it was not his mother or the others coming. Frevisse smiled at him and bent down to feel his forehead. It was only slightly warmer than it should have been and the fever brightness was out of his eyes.

"How are you feeling?" she asked.

"Hungry, my lady," he said, croaking only a little. He looked at her expectantly, as if she might have something edible up her sleeve or in a pocket.

Frevisse regretted she did not, but only said, "That's a good sign. Would you like a drink?"

"Milk?" Piers asked hopefully.

Frevisse shook her head. "Water."

Piers sighed and nodded. Frevisse fetched the cup from the bucket for him. While he drank, she asked, "Shouldn't you be trying to sham illness a while longer, so you can all go on staying here?''

Piers looked at her scornfully as he handed the cup back. ''What's the use of that?'' he asked. ''There's money to be had in Oxford, and good times at the Rose and Crown, and not much of either here. There's better places than here to be, and not much use in staying in one place for very long.''

What Frevisse could have answered to that was forestalled by the players' noisy return from the village. Their loud voices dropped as they crossed the threshold but their arguing went on, intense and maybe not completely cheerful, with Bassett saying, ''So couldn't you have found someone else to flirt with that didn't have her sweetheart lowering over her shoulder, and him already angry with us?''

''Am I supposed to care about that clod-witted lout?'' Ellis asked. ''She was the best of the lot, as pretty a thing as I've seen since Michaelmas.''

''And willing as well as lovely,'' Joliffe added.

Ellis grinned. ''Yea, you were quick to notice that, I noticed. And left me to handle her angry clod while you looked for a chance to handle her.''

''Well, it didn't come to handling for either of us, did it? So there's an end of it.''

''That's enough,'' said Rose. ''Here's Dame Frevisse, who doesn't need to hear your nonsense.''

Piers lifted his head out of his nest again and asked, ''Was Ellis in a fight again?''

''Hush, pigsney,'' said Rose, stooping to lift the blond thatch from his face and feel his forehead.

''I'm almost better,'' Piers said, ducking from her hand. ''Dame Frevisse says so. Ellis, did—''

''Look here, Piers,'' Bassett interrupted deftly, holding out the half loaf of bread and end of bacon.

''Ah!'' Piers's enthusiasm quickly changed direction. ''Is that for eating now?''

''No better time,'' Bassett said, and broke a generous chunk from the loaf to stuff into the boy's mouth. Then he held out a cap and jingled it under Piers's nose. ''We're set for our journey to Oxford, too. We can have Tisbe shod.''

Piers removed the bread wad from his mouth. "Then can we leave now? I'm nearly well. Well enough. I could have gone with you to see Ellis start that fight in the village."

"I never start fights," Ellis said. He sat down on his heels beside the boy and pushed the hair back off his forehead, making a playful gesture of feeling for a fever.

Piers, clearly bored with being sick, pushed his hand away. Sucking on the chunk of bread, he said, "I'm thirsty." He thrashed at his blankets, making a tangle of them. "Was it a good fight? Who did you fight?"

Rose handed him a cup of water while Ellis patiently untangled him and said, "Nobody. I just sat this villein down on the ground to think about the error of his ways. It's Joliffe I'm going to fight with if he doesn't stop stealing my girls."

"I can't steal what isn't yours," Joliffe said. He had taken the bread from Bassett and was slicing it into five equal pieces. His dagger sliced through the thick crust and tough brown bread effortlessly, Frevisse noticed; and when Ellis drew his own to reach across the distance and spear his share, Frevisse said in surprise, "Your knives match, yours and Joliffe's."

Bassett drew his own and held it out for her to see. "And mine, as well," he said.

The blades were an identical shape and the handles, of wood with copper wire inserts, also matched.

"And my mother's," Piers added around a mouthful of bread. "And mine, too. Only they won't let me have it yet. They say I'm too young." His tone scorned that notion.

"We played at a wedding up Sheffield way," Bassett said. "We were a little larger company then and did one of our better plays—"

"Not," said Joliffe, pressing a hand over his face and shaking his head in mock shame, "*The Statue of St. Nicholas.*"

"Don't be complaining," Rose said. "St. Nicholas brought in a pretty number of pence." She dumped the coins into her lap and tossed the hat at Ellis. "I'd not have thought there were so many to be had from the place. A whole penny," she added in admiration. She looked at it close up.

"From Henry the Fifth. Probably in the peasant's pouch these twelve years and more since his grace died, I'd not be surprised."

"They'd not seen players in a while. And it's the holidays so they were ready for a bit of sport," Bassett said. He had dropped wearily onto a bench and was surveying his group with fulfilled pleasure. "All in all a good morning's work." He looked at Frevisse. "I don't suppose there are any more villages near to hand?"

"The nearest is two hours' walk away," Frevisse said.

"And two hours back. Too far for a short winter's day," Bassett said regretfully. "But as to the wedding that brought us our daggers, we did so well that the bridegroom—he'd made his fortune forging steel—gave us these, being his specialty, beyond our agreed fee. A gentleman, and generous. Somewhere there's three more like these loose in the world, but they went when our company broke." He brooded into some distant thought, his mouth grim. "But that's another story."

"And not for here and now," Rose added. "Is anyone going to cook that bacon, or are we going to sit here staring at it until it rots?"

"It's not likely to rot in this cold," Joliffe said. "What happened to mild winters? I don't suppose anyone could arrange for spring to come next week and warm the world for a while?"

"I don't suppose you could arrange for me to warm that girl you filched today?" Ellis returned.

"It's not my fault she prefers my charm to your brawn."

Frevisse, smiling inwardly, left them to what were clearly their familiar ways and went about her own.

Meg's tasks kept her at the priory until the sun was going down. It was New Year's Eve and there were special little things to be cooked, not just for tomorrow but for afterward because the day after New Year's was going to be given over to killing and readying the chickens meant for the pies Domina Edith had said the nunnery would have for Twelfth Night.

''So there's more than enough that has to be done if we're having holiday tomorrow and there's going to be dead chickens all over here afterward,'' Dame Alys had declared. ''Nasty, messy business, and I hope there's sage enough to see us through—someone's been wanton fisted with it again—or the pies won't be worth eating. Don't thump that pan down like that, you'll kill the pudding and then I'll thump you.'' Narrow-eyed with hostility but still tired from her cold, she did not rise from her stool but contented herself with pointing her spoon like a sword at the offender, who out of habit ducked. Anyone who worked in her kitchen quickly learned to keep clear of her if possible. But there was no keeping clear of her temper and when the day was over, Meg dragged herself out of the kitchen into the quiet of the back passage from the cloister in a weariness too deep even for thankfulness.

Out of the kitchen's heat of ovens and cooking, the air bit deeply into her thin flesh. From habit, not from any hope of it doing any good, Meg huddled her cloak more tightly around her and let herself out the back way into the side yard that ran between the nunnery and its outer wall and opened by another gateway into the courtyard at the front, from where she could take the road until she reached the field path again.

The sun was a deepening gold, swollen in the cloud-clear sky as it dropped to setting. Across the fields under the sweep of sunset light, darkness was already gathered in the grass and along the hedge line, waiting to take the world as soon as the sun slipped away; and Meg hurried, driven as much by the coming darkness as the cold, wanting to be home and close to her own fire.

If someone had bothered to bring in wood. If someone had bothered to feed it to the fire.

There was no one in sight as she came past the church and along the frozen ruts to her house. The sun was gone and everything in twilight shadows. Yellow light showed here and there at cottages where a window's shutter did not fit close enough; but there was only darkness at her own, she saw as she came to it, and her faint hope of a fire and warmth sank lower.

But after all, as she opened the door, there was a glow on the hearth from wood burned down to coals but still alive. Warmth, and familiar smells of woodsmoke and animals wrapped around her as she closed the door at her back. Hewe was there. He turned from laying hay in front of the goat. In the half darkness she could not see his face clearly but his voice was cheerful. "I made the fire, Mam. Only I've waited to build it up again so it wouldn't be gone before you came."

"And brought in Nankin," Meg said, letting approval come into her voice. "You're a good son, Hewe. And the chickens?"

"They're fed and watered." His voice fell, waiting for her to be angry as he added, "But I've not cleaned their mess yet."

Meg was too glad of the fire to care. "That can bide. Come to the warmth now."

"And one of them's dead," Hewe added in almost a whisper.

Meg sighed and sank down on one of the three-legged stools close to the hearth, opening her cloak to the warmth, holding her hands out over the coals. "That can't be helped," she said wearily. "Maybe I'll set it to boiling tonight and we'll have a New Year's feast of it. Come lay wood on the fire for me. My hands are that stiff with cold I don't know if I could."

Hewe came and with great care built up the fire until it danced, throwing shadows and light around the room and over his face. Meg fondly watched him watching the flames, and after a while said, "Where's your brother? Why isn't he here helping you?"

Hewe did not look around from the fire. "He's at the alehouse, or near it, I'd guess." Sym was willing to do for others the chores he neglected at home, because of the few coins he could earn to drink away at the alehouse. "And like to be out for a while."

The shabby cottage that served as gathering place for idle men and dishonest women had been his father's place and he looked like making it his own, too. Then, like his father, let him take the consequences. "There's something in the flour kist," Meg said. "You bring it to me."

"Something besides flour?" Hewe asked in surprise.

"Besides flour." Though precious little of that there was. She must be making some deal with the miller, or finding a way to buy or barter some from Dame Alys.

"What's this?" Hewe asked, puzzled, holding out the orange that Barnaby had brought from Lord Lovel's feasting.

"A treat for us," said Meg. She had kept it in her apron until she had come home again; and put it in the flour kist for safekeeping. "Look you." She wiped the flour off of it with her cloak and held it out into the firelight so its color glowed and its strangeness showed.

Hesitantly Hewe reached out a forefinger to touch it, stroked it cautiously, and then drew back. "What is it? Where did you find it?"

"Hold it," Meg said. "It's not tender. Go on."

Hewe took it, turning it around and around in his hands while she told him where it had come from, how his father had earned it.

"By singing for the lord?" Hewe asked.

"Noble folk like to be entertained when they're feasting," Meg said. "And do you know what we're to do with it now?" Hewe shook his head. "Eat it!" she said triumphantly.

Hewe prodded at its hardness doubtfully, as Meg had when she first held it. But she had seen what Dame Frevisse had done, and held out her hand for it. "Give it to me. I'll show you."

It proved to be more messy than she had thought. The thing was no more like an apple under its rind than it was without, but they managed it at last, pulling it into the slices already formed, once they understood how it was put together. They shared the pieces between them, laughing and delighted at the tart sweetness and juice and surprise of it all, until the orange was all gone except for its peel, and they were themselves fragrantly messy, hands and faces both.

When they had washed the stickiness away, and Meg was on her stool again with Hewe sitting beside her, his head leaning on her knee, he sighed. "That was grand. All that, just for singing for Lord Lovel."

"Umm." Meg was not much listening. Warmth and weariness were overtaking her. She had meant to think about Gilbey's offer tonight, but thoughts did not seem to want to come.

"I could do that," Hewe said.

"What?"

"Sing for Lord Lovel. Or dance, maybe. I can dance, you've seen me. So they would give me things. Or pay me. Like the players did today. They did their play and then people gave them money."

Meg had hardly thought of this morning's nonsense on the green since it had ended. A little sharply she said, "That's not man's work! Dressing up and pretending some foolish tale. And look what sort of folk they are. Not decent, wandering the roads and belonging nowhere."

"It looked as good a sort of work as any I've seen," Hewe said warmly, sitting up away from her, his face taking on all the rebelliousness he otherwise saved for saying he did not want to be a priest.

Meg opened her mouth, wanting a sharp reply to put sense in his head, but the door fell open from someone's heavy thrust and in a draft of cold air and night's blackness, Sym lurched into the room.

He was drunk. That much was immediately clear. He staggered against the doorpost and stayed there, gaping at her as if not remembering where he was or why. And sometime he had fallen; one knee of his breeches was torn through its patch and where she would find another piece of cloth to mend it again, Meg did not know. That, added to Hewe's foolishness, made her angry, all the contentment of hardly a moment before gone in a frustrated urge to hurt him back the way he was hurting her.

"If you're that drunk, Sym, take you off to someone's sty and sleep it off," she snapped. "You're not to come in here to be sick."

He slurred, "Mam . . ." and swayed forward from the doorway, leaving it open behind him.

"He stinks," Hewe said disgustedly, moving away from him. "He stinks like Da did."

"You stink, brat!" Sym snarled. "Of mother's milk, baby. I'm going to rub your head with knuckles till it bleeds, you come in reach of me!"

"Hewe, close the door. There's no need we have to freeze because he's drunk."

Hewe circled his brother to obey. Sym lurched for him but Hewe was too used to that to be caught. He deftly avoided him and in the doorway said over his shoulder to Meg, "I'm off to Peter's for the night. When I see Sym's sober I'll be back."

Meg cried out, "Hewe!" but he was gone, pulling the door shut behind him, leaving her alone with Sym, whose lurch had carried him on sidewise to fetch up against the table where he leaned, resting his weight on one arm, his head bent down. His other arm had been wrapped across his stomach. He moved it, held out his hand in front of him and frowned at the dark gleam of it in the firelight. "Mam." He sounded bewildered. "I'm bleeding."

Chapter 13

FOR THE DAY'S last prayers at Compline, St. Frideswide's nuns were spared the cold rigors of the church. At the bell's ringing of the hour, they laid aside their reading and handwork in the warming room, Dame Alys put out the candles, and in the gentle glow of the firelight Domina Edith led them in their prayers.

Frevisse enjoyed this brief while between the ending of each day's tasks and the going to bed by twilight in summer, in darkness in winter. Even marred this evening by coughing and snuffling, the prayers held their promised peace for a day done and a night of rest to come, and ended as they always did with, "The Lord Almighty grant us a quiet night and a perfect end. Amen."

As they finished, Sister Lucy sneezed heavily, Dame Perpetua coughed until it seemed she must suffocate, Dame Alys trumpeted into her handkerchief, and Frevisse thought with a private sigh that a quiet night did not seem likely. But two women from the kitchen bustled in with a pitcher of hot spiced wine and cups and such bread as was left over from supper, and Frevisse let go future woe for the present pleasure of that warmth before the cold walk through the cloister to bed.

By rights, when the time came to make their soft-footed, skirt-whispering way along the dark cloister walk, Domina

Edith should have led them, and left them at the foot of the dormitory stairs to go with her servant on around the cloister to her own rooms. But the prioress was well aware of how slowly she moved these days, and of how cold the nights were. So tonight she gave her nuns leave to go on ahead of her, smiling gently and bowing her head to their curtsies before they hurried out the door into the darkness between the warming-room door and the lantern left lighted by the dormitory steps.

They were already on the stairs when they heard the rabble of sound from the courtyard. Where there should have been only the night's thick black silence, there were voices rising in anger. Raggedly, losing their haste, the nuns stopped, turning toward the noise, startled.

"Outlaws!" Sister Amicia whispered. "They're breaking in! We'll all be raped!"

This might have started a panic among the nuns, except that Dame Alys likewise broke the rule of silence. *"Hold!"* she bellowed, and such was her authority, and volume, that the nuns froze in place.

Sister Fiacre made the sign for church and began to push herself feebly against the nuns in her way. But one of them was Dame Alys, and she was not to be moved. Her large, steadfast presence was a rock against which the tide of frightened women broke uselessly.

Dame Claire raised her hand in signal to Frevisse, who nodded, and the two stepped the other way down the cloister walk toward the gate that led to the courtyard. Dame Alys watched them go with such concentration that the others began to notice the direction of her gaze and, seeing two nuns who were not afraid—who were in fact moving toward the danger—their own courage was restored. Only then did Dame Alys begin to lead them toward the church in a silent, orderly procession.

As Frevisse and Dame Claire reached the outer door, it was clear from the noise that whatever was happening was directed at the older guesthall, not at the cloister door. As Frevisse reached for the latch, the voices rose in a kind of animal triumph. Dame Claire crossed herself. By the sound of it, there were going to be people hurt. Frevisse lifted the latch and went out.

Confused for a moment in the suddenness of torchlight, she paused. There were perhaps a dozen men struggling in a knot outside the old guesthall door. Some were carrying torches whose spasmed light jerked and flared and hid almost as much as it showed as the men wrestled and struck at something in their midst. Only one of them she recognized surely—Roger Naylor, the steward. At the edge of the melee, he was trying to drag men back, yelling at them to stop.

Frevisse grabbed her skirts out of her way and crossed the courtyard at a deft-footed run, adding her voice to Naylor's. "Stop this! You've no right here! Stop it!"

She was unheeded, but as if spurred on by her presence, Naylor shoved in among the men, dragging first one and then another back from their violence until he was wedged well in among them, still shouting for them to stop. Frevisse tried to follow. These were village men; once they knew she and Naylor were there, they would stop. But they were too furious to notice anything but their goal, struggling against each other toward the center where more men were bent down holding and striking at someone under them.

Naylor drove a hard fist sideways into the ribs of a man to his left. The man, clutching a torch, reeled backwards. Frevisse caught at his elbow, shoving it up to keep the fire from her face, and shook him, demanding, "How dare you come here like this?"

The man gaped at her, seeing in a single glance who and what she was, then jerked free and backed off, throwing the torch to the cobbles before he turned and ran blundering off into the darkness.

"Naylor!" she called. "Are you all right?"

Naylor was too busy to reply. He dragged another man back by his tunic neck, pushed him aside, and grabbed for a third. The first man, staggering to balance, went snarling at Naylor's back. Frevisse stepped forward and kicked hard at his knee. Her swing, shortened by her skirt, staggered him without bringing him down and he swung around on her furiously, fist rising. Frevisse flung up her arm but fright doused his anger before he struck. He pushed back from her, mumbling, "Pardon, lady, pardon." He turned to run, shouting, "Look, men! The nuns are come!"

"And you might take note of Master Naylor, too," Frevisse said acidly, unheard.

Distracted, the men began pulling back from their victim, helped by Naylor's final shoves and curses. "It's enough, damn you," he snarled. "Pull back. You've done enough."

"More than enough," Dame Claire said. Frevisse was suddenly aware that Dame Claire was directly behind her. Now with a reined anger and unshaken nerves, the infirmarian went in among the men. They readily yielded to her passing, and she went to her knees beside the man they had been pummeling.

At her voice he warily uncurled from the ball he had made of himself. Naylor grabbed a torch from someone and held it for Dame Claire to see him better.

Frevisse, with dismay, recognized Ellis.

But he seemed little hurt. A smear of blood from some cut hidden in his hair was trailing down his cheek in front of his ear, and he was holding one hand to the back of his head and the other to his ribs, but he looked up at Dame Claire with a grimace and said, "Thank God there were so many of them. They might have made a competent job of it otherwise."

"Let me feel," Dame Claire ordered, pulling his hand away from his side.

Frevisse, leaving her to it, turned savagely on the men around her. "So what do you mean, coming like this, laying hands on a guest of the priory?"

The man who had nearly hit her, squarely built, with a blunt face and blunter manners, said, "He's stabbed young Sym. We come to get him 'fore he can be away."

"You pursued him even into here?"

"Pursued be damned," Ellis said. He winced from Dame Claire's probing at his ribs. "They dragged me out of the guesthall. Where I've been since well before sundown and nowhere near this Sym."

"It were a player done it. His mam said so. Said he said so. And it's you he fought with this morning," the man said.

"That doesn't mean I did it." Ellis flinched as Dame Claire parted his hair to find his wound. "I haven't left here tonight and I've not been stabbing anyone."

"No," Joliffe said with dispassionate arrogance. "But I probably did."

He was standing in the guesthall doorway, with darkness behind him and the red flare of torchlight in front, catching and losing his finally drawn features as he added, as if lightly amused, "But you all came in so sudden and grabbed so quick without saying why, you never gave me chance to say, did you?"

"You bench-bred cur—" the blunt-faced man said, starting to move toward him.

Roger Naylor stepped in front of the man, facing Joliffe, and said the same thing that was in Frevisse's mind. "So what do you mean, saying a fool thing like it was 'probably' you who stabbed him? You don't look drunk enough to not know whether you knifed a man or not."

"I'm not drunk at all," Joliffe answered. Frevisse had seen his mouth tighten at the villager's insult but his voice was still as casual as before. Only the glint in his eyes was dangerous, telling her he knew exactly what he was doing in drawing the men off Ellis to himself. "I went to that little rathole of an alehouse but I'd hardly sat myself down when this Sym of yours decided he didn't want me there. I never had chance to drink."

"And why would he be minding you there, if it was this fellow here he fought with today?" Naylor demanded, gesturing at Ellis.

"Maybe because of the girl I was sitting by. She didn't mind but he did."

Ellis, ducking away from Dame Claire's probing fingers, said indignantly, "That's why you were so set on going? That's what you did while I was laying him out this morning? Arranged to meet her there?"

Joliffe shrugged. "She said she'd be there. Said she'd not mind if I came. So I went."

"But Sym objected," Frevisse said.

"Very much." Joliffe matched her dry tone. "And he'd

had ale enough to make up for what I never had a chance to drink. He wouldn't take talking to, not by me or the girl, and when I went to leave he came for me."

"So you drew your dagger in defense," Naylor said.

"I never drew my dagger at all. There wasn't time. He had his knife out when he came for me, and I grabbed his wrist and kept hold if it, that's all. We lurched around and fell over a bench, twisting as we went so he was on the bottom. I sprang clear, told some of his friends they'd best hold him there until I was gone, and I left."

"And came back here," Naylor said.

Joliffe hesitated, then agreed, "And came back here."

"Or lay in wait to knife him in the dark!" someone yelled from the crowd.

"I could have," Joliffe returned as loudly. "Only I didn't."

"Easy to say!" someone else yelled. Drawn off Ellis, they were stilling wanting vengeance and Joliffe would do as well as any other stranger. Frevisse eased sideways around someone, meaning to put herself between them and Joliffe. But Naylor moved more openly, stepping directly out into the space between him and the villagers, and said in a voice as roused with anger as their own, "And understand that talk is all that's going to happen until we've had a chance to ask Sym himself. Were any of you at the alehouse, to say if what he's said so far is true?"

With a grumble and shuffle, six of the men showed they had been there.

"So," Naylor demanded, "did it happen the way he says? Sym drew on him and they fought and fell and then he left?"

The men shifted and looked at one another, twitched elbows at each other's ribs, until finally one of them said, "Aye. That was the way of it. Just like he says."

Frevisse was at Naylor's side now, between the crowd and Joliffe, a naked place to be, the small torch-glared space between one man and the crowding, anger-harshened faces, but she set her voice bold as Naylor's to ask, "So was Sym's knife still in Sym's hand when he got up?"

One of the three men caught her thought. "That's right. He still had it. He put it back in its sheath. I remember."

General nods from the others agreed with him.

"So whatever happened, if he was hurt then, it was an accident," Frevisse said, "and of Sym's making."

There was nodding to that, too, through the whole crowd; but then the blunt-faced man said, "So it was maybe afterwards, in the dark outside, he did it."

The crowd readily grumbled back toward anger. Frevisse swiftly turned to Joliffe and said, "So tell us where you truly were after you left the alehouse. You didn't come straight here."

She was guessing but already knew Joliffe's face well enough to read, despite his control of it, that she had guessed right. Knowing only he could see her own expression, she willed him to understand it might be his life to answer her rightly; and maybe Naylor's and Ellis's lives, too. She and Dame Claire were almost surely safe enough; they would only be dragged aside if it came to fighting again; but she thought Naylor was not the kind of man to leave him to the crowd unfought for, and Ellis was already in the middle of it.

Joliffe met her look and read it. Or already knew the stakes as well as she did. With a penchant for survival and wry humor both, he answered, "I went from the alehouse into the arms of the pretty girl. She left when Sym turned ugly, and waited for me at the church porch. We saw him go stumbling past on what I suppose was his way home. Unfortunately," he added carelessly, not seeming to hear the stir and mutter among the men, "all I could charm from the girl were kisses and sweet words, but surely we were there long enough for even Sym to have reached his door."

"And that's something Roger Naylor can ask about tomorrow," Dame Claire cut in before anyone else could say more. "Tonight he can lock you up and be done with it, but Dame Frevisse and I need escort to the village if there's someone hurt there. How bad is the wound?"

The men looked vaguely at each other and shuffled uneasily. Dame Claire stood up with a disgusted look, but it was Naylor who said, letting his aggravation show, "You came storming up here, breaking our peace and beating our guest without even knowing how bad the hurt is? You don't have any idea of it?"

One of the men shrugged and muttered, "Meg came in t'alehouse. Said Sym'd been stabbed by one of the player folk. And we—" He looked around at his fellows and shrugged. "We called up some of t'others thereabouts and came up here to make sure the man wasn't trying to leave without he paid for what he'd done."

"Only you didn't bother to grab the right man, and the right man hadn't done it anyway," Naylor snapped. "A fine lot of fools you've made of yourselves."

Their looks said they agreed with him. Ellis had climbed painfully to his feet and went now to join Joliffe in the doorway. Dame Claire said, "So that's settled. But we still need to go to the village. Who will . . ."

But she was interrupted. Torchlight and voices from the priory gateway turned them in that direction as four more village men trod heavy-footed in, carrying a piece of fencing flat among them, a blanket-covered body on it. Meg walked beside it, unsteady on her feet, clinging and leaning on Hewe, who was white faced, tear stained, dazed. Father Henry came behind the sorry little group, his head bent in prayer. There was no need to ask who lay under the blanket, and no one did.

Chapter 14

FLATLY TURNING TO business in the face of death, Naylor said, "We can put him in the outer cowshed. It's empty and he'll keep there until the crowner comes."

It became the King's business whenever any of his subjects died in an unexplained or violent way. His representative in such matters, the crowner, must come to look and question and collect evidence until he was satisfied he had the facts of the case. If there was guilt, he made an arrest. If the death had been by accident or from natural causes, everyone was released to go about his business. Sym's body could not be buried until it had been viewed by the crowner.

By custom, the body should go to lie in the village church, but there was no priest there now; and the priory's church was not the place for one of Lord Lovel's peasants. Indeed, the matter should have belonged altogether to Lord Lovel's steward, but there was no telling where he was among his lord's properties just now; it would take time to contact him, and he and Naylor had long since fallen into helping each other when either was in need or gone.

So for the time being the priory was the place for Sym's body. But Frevisse said with quiet authority equal to Naylor's, "Rather, put him in the new guesthall. It's readier to hand for what needs to be done." And better the guesthall than a cowshed.

Dame Claire had gone to Meg and was murmuring to her with the deep, ready sympathy she had for anyone in any kind of pain. But the blunt-faced man was not done yet and said loudly, still ready for trouble, "So it's murder now maybe."

"Ah, Jankyn, let it go for now," someone said. But others rumbled.

Ellis and Joliffe still stood together in the doorway. Frevisse prayed they would have sense enough to fall back inside and throw down the bar across the door if the crowd turned ugly again.

But the ugliness was past. There was only the grumbled certainty of wrongs and a wanting of explanations. Frevisse, careful to seem unhurried, moved to Meg's other side, took her hand—dry, callused, limp in her own—and asked, "What did your son say about his hurt? Did he say who did it to him?"

Meg did not raise her head. In a remote, weary voice, she answered, "He said the player stabbed him. In the alehouse. That's all he said. It was another useless fight. Like Barnaby used to get into. Sym was always starting fights, like his father."

Her voice trailed off, but it had been enough. Naylor raised his own voice to say, "There. You've heard it. It happened in the alehouse, in the fight, and enough of you saw what happened there to know there's no one to blame but Sym himself. There's naught else for any of you to be doing now until the crowner comes. Go on home. It's a cold night to be standing about."

Unpurposed now and aware of the hour and the cold, the men began to drift away out the priory gateway. The four bearing Sym's body waited for Father Henry to lead the way to the new guesthall. Meg looked at Dame Claire, who said, "You come with me, Meg. You can stay the night here. There's no need for you to go back to your house tonight, not alone."

"There's Hewe," Meg said vaguely, looking around.

"I'll see to him," said Frevisse. The boy was standing where he had stopped, dazed, past tears for now. Meg did not look at him, only nodded and let Dame Claire take her from the women and lead her away toward the cloister door where cautious heads were brave enough to peer out, now the noise was over.

"You'd best tell Domina Edith what has happened," Frevisse said.

Dame Claire nodded. The curious faces disappeared inside with her and Meg, and now the only light left in the courtyard was from the open guesthall door and a lantern sitting beside the mounting block. Naylor went to pick it up and held it so its yellow glow fell on Joliffe's and Ellis's faces where they still stood in the doorway.

"You were luckier than I'd have thought was likely," he said. "But you're not to leave here. Master Montfort will be wanting to talk to you when he comes."

"They'll stay," Frevisse said. "There's a sick child, and they're to play for us tomorrow or next day."

Naylor nodded acceptance of that, his attention changing to her. "You were overbold in taking on those men with me. But I thank you for your help."

His ungrudged honesty surprised Frevisse into a frank answer. "You were bold enough yourself. I couldn't leave you alone to it. Besides, they didn't have the mindless sound yet of a mob that kills without thinking. They were angry at one man in particular and not past knowing a nun when they saw one. I thought it safe enough."

"Your notion of safe is somewhat broader than most," Naylor said. "Well, I'll be finishing my rounds now and go home, please you, my lady."

Frevisse nodded and he left, taking his lantern with him. Frevisse went to Hewe and took hold of his arm. "You're cold," she said. "Come in now. We don't need you falling sick along with all else that's happened."

He came, less because her words made sense than because he was ready to do anything he was told just then. Joliffe and Ellis were still waiting in the doorway, Bassett with them now. They all drew back as Frevisse brought Hewe in, and followed as she led him down the hall to the farther hearth were Rose was building up the fire. Piers, obviously under orders to stay where he was no matter what, peered out from among his blankets with wide-awake, wary curiosity. But they knew the immediate danger was past; only some of Rose's tension was still betrayed in her movements as she glanced at Hewe and then at Frevisse, questioning.

It had been plain instinct to bring him to Rose. While Barnaby had lain hurt there, no one had come visiting; Frevisse had no idea who in the village he could go to tonight. Father Henry had enough to see to with Sym's soul and body, and if she gave him over to the priory servants, they would give him no peace with their questioning. That seemed to leave only Rose. Frevisse said, "His father was buried yesterday. Now his brother is dead. Dame Claire is caring for his mother and I don't think there's anyone he can go to."

Rose shifted her look back to Hewe for a considering moment, and then nodded. "He's welcome here. Set him close to the fire. He looks in need of warming."

Over their heads Joliffe answered something Bassett had said. "You would have been a fool to follow me out there. The matter was mine. And if I didn't set it right with the oafs, if it went wrong for Ellis and me, then Rose and Piers would have been needing you indeed." He asked loudly, "So what's in the pot for my supper, Rose?"

"You've had your treat for tonight, my lad," she said, and handed the bowl toward Hewe.

He blinked at her uncertainly, not taking it. "My brother is dead," he said.

All the gentleness there had not been for her own menfolk was in Rose's voice as she answered, "I know." She shifted to sit in front of him. "And that's a thing sad beyond saying. But your mother is going to be needing you, and you have to stop your shivering or you'll be sick and that would be a pity, too. Here."

She held the spoon out to his mouth. As if he were no older than Piers, he opened for it obediently. Rose looked over his shoulder to Ellis, who picked up a cloak and draped it over the boy's huddled back as she fed him another spoonful.

Frevisse backed away. Hewe would be cared for now; she should go see what help Dame Claire might need. She found Dame Claire was still in the infirmary, sitting on the edge of one of the beds beside Meg. Dame Claire rose when Frevisse came in but Meg did not even look up, only went on sitting there huddled in on herself, dry-eyed, her hands clenched tightly together in her tense lap.

"She'll stay here the night," Dame Claire said, coming to Frevisse. "There's no point in her going back to her place alone."

Frevisse nodded agreement, but Meg stirred herself enough to say, "Hewe?"

"He's with friends," Frevisse said. "He's warm and he's fed. He's fine." She nearly went to take the woman's hands, to make some sort of contact with her to be sure she was still there enough to hear, but instead she asked Dame Claire, "She needs some rest. You'll give her something?"

"The strongest draught that I can make. Then I'll stay with her until I'm sure she's sound asleep."

Meg did not even look up at this conversation going on over her head. She had lost a husband and her son in scarcely three days with not even a sickness to warn her it was about to happen. Sleep would help but it could not stop the full weight of the grief that was going to come when the first numbness of shock went out of her.

Meg raised her staring eyes from her hands to Dame Claire and said hopefully, "He was frightened, Sym was. Said he was afraid he might die. So I helped him say, 'O my God, I am heartily sorry for having offended Thee,' like after confession. He said it slow and good, with tears. And he begged the Virgin to help. He wanted Heaven at the last, just as he should. I blessed him in God's name before I went for help. Was that enough? Will he be all right?"

"If it happened just as you just told me, his soul is saved," Dame Claire assured her. "All who ask for God's mercy receive it. You did well to remind him and pray with him. He's safe now."

Meg nodded, and looked back at her hands. "He's safe now," she murmured.

Dame Claire, lower voiced, said to Frevisse, "Talk to her, will you, while I go make the sleeping draught?"

"Yes," Frevisse said, not wanting to. Meg looked at her

and said again in a vague and worried voice, "Will it have been enough? He'll be all right? Father Clement said once, when there was plague and he couldn't be with everyone at once, that that could be enough. Sym will be all right?"

"He's fine now," Frevisse assured her. "Happy and at peace." Sym's corpse was lying empty under a blanket, but Dame Claire was right. If his mother had done all she said she had done, then his soul was safe, and that grief at least she could let go of. "You did all you could. Father Henry will say a proper funeral Mass for him, and that can only help. So don't worry. How did this happen?"

Meg stirred a little. "It was a fight. Another of his fights. At the alehouse, he said. With one of the players. He didn't even know he was hurt until he was home. He was so surprised, he looked and there was blood. I made him lie down. On my bed. And I looked at it, and I was scared, and that made him scared and he started begging for the priest because he didn't want to die unshriven. He was so scared." Her voice and face echoed his fright, reliving it. Frevisse patted her shoulder distantly. Meg went on, unable to let go of what was running steadily through her head. "I didn't leave him until I'd done all I could. I remembered what Father Clement said and I did it. But there was no one else so I had to leave him. To find help. But he's safe now. No more hurting. No more angers. He's safe?"

"He's safe," Frevisse repeated, wishing Dame Claire would hurry.

Meg made as if to rise. "I have to go watch by his body. He can't be left all alone tonight."

Frevisse laid a hand on her cold arm and pressed her to stay where she was. "Father Henry is with him. He'll pray beside him through the night. There'll be time enough tomorrow. You're staying here tonight."

Meg looked around herself. "Here?"

Dame Claire came with the cup and its medicine. "You're going to stay here and you're going to drink this."

Meg took the cup and stared into it without drinking. "It's different here from everywhere else."

"Drink your drink," Dame Claire said.

Meg obediently drank a little, then said, staring at the dark liquid again, "They made me marry him. And then Sym was just like him. Just like him." She raised her dazed eyes to Dame Claire. "I can stay here?"

"For tonight, at least. Drink all of it."

Meg did, in a long, steady draught.

"Now lie down," Dame Claire said, "and sleep. That's what you're to do now."

"Hewe?"

"Hewe's in the guesthall with friends," Frevisse repeated patiently. "He's taken care of."

Meg's eyes closed. "There's no hurting in him. He's not like his father. He'll be all right." Her eyes closed and probably as much from exhaustion as Dame Claire's medicine her breathing evened into sleep as they watched her.

The clear weather held next day, and the cold with it. The services were blurred with snuffling and the chapter meeting with coughing; and Frevisse, who had been nearly over her own rheum, found it was come back, probably from her short sleep and being out in the icy night. Handkerchief in hand, she went about her duties until, as she was crossing the courtyard back from the old guesthall to the cloister, Father Henry intercepted her.

"Dame Frevisse, Dame Claire asks if you could come to her in the new hall," he said.

Busy with her running nose and her aches, she did not ask why, but with a resigned sigh, only nodded and turned from her way to fall into step beside him, back across the yard and up the stone steps to the new guesthall, built for their higher-ranking visitors, with separate chambers and its own kitchen.

Sym, alive, would likely never have entered it. Now he was laid on a blanket on one of the hall's trestle tables. Dame Claire was there, with a basin of warmed water steaming into the cold air on the table beside him, and a pile of clean rags and a folded cerecloth showing she had come to clean the body and ready it as far as might be for burial before the crowner came.

‘‘Where are his mother and brother?’’ Frevisse asked.

‘‘The boy is with the players. Meg was still sleeping when I left her,’’ Claire answered. ‘‘Which is just as well.’’ She made a small gesture toward the body. ‘‘There’s a problem.’’

Probably with Father Henry’s help she had begun to strip it for washing but had gone no further than beginning to remove the doublet and shirt. Sym’s chest and side were laid bare, and the ragged cut along the right side of his waist, smeared with dried, blackened blood, showed plainly. To Frevisse’s eye it looked no more than a shallow scrape that in the heat of his temper and the fight, Sym could quite possibly have not heeded right away.

It was the other wound, the smaller one, on his side between the lower left ribs and almost unbloodied, that held Frevisse once she saw it. She looked and went on looking, her mind knowing but not ready yet to admit what it meant. Only after a long pause did she say, knowing that Dame Claire knew as well as she did, ‘‘That went into his heart.’’

‘‘Directly in,’’ Dame Claire agreed.

‘‘And if it did . . .’’

She did not finish. There was no need. From a dagger thrust like that, into the heart and out again, and no more blood around it than would have followed the exiting blade, Sym must have died almost on the instant. Would have fallen and probably been dead before he was down.

Chapter 15

FATHER HENRY, LOOKING from Frevisse's face to Dame Claire's, said, "I don't understand."

Frevisse waited for Dame Claire to say something but she went on staring at Sym's body, brooding over a death that should not have happened. At last, instead of answering the priest's question, Frevisse asked, "You were in the village last night when Meg went looking for help?"

"One of the women was sick and had asked for me and—" Father Henry betrayed embarrassment. "—and I stopped at the alehouse before I came back here. To warm myself. It was cold out."

"And Meg came there and said Sym was hurt?"

Father Henry nodded. "All afraid, she was, and glad to see me. She told the men her boy was hurt, that the player had stabbed him, she needed help. And then, seeing me, she begged me to come."

"She'd left his brother with him and come looking for help?"

"The other boy was gone. She'd had to leave Sym there alone. That was part of her fear. That she had left him all alone. She kept saying we had to hurry so he wouldn't be alone."

Dame Claire raised her eyes from the body. "He must have died almost immediately. With hardly any pain."

Frevisse lifted the boy's hand. Or had he been old enough to be called a man? she wondered. In the quiescence of death his face was younger and more vulnerable than she remembered it being in life. Not that it much mattered now, she supposed. Young or old or in between, he had been murdered. That at least was certain. She went to his doublet and shirt lying at the far end of the table, turned them over, held them up. A ragged tear on the right side showed where one dagger blow had slid in and torn out. There was no other rend.

"His mother must have pulled these up from his chest and side, to better see how he was hurt. And left them open when she went for help."

"Then someone came in after she was gone," Dame Claire said.

"Someone he didn't fear. Or didn't fear enough to be wary of. He was lying flat and quiet when the dagger went in the second time. Or would he have lost enough blood to be unconscious, do you think?"

Dame Claire shook her head. "No. That first wound is messy but shallow. Even bleeding, it took so long to soak through his doublet, he was home before he knew he was bleeding, didn't Meg say? There wasn't enough lost for him to faint. Unless he was the sort who does when they see blood."

"He was aware enough to be afraid and plead for help. His mother said so. And ask for absolution and the rest."

"How do you know he was lying down when he was struck?" Dame Claire asked.

"The angle of the blow. In a fight a dagger coming into someone's side like this one seemingly did has to be held underhanded, and comes almost always in at an upward slant. But this one went straight in. I'd guess the person had to have been standing directly at his side when they did it, and Sym not expecting it at all." Frevisse turned to Father Henry. "How was he lying when you came in?"

The priest had been looking from one to the other of them while they talked, his large features registering his bewilderment. Now, glad of something plain that he understood, he said, "On a bed by the far wall, on his back, his hands folded on his chest. Like he was asleep and peaceful. I thought he was until I touched him."

"Was he covered?" Frevisse asked. Father Henry nodded, and she prodded, "How? With what and how much?"

"A blanket. It was pulled up to his chin."

"And his hands were outside of it, folded on his chest?"

"Yes."

Frevisse came back to the corpse and carefully folded the arms so the hands rested one on top of the other on his chest. "Like this?"

Father Henry nodded.

Dame Claire met Frevisse's look. In that position Sym's arm completely covered the fatal wound in his side.

"Oh, no," Dame Claire said.

"Oh, yes," Frevisse answered. "A murderer not only sure of his blow but very considerate and respectful afterwards."

"Murderer?" Father Henry asked. "It was accident. That's what was being said last night."

"What happened in the alehouse was an accident. It wasn't that wound he died from. It was this second wound, here, directly into his heart, that killed him. At home, while he was lying on his bed."

That seeped with some degree of slowness into Father Henry's understanding, but as it did, his eyes widened. "Someone killed him while he lay there hurt and needing help?"

"It seems so, yes."

Father Henry crossed himself. "That's horrible."

"Maybe more horrible is the fact that we don't have any idea who might have done it. Or why."

Dame Claire wrung out a cloth in the cooling water. "He was quarrelsome, I gather, from what his mother said."

"And by what the men said last night," Frevisse agreed. She watched as Dame Claire began to wash the body.

She knew Roger Naylor had already sent for the crowner. The messenger had gone that morning; but there was no certainty as to where Master Montfort might be at this holiday season or of how long it would take the messenger to find him, and so no way of knowing when he would come.

Nor any assurance that his coming would aid in finding the truth. Master Montfort had been to St. Frideswide's before, and to Frevisse's mind he was an arrogant fool who resisted any help anyone tried to give him, especially women, and most especially cloistered nuns.

Frevisse said, "There's no one knows this is murder except us. Can we keep it so?"

Dame Claire paused. Like Frevisse, she felt that Montfort could be a menace to the truth. She nodded.

Father Henry, a worried frown of thinking between his eyes, worked at it a little longer before saying, "You mean keep secret that he was murdered?"

"Until the crowner comes. To give us time to question and learn things before the murderer knows we know and are looking for him." She picked up one of the cloths, dipped it into the water, and wrung it out. "It was someone that knew Sym was hurt and where to find him."

"It may be just as well his mother was gone," Dame Claire said.

Frevisse joined her in the task of cleansing Sym's body. It was not hard to think that whoever had killed Sym and coolly taken the time afterward to arrange his body, might well have killed Meg, too, if she had been there.

"Father Henry, are you free this morning to go down to the village and spend time in the alehouse asking questions? And to listen to what's being said? For surely the talk will be rife about last night."

Father Henry did not need to consider on that. He nodded readily. "I can spend the whole day if need be, until I'm sure I've heard everything there is to hear."

"And remember it all and bring it back here to me," Frevisse said. "Can you go now?"

Father Henry looked doubtfully at the body.

"We'll see he's not left," Frevisse assured him. "He'll be well prayed for. And finding his murderer is a service to him, too."

Father Henry nodded agreement with that. "I can go now."

"Try to learn who he's fought or argued with lately. And

where they were after he left the alehouse last night if that's possible. But don't let people know you're after more than only gossip,'' Frevisse warned.

Father Henry nodded. ''They're used to me gossiping. That will be no problem.''

When he was gone, Frevisse put down the cloth. ''I'm going to bring Joliffe's dagger and see if it matches the wound. He's still going to be the first suspected when word of this is out.''

''And the other player's, too. The one who fought with Sym.''

''Their daggers are all the same.'' But she would check to see if they had other knives beside the daggers they had shown her. She would need to have the players cleared beyond any doubt before Montfort arrived; he was ever willing to take the easiest path to a solution, and the players were a very obvious choice.

It did not signify, for example, that Ellis had said he'd never left the priory last night. She would need to find out that no one saw him leave, or, better, that someone, not Bassett or Rose, saw him asleep in the guesthouse at the right time. And Bassett and Rose would have to be proven innocent as well. And Joliffe. She hoped Father Henry had the wit to seek out the girl Tibby.

''What if . . .'' she began, thinking out loud.

Dame Claire, looking past her, shook her head.

Meg was coming into the hall. Her hours of sleep from Dame Claire's drink seemed to have brought a little more life back into her body and mind. She looked less shrunken, less bewildered as she came to stand beside Sym's body. She gazed at his face, then tenderly laid a hand over his own resting on his chest and looked up at Dame Claire.

''He's gone to Heaven,'' she said. ''He's not hurting nor angry anymore. Never angry anymore again.''

''Never again,'' Dame Claire agreed gently.

A single tear moved down the lines of Meg's face. ''He's better where he's gone.''

''It's what we pray for, each of us,'' Dame Claire said.

Meg turned her look to Frevisse. ''You said you'd seen to

my other boy? He needs to go home to see to things there, if he hasn't already. Has he, do you know? He doesn't always remember the stock needs tending, come what may."

"I'll see if he's gone," Frevisse said, "and send him to you if he hasn't."

"Nay, then. This is women's work here and none of his," said Meg as she reached for the cloth Frevisse had laid down. "We'll see to Sym. Just tell him to go on home, pray you, but I want to see him later."

"I will," Frevisse said, thinking as she went that Meg was on the body's right side and that Dame Claire could be trusted to keep her from seeing his left side and the second wound if it were at all possible.

The cold had a crisper edge to it as she crossed the yard but the sky was still shining, barely wisped with far-off clouds. Frevisse huddled her habit around her as she hurried and indulged in a moment of covetousness, wishing for Domina Edith's fur-lined cloak.

The players were gathered around their hearth. Hewe was with them, leaning forward on a bench to listen to something Bassett was saying while Ellis and Joliffe, working at a piece of leather harness, sat across from them, looking amused. Rose was on a cushion near the fire, sewing at something bright and threaded through with gold on her lap, with Piers wrapped to his ears in blankets and looking pallid but unfevered, leaning against her. He was the first to look up at Frevisse's coming, and he smiled as brightly as a young angel. Rose, following his look, made a reserved greeting. It appeared, Frevisse thought, that the warmth and strength of her affections were saved for her menfolk.

"Mending?" Frevisse asked, gesturing to the sewing.

Rose held up a pennon whose hem was ripped. "We use it for St. George. Bought from a town's pageant when they decided they needed something better, but it does well enough for us, although travel is hard on it."

"And on people?" Frevisse asked.

Rose smiled. "Travel is hard on everything, one way or another."

She was a strong-featured woman, her mouth and eyebrows and nose drawn in bold strokes, but she was not grown coarse with spending her days on the roads and in uncertainty. Except that her skin was marked by being out in too many sorts of weather and her hands showed that they did hard work, she might almost have been a lady in her bower sitting there, deft at her sewing. And her voice, though not nobility's, had not come from a peasant's cottage.

Frevisse wondered about her, and asked, "How does Piers?"

Rose left her sewing long enough to stroke the boy's gold hair back from his forehead. "He's mending."

Piers ducked out from under her hand. "I'm bored."

"But you're better," Rose said, and retucked his blankets.

"Well enough to sing, say, tomorrow?" asked Frevisse.

"Easily!" Piers declared.

"Quite probably," his mother corrected. Piers smiled up at her and snuggled closer.

The men and Hewe had acknowledged Frevisse's coming with brief looks and nods. Now Frevisse moved toward them to draw their attention. "Hewe has been no trouble?" she asked.

"A grievous pain and unending trouble," Bassett declared, then relented at Hewe's startled, stricken look, and rumpled his hair casually. "No. None at all. He slept, and we've fed him, and told him he could stay until someone came looking for him, if he wanted."

"And he's one reason I've come," Frevisse said.

Hewe already knew that. And he was remembering why he was here, and that he was supposed to be in grief. But it was an effort.

Had life with Sym been so unpleasant, Frevisse wondered, that his own brother had trouble grieving for him? But all she said was, "Your mother says you should go home to see to your animals for her. Later she wants to see you here."

"But not now?" Hewe asked.

"Not now. She's tending to your brother's body and will want you afterwards. Is there anyone in the village who can come help her?" she asked as an afterthought.

Hewe, gathering up his cloak from the far side of the

bench, shook his head. "She doesn't have any friends to mention. Someone will likely come if she asks, but she won't."

He seemed to take that as a simple given of life, ducked a bow to her and to the players, but added a suddenly shy smile for all of them and said, especially to Bassett, "Thank you."

Bassett inclined his head in acceptance. "And to you, youngling. You have been both a good guest and a good companion."

Hewe flushed with pleasure, ducked another bow, and quickly left.

Bassett grinned after him. "A likely enough lad and as different from his brother as cheese from chalk."

Joliffe leaned toward Ellis and said in mocking conspiracy, "He says that because the boy listened to all his stories and thought they were wonderful."

"Well, they are," Ellis said indignantly. "Until you've heard them three dozen times. Or four. Or more."

Bassett pulled a face at them, unoffended.

Frevisse put down her rising amusement at their banter, and came to the heart of her reason for this visit. But she kept her tone light. "Joliffe, may I see your dagger?"

With a slight puzzlement, he drew and held it out to her hilt first. She took it, appreciating the good weight and easy balance of it in her hand. "Yours, too?" she asked Bassett and Ellis.

They drew and held out their own, not questioning what she wanted but with an undertone of wariness that Rose's sudden watchfulness reflected. Frevisse did not take their daggers, but contented herself with comparing them to Joliffe's. As they had said, and she remembered, they were all of a kind, perfectly matched. She nodded them away, but said to Joliffe, "I need yours for a while," not asking his permission, simply telling him.

Quite still, he met her gaze with a knowing she could not read. In stillness his face was older, the boyishness gone out of it. Frevisse turned and left, taking the dagger with her, feeling their silence at her back.

* * *

Dame Claire and Meg were still beside Sym's body. With Dame Claire at his feet and his mother at his head and shoulders, they were lifting him sideways onto the white cerecloth he would be wrapped in for his burial, moving him as tenderly and smoothly as if afraid of waking him. It being New Year's Day and Feast of the Circumcision, there would be no coffin made until tomorrow, but there was no need for haste. He could lie here until it could be made; the body could not be buried in any case until the crowner had seen it, and would keep in the unheated hall.

Frevisse had hidden the dagger up her wide sleeve as she came. She waited while Dame Claire and Meg wrapped the cloth over the body. When they were done, Dame Claire asked Meg to take the wash water away, to dump it before it could be spilled. Eyes down, Meg took the basin without questioning and disappeared toward the garderobe.

Frevisse stepped quickly to the table, drawing the dagger from her sleeve to compare it to the wound.

"The blade is too broad," Dame Claire said. The neat-edged hole between Sym's ribs was too narrow by the width of her widest finger for the dagger's blade.

"And too short," Frevisse added. She laid the dagger on Sym's chest to gauge how deep it would have gone. "Striking from the side, the blade has to go in a fair ways to reach the heart and this is hardly long enough. It wouldn't reach." She tucked the dagger out of sight again with concealed relief. Whatever had stabbed Sym, it had not been one of the players' daggers.

Unless they had others, she forcibly reminded herself. That was still a possibility, though not one easily pursued.

But, her mind insisted, if one of them had deliberately used some other dagger than the one he usually carried to give the deathblow, then the killing had almost surely not been the mere taking advantage of a happenstance; it had been deliberately planned and purposed beforehand. Which was impossible, no one could have known Sym would go home and frighten his mother into seeking help.

So who then might have done it? Someone watching for a chance and ruthless enough to take it.

While she thought, she tucked her hands into either sleeve. It was a habitual gesture; now it warmed her hands and hid the dagger from Meg coming back. Belatedly Frevisse remembered and said, "I saw your Hewe. He's gone back to the village to do what needs doing there. He said he would come to you later."

"Thank you, my lady," Meg said, looking at her feet.

The cloister bell began to ring for Nones. Meg raised startled eyes toward the band of sunlight from the nearest window. "Midday?" she asked, completely bewildered. "How did it come to be midday?"

Dame Claire laid a gentle hand on her arm. "It was the drink I gave you. It made you sleep a long while."

And so heavily she had not even noticed what time of day she had awoken. Meg looked around a little frantically, as if to find the lost hours. "My work," she said. "I was supposed to be in the kitchen. Dame Alys . . ."

Dame Claire said, "She knows what's happened. She understands and isn't expecting you today. Or tomorrow either. It's all right."

Meg began to say something, stopped, looked to Frevisse, back to Dame Claire, then seemed to collect herself and turned away to her son's body. So low they could barely hear her, she said, "I'll stay here and pray then, please you."

It was probably the best thing she could do, both for herself and Sym. Leaving her to it, Frevisse and Dame Claire hurried away to church.

The service of Nones was fairly brief, consisting of a hymn, lesson, and verse in addition to three short psalms sung straight through. Frevisse's cold had given her a headache, made worse by the way one person's cough set off a noisy chorus of them, by the shuffling of impatient feet, and the frequent exchange of bored or exasperated glances. It was painful to hear this group of sufferers croak, " 'Then was our mouth filled with laughter, and our tongue with singing. . . .' " Frevisse was startled to realize near the end that she had let Joliffe's dagger slip down into her hand, and that she had taken it with a grip so tight her fingers were cramping.

In the original Rule, St. Benedict spoke of two meals a day, the main one at midday and a light supper in the evening, with variations, including fasts and late dinners, with never the flesh of four-footed animals to be served. The only part strictly observed at St. Frideswide's was that they ate their main meal at midday. Today they were served mincemeat pies and cabbage boiled with caraway seed.

Sister Thomasine, whose voice alone remained clear, had volunteered to be the reader at dinner until someone else recovered enough to take her place. They were reading from a borrowed book, St. Bede's *History of the English Church and People.* They had arrived at the late seventh century and were hearing of the death of St. Chad, Bishop of Mercia, and of miracles associated with his burial place in the Church of Blessed Peter, Prince of the Apostles. " 'Chad's tomb is in the form of a little wooden house,' " read Thomasine slowly, " 'with an aperture in the side, through which those who visit it out of devotion to him may insert their hand and take out some of the dust. They mix this in water, and give it to sick men or beasts to drink, by which means their ailment is quickly relieved and they are restored to health.' "

Ugh, thought Frevisse, *I would have to be sick indeed before I would drink anything flavored with spiderweb and dead man's dust.*

At the end of the meal, Domina Edith declared that everyone not so sick she must take to her bed was to come to the church and help Dame Fiacre sweep and dust.

The priory's sacrist had been slowly declining for some months. Now she had caught a cold like everyone else, and though she kept to her feet, she could not perform all her duties. This afternoon she sat on a stool at the foot of the altar and pointed to what needed doing. Frevisse found the dagger's keen edge very handy for cleaning melted wax off the altar's two brass candlesticks, a task she performed with grim thoroughness.

When it was all done to Sister Fiacre's satisfaction, they

were dismissed. Frevisse went out to discover that Father Henry had returned from the village.

She went to find him in his little house eating a late dinner. She sat down at his table and said without preamble, "What did you learn?"

"Sym wasn't much liked. He was given to quarreling. Little quarrels all the time, one after the other, for no real reason mostly."

"Any great quarrels? Or new quarrels just around now?"

"There's a girl, Tibby, whose folk weren't happy he was showing her attentions. Nor did she care for him much either, it seems, but that wasn't stopping him. There'd been pushing between her brother and him, and a few words, but nothing more."

"No daggers drawn?"

"No. He was not known for daggering. All words and fists, was Sym, from what I've seen—from what they say."

"But he drew on Joliffe last night."

"Joliffe? You mean the player, in the alehouse? Yes, he did. But he was being goaded some, I guess. Too many words and the way the player was saying them and that the girl wasn't minding. It went past what Sym would take."

Frevisse could see Joliffe deliberately outwording him, with a mocking smile and goading tone, until Sym was past wanting anything except to silence him. "But no great particular quarrel with anyone else?" she asked.

"The talk is that there looked to be one shaping up with Gilbey Dunn. He holds the croft by theirs and has been wanting to take claim to their field strips. Talk is, Lord Lovel's steward has been thinking maybe of letting him."

"Could he?" To give one villein's share of the fields to another was no little thing and not easily done.

"Oh, maybe yes, since Barnaby was going these past years the short way along to ruining them and Lord Lovel's steward was none too happy with him for it. Yes, there was a chance."

"But now with Barnaby dead, Sym would have been given his chance to prove himself before anything was done about taking the land away."

Father Henry shook his head heavily. "Maybe not. Sym has been looking to go much the way of his father already and patience was pretty well out with him. But that wasn't the whole of it. Seems Gilbey Dunn has been at Barnaby's widow, wanting to marry her, and the general thought is that she will since she's a poorly little thing who'll be needing someone to see to her and her matters. He might not have been able to talk her around with Sym in a rage about it, but now with Sym dead, he'll have no trouble with her. That's what they're saying. They quarreled badly yesterday, Sym and Gilbey Dunn, in front of the whole village."

"About the marrying?"

"Yes."

"What did Gilbey Dunn do?"

"Nothing much." He shrugged.

"What about the girl? I've heard she went off with the player after the fight with Sym."

"And her folk are none so pleased with her about it," Father Henry said. "She's shut up in the house for so long as the players are here and apparently had best be thankful her father only gave her a small beating when she came home last night."

"Can you talk with her tomorrow?" she asked.

Father Henry looked surprised and then nodded. "I should tell her to be a more dutiful daughter?" he suggested.

"Surely. And ask her if she has any way of judging how long she was with Joliffe, and where they were, and—but not until you have the other answers from her—if he ever asked her where Sym lived."

Father Henry's mind moved at its own steady pace but had the grace of holding on to what it was given. He thought for a moment, nodded again, and repeated, "Ask her how long she was with Joliffe, where they were, and then if he asked her where Sym lived."

"Yes. Exactly so."

"You think he did it?"

"Maybe. I don't know." She was certain he had not, but it seemed better not to say so. "But if I can show he couldn't have done it, then I can look elsewhere, do you see?"

Chapter 16

SORE-NECKED AND ACHING, Meg raised her head from the table. Dimly, as her mind stirred back to awareness, she realized she had been sleeping. By the faint gray web of lesser darkness at the guesthall's windows she guessed that dawn was nearing; and then she remembered where she was. And why.

Slow with stiffness, she straightened on the backless bench, forcing herself to move. She reached out her hand to Sym's wrapped body in front of her and stroked where she knew his arm to be. Father Henry had been with her a while last night; he too had promised her that Sym's soul was safe, so surely it did not matter that she had fallen asleep at her praying. She had not meant to, had not known she was so tired, or she would not have told Father Henry that he did not need to stay, that she and Hewe would keep the watch. She had even said that maybe someone would be coming from the village, though she had half known that was not true. Some might have come if Sym were laid out at home, but the priory was not a village place and no one was friendly enough with her or Sym anymore to come there, where he had to stay until the crowner came.

So Sym's watching belonged to her and Hewe, and they had both slept.

Meg smiled down at the curled dark shape in the rushes by the bench that was Hewe asleep. She had not expected him to stay awake with her. He had been a good boy yesterday, going to the village and back again twice over, seeing to things there so she could stay here. And he would do it again today, so she could go back to working for Dame Alys for her halfpence. They couldn't afford to lose any more of those, or let Dame Alys think Meg was not needed here.

Under the rough skin of her fingers the cerecloth was smooth and cool. Meg had never owned so large a piece of cloth in her life. And would never have given it away if she had, the way the nuns had simply given this one for Sym. That was a blessing, at least, because the only spare blanket had gone to wrap Barnaby for his grave. The nuns' pity was a blessed thing.

But then, they had more cloth where this had come from. More of everything. Meg had seen what they had folded and stacked away in chests in one of their storerooms. And that had been just one storeroom. They had others. What was it like to have so much?

In her mind she heard the nuns begin their singing in the church. She had heard them singing, when working in the cloister, and the unworldly beauty of their voices had stirred her mind. Singing and praying seven times a day, even in the middle of the night, every day, all the year round, was to her mind what the angels did in Heaven, too. How wonderful to be so close to Heaven here on earth! She rubbed at her tired eyes. Sometimes the beauty of the life they led tempted her into the sin of envy.

The dim light was growing. She turned a corner of the shroud away from Sym's face. She could not see his features yet, but remembered how they had been in the lamplight last night. A young face. Younger than he had looked for the last few years as his sullenness and temper had grown. Not a man's face taut with tempers and desires and needs, but her sweet son's face, all quiet and at peace.

She stroked a finger along his cheek. The stubble of his beard pricked at her flesh, but his own flesh under it was cold and strange, not Sym at all. Meg took her hand away. She did not want to touch him anymore, just look at him while the day grew slowly into light in the hall, and think of what might have been if things had been some other way.

She only knew that she was crying when a tear left a warm trail down her chill cheek.

Hewe stirred to wakefulness a while after that. He huddled against her for a while, like a little boy again, until he was awake enough for Meg to tell him to stir up the fire. One of the servants had built it for them against the long night's cold. It had burned down to a few coals while they slept, but enough was left that Hewe shortly had it roused. He crouched beside it, hands out to its heat, and said, "I'm hungry, Mam. Isn't there food?"

"We're not guests here," Meg said wearily. "Just biders-by. There'll be something you can eat at home when you go there."

Hewe looked at her guiltily.

"Did you eat what was left from the funeral foods?" Meg asked.

Hewe nodded. "Yesterday. I was hungry."

Meg sighed. "I'll find something in the kitchen here today for you."

"And come home soon?" Hewe asked hopefully.

"Tonight," Meg said. "I'll do my day's work and come tonight and bake. If I can find someone to watch by Sym."

"Father Henry will, if you ask. Or he'll find someone. Then you can come."

"Then I can come," Meg agreed, and added, "He's a good man. A holy man."

Hewe faced the fire again with a calculatedly indifferent shrug. Meg patted absentmindedly at Sym's shrouded arm, wondering why Hewe would not see what she saw in his becoming a priest, why he did not understand how right it would make everything.

Dame Frevisse came a little while after that. Meg and Hewe both rose to their feet and Meg curtsied, saying, "My lady."

"Good morrow, Meg." Dame Frevisse swept a sharp look around the hall. "You have wood enough. Has anyone brought you food?"

Meg was surprised. "No, my lady."

Hewe made an eager movement and Dame Frevisse turned a smile toward him. "I'll see that someone does," she said.

"Thank you, my lady," Hewe said with undisguised grateful eagerness. Emboldened, he moved a little toward her and asked, "The players, my lady. Are they leaving today?"

"Not today. They're to do a play for us tonight. Nor I don't think they can go until the crowner has come and talked with them."

Meg wondered at Hewe being so plainly pleased with that, but was distracted by someone else entering the hall; and more distracted to see it was Gilbey Dunn, with Peter and Hamon at his back.

So far as she knew, Gilbey had never been so far into the priory before. Certainly Peter and Hamon had not; they were gawking to one side and another and up at the wide-beamed roof and at the glassed windows; and when they realized Dame Frevisse was there, they dragged off their hoods with clumsy haste and bowed at her nervously.

Gilbey on the other hand, drew off his own hood smoothly and bowed as if well sure of himself, first to Dame Frevisse and then to Meg. Nor did he gawk; his look around the hall was quick and assessing, and when he spoke to Dame Frevisse his tone was confident behind its respect. "Asking your ladyship's pardon, is it allowed I speak with Mistress Meg here, by your leave?"

"Assuredly," Dame Frevisse said. "She's welcome to speak to whom she will. And I'm just leaving, so you may speak freely."

"And I've brought two friends of Sym to watch by him so young Hewe needn't stay," Gilbey added. "And you can step aside, Meg, so we can talk more private."

Meg wanted to deny him, to tell Hewe to stay and Dame Frevisse to make Gilbey go. But she lacked the nerve to be so bold and only watched helplessly as Dame Frevisse said, "That's kindly done. Come, Hewe. I'll see to your being fed. Meg, if you need aught, have one of the servants tell me."

"Thank you, my lady. And Hewe—" She caught at his

attention as he went willingly away. "Don't be biding here. You go on home and see to things."

He jerked his head in a grudging nod and left behind Dame Frevisse.

Outside, at the head of the stairs leading down to the yard, Frevisse stopped and turned to Hewe. "That man. Who is he?"

"Gilbey Dunn. He's our neighbor and he's been making trouble, and now I think he wants to marry Mam."

He said it so readily, with no particular caring one way or the other, that Frevisse was taken a little off stride. "Indeed," she said. "And what do you think of that?"

Hewe shrugged as if it did not matter much. "He'd treat her better than Da did, and so long as I stayed out of his way he'd not bother me."

"Your mother wants you to be a priest."

Hewe made a face like sipping vinegar. "And that I won't be doing. But she won't listen to me." He brightened and pressed a hand over his belly. "Do you think I could eat with the players and save you the trouble of getting me something? I'm fair growled with hunger and it's a long walk home."

Frevisse repressed a smile. "Yes. I'd think that would be all right."

"Thank you, my lady."

He remembered to bow and then was gone, leaping down the stairs and running across the yard to the other guesthall with far more eagerness than he had shown at any word from his mother.

Frevisse watched him go and then the yard was empty. No one was out in the cold and deliberately she stepped backward, nearer to the closed door behind her. Its thickness muffled what was being said but close to it inside—well away from Peter and Hamon, she suspected—Gilbey Dunn was in earnest talk with Meg. At least she assumed it was Meg. She could only be certain of Gilbey's voice, going on at length and strongly. If Meg was answering him in the occasional pauses, her voice was too low to be heard at all.

Because she was not learning anything beyond the fact that Gilbey Dunn was come well out of his way to talk to Meg, and because she did not want to be caught eavesdropping, Frevisse left, not hurrying, but descending the stairs and crossing the yard with the outward purpose of seeing how matters were in the old guesthall but going as slowly as she might without actually stopping. She had finally stopped near the door of the old guesthall and was, in desperation, bending to check her shoe strap when Gilbey came out at last.

To her surprise he did not go to the gate but across the yard diagonally, to the small wicket gate into the walled way that hid the storage and work sheds built along the inside of the priory's wall between the guesthalls and the priory's kitchen and back gate. Hidden from the courtyard but handy to the main life of the nunnery, it was usually busy with servants, but these were the Christmas holidays and not much in the way of usual work was being done. Frevisse, following Gilbey through the gateway at what she meant to be a discreet distance, found the area deserted. She paused. Gilbey was out of sight and there was no one to ask which way he had gone. The only movement was a white drift of smoke from the laundry's roof hole, showing that someone was there at least, and that cleanliness—like prayers—went on no matter what.

So, too, did human anger, to judge by the roused voices Frevisse heard as she approached the laundry door. And one of the voices was Gilbey Dunn's.

The other's, unsurprisingly, was Annie Lauder's.

Frevisse smiled narrowly. Gilbey was a bold man if he chose to quarrel with the priory's laundress. Her will was as strong as her arms and she brooked no interference in her work or her life from anyone.

Not needing to go too near the door to hear them, Frevisse stopped at the corner of the building. It helped that the door stood partly open, the laundry's escaping hot, damp air roiling into a cloud as it met the outside's chill.

Annie was saying loudly, "Don't go honeying to me, Gilbey Dunn! All the village knows you've asked her to marry you. You're as great a fool as that son of hers was, God keep him, if you think I want to hear you wooing me again."

"What's marriage got to do with us, girl? You know as

well as I do that I'm not asking her for love. There's sense to our marrying and that's all there is to it."

"Does she know that?"

"As surely as I do. She wants to better herself and so do I, and here's the way to do it."

"You're always out to better yourself." But she said it less angrily. "You've gotten what you want from me, and now you'll have what you want from her, and that's the end of it between us."

And Gilbey answered, "Why should it be over between us? Don't you like what I bring when we're together?"

"It's little enough you bring me," Annie returned, but playfully now.

Gilbey answered her in kind, his voice lower as if he were nearer to her. "Little enough maybe, but sweet."

The silence after that was weighty with possibilities that made Frevisse consider leaving, but she chose not to; there might be more to learn from these two.

But there was not. And when, in a little while, Annie asked, "Know what I want right now?" and Gilbey answered, "I know what I can give you. Same as always," Frevisse moved away, knowing she must not hear more.

But what she had heard put both Gilbey and Annie in the priory's mercy. There was a fine imposed on any unfree couple who carnally indulged themselves outside of marriage. A fine Gilbey and Annie had clearly incurred. He would pay his to Lord Lovel, who owned two-thirds of Prior Byfield, land and villeins. Annie belonged to the nunnery, and her coins would go into the priory coffer. But it was not coins Frevisse was interested in. She wanted information and the means to it had been put into her hands.

She was feeling the cold through her sheepskin-lined shoes before Gilbey came out of the laundry. She had counted on him leaving by the priory's back gate, the one most villagers used when they had business at the priory. She was waiting in the doorway of the storage shed across the narrow way from it, and nearly let him reach it before she stepped out into his way.

He jerked to a halt, startled, and glanced back over his

shoulder, plainly wondering if she knew where he had come from. But almost as quickly his expression went smooth and innocent, and he said with a respectful bob of his head, "God's good day to you again, lady."

"And to you, too, Gilbey Dunn."

That startled him again, because he had no reason to think she knew his name. Meaning to keep him off-balance, she said, "Show me your dagger."

It did not please him. But he had nothing to gain by being rude to her. His being Lord Lovel's villein instead of the nunnery's would not serve as excuse for anything.

But he paused, a momentary shadow of a frown between his eyes, before he unsheathed his dagger and handed it to her, hilt foremost.

She took it and laid her fore and middle fingers together along its blade, measuring its width against the width of Sym's mortal wound, and found that at its widest Gilbey's blade was near enough a match as made no difference. Measuring the blade along her forearm, she saw it was longer than Joliffe's dagger. Maybe long enough.

She gave it back, looking directly into Gilbey's face as she did. Expressionless, he took it without meeting her gaze. And that told her nothing; villeins were not supposed to presume so much on their betters as to dare look at them eye to eye, but she had already overstepped her own propriety in talking with him alone this much.

Gilbey, his dagger back in its sheath, said "I'd best be getting back to the village."

Frevisse gestured at the gate to indicate that he could depart. But she stood there alone a while longer, considering what she had discovered, before going on her way, wiping her nose, harkening to the bell calling to Tierce.

The only way Tierce that day differed from what was expected of it was that Domina Edith was not there. She had suffered a mild relapse—nothing dangerous, Dame Claire said—but she should keep to her chamber.

After, the other nuns bustled away to their various work and to be out of the cold. Frevisse, with the smothered feeling of being too enclosed, stayed in the cloister walk, pacing a while before finally sitting down on the low columned wall that ran around its inner side, between the roofed walk itself and the little garden in its center. There were other things she should be doing, and she would be called forward in chapter meeting if she were seen so apparently idle, but she needed to gather her thoughts and so far as she was concerned that was work indeed just now.

For one thing, she discovered she did not have much in the way of thoughts. What she had was a head that felt full of porridge—dull, lumpy porridge, lying on her thoughts like a dead weight.

She leaned against a column, feeling its carved spiral of vines and leaves pressing at her flesh through the woolen and linen layers of her habit. The stone's chill would creep through soon, but for just now sitting felt very good while she tried to sort out what facts she had.

Sym was known in the village as a quarreler and a fighter so there was nothing special in his discord with Ellis and Joliffe; the players were only the latest people to have reason to be angry at him.

Nor were Tibby's relatives happy with Sym's attentions, according to Father Henry. Maybe, wary of his temper, one of them had wanted him out of the way for better reasons than either Joliffe or Ellis had.

And there was Gilbey Dunn, of course, the pushing neighbor who could not leave the widow and grieved mother alone a decent while. Though Gilbey Dunn did not strike Frevisse as the sort of man who cared for risks he could avoid.

Sym had not been badly hurt in the fight with Joliffe; apparently he had not even known it, or else thought it no more than a scrape, until he reached home. It had been his mother's fright that had frightened him into wanting to be shriven. With his father's death so new in his mind, he had probably been especially afraid he was dying, and his mother in her own fear had done all she could before she left to find help. That was maybe the only comfort the woman could have from his death: that she had helped make his soul safe before she left him. Because then, before she had returned, someone had come in; and either Sym had been lying with his eyes closed and did not hear him, or it had been someone he was easy enough with that he did not stir when they came. He possibly had not even had time to know what they were doing before they thrust a dagger between his ribs and into his heart. The wound had been too clean and simple for him to have struggled at all. He had probably died barely knowing he was hurt.

And then whoever had done it had folded Sym's hands on his chest and covered him and gone away. Had they hoped his mother would only think he was sleeping when she came back and so put off the outcry for a while?

But why had they wanted him dead at all? What little she had seen and now knew of Sym, he seemed to have been more his own worst enemy than anyone else's. It was only his death that told that someone else had felt very differently. But why? That was the question she found herself holding to now. Gilbey Dunn had reason; he could be more sure of the marriage and the land if Sym were out of the way. But murder was a desperate act, and a final one for the murderer as well as his victim if he were caught. She had the distinct impression that Gilbey was a man who liked to keep his options open. And very likely he had someone to say where he had been that night, it being New Year's Eve and people gathering for festivities of one sort or another.

She found that her hands, tucked up either sleeve for more warmth, were pressed against Joliffe's dagger in her belt. There was where the next real danger lay. Master Montfort the crowner would come sooner or later, and from past dealings with him, Frevisse knew him well enough to know that he favored the easy solution over the harder. In this matter Joliffe was the easier solution. A stranger of the less desirable kind, with no protector, and a tongue that he would not curb even if his life depended on it. She could already hear Montfort's quick summation of the facts that would make his work simplest; and she could imagine Joliffe in his hands, hauled off to Oxford and a quick hanging.

Frevisse shivered from more than the day's cold and the stone's chill. She stood up. There were still her daily duties to be done, including returning Joliffe's dagger to him, and she had best see to doing them. She had thought as far as she could with what little she knew, and could only hope Father Henry would return with answers that she needed.

Chapter 17

MEG KNELT IN the shadows at the back of the church, beyond the choir. She was not sure she should be here. This was where the nuns prayed; her own church was down in the village. She had meant to go directly from the guesthall to the kitchen, but the nuns' singing had drawn her as she went through the cloister, and when they had left she had slipped in and along the nave to kneel here with her thoughts that were not quite prayers, only a seeking to know what God wanted of her, and if He was pleased with what she had managed for Sym and Barnaby.

Beyond a numbness in her mind and heart, she knew that she was grieving for Sym. But she was past tears. Her only strong feeling seemed to be the dim joy of knowing he was safe from Hell, that he would someday go from Purgatory into Heaven's golden light. She had done that for him. So while there was the stone-hard weight of losing him on earth, she also had the certainty that he was safe, and the comfort of that was great.

"My child." The voice beside her was so soft and Meg so far into her thoughts that for an instant the words seemed a part of her own mind, come to answer her from wherever prayers went for answering. Then she realized a nun was standing beside her, and she struggled up from her stiff knees to curtsey unsteadily. She knew the sister's face but not her name. It was hard to learn the nuns' names when most of them never spoke at all, or so it seemed. The soothing lack of clacking chatter inside the cloister was one of the things she loved about the priory, so different from the village.

Now this sister put out a gentle hand toward her shoulder, not quite touching, and said softly, "I only wondered if you would rather come kneel at the altar instead of back here."

Meg turned her wonder-widened eyes toward the altar, the heart of the church. Covered by a damask cloth of spotless white, set with the golden-clasped prayer book, the gleaming candlesticks, and little golden house enclosing the bread and wine that were Christ's living body and blood, it had a special light of its own, kinder than sunlight, as mysterious as the undying flame in the red-glass lamp hanging above it.

"I couldn't go there," Meg whispered. "Not there."

"Yes, you can. I'm Sister Fiacre. I'm sacristan here and the church and everything in it are my duty. I promise you can go to the altar's very step if you want. Come with me."

With her hand under Meg's elbow to guide her, she drew her toward the three steps that led up to the altar. At the bottom one, she said softly, "This is where I pray when I can. When I'm here, and it's quiet, I can feel Lord Jesus's comfort all around me, almost hear his words, and know God is pouring himself over me like healing ointment and the Holy Ghost is waiting to enter my soul with peace."

Meg began to pull back. She did not understand the words but they sounded as holy as anything any priest might say. At the same time, she felt the sister's fragility, and was afraid of how easy it would be to hurt her. But she protested, "I shouldn't be here."

"You're one of God's children. The blessed Mary, mother of Jesus, stood at the foot of the cross and watched her own son die. She has a special care for any mother who suffers a son's loss. Kneel here and ask her to ask her resurrected son to comfort you."

Meg thought for a panicked moment that Sister Fiacre meant she was to ask for Sym's resurrection. Then she understood, and even found the word for it. "Intercession," she said.

Sister Fiacre's pale lips parted in surprise, even respect. Then she nodded and said, "That's right. Ask the blessed mother's intercession. And how can so perfect a son as Jesus deny what his own mother asks of him?"

Meg's uncertainty went away. Sister Fiacre must have seen her acceptance because she said with a kind smile, "So you can pray here as long as you want. You'll not bother me at my work."

Awed at the thought of working in a place where she herself hardly dared come at all, Meg asked, "You work here? What do you do?"

Sister Fiacre's smile made her whole face wistful with remembered pleasure. "I see that the church is swept, the altar cloths clean, Father Henry's vestments ready, all the gold and brass and glass polished, the candles trimmed to burn their best, the prayer books marked to the right text, new herbs strewn to freshen the air. If needed, I see that things are repaired or replaced. Everything must reflect God's glory and aid our worshiping here. And then . . ." She looked around at everything. "And then when all is done and if I have a little time, I kneel here and pray, and if I've done very well, I sometimes feel St. Frideswide is thanking me for what I've done to keep her church lovely."

"The saint comes to you?" Meg breathed.

Warming to Meg's admiration, Sister Fiacre said, "Not to be seen, of course. That's not been granted me. But I can feel her presence. Her veil is in the altar, you know. And one of her fingernails. You know her story? She refused to marry a prince in order to be a nun. The abbey she founded is in Oxford, and so is her tomb, but a part of her is here, too. And I can feel the warmth of her love wrapping me all around and her pleasure that I've done well. It's like nothing of the world at all. Maybe she'll come to you, too, while you're here, and ease your heart."

Meg, wrapped in a kind of holy enthusiasm, said, "Maybe, if . . . Could I help you with your work?"

Sister Fiacre hesitated, looking doubtful. "Instead of praying?"

Meg clasped her hands. "Isn't work a kind of praying?

Father Clement in the village used to say that. That we should do our work as a kind of prayer to God instead of complaining of it. Surely, taking care of God's holy church must be prayer of the best kind. And it would ease my heart."

As soon as she said it, she knew that was the best plea she could have made. Sister Fiacre nodded. "Of course, child," she murmured, though she was probably barely older than Meg herself. "Of course. Come and help me."

The little while then was a treasure to Meg. Humbly aware of the blessing she was given, she swept the tile floor in the choir and ran a polishing cloth over the already gleaming wood of the nuns' choir stalls. Here was where they stood all those times every day and in the night with their prayers and singing to God. Except for the altar itself, there must be no more holy place in the priory. She moved with conscious silence and deep reverence, leaving reluctantly, returning gladly when Sister Fiacre gave her a bowl of rosemary and meadowsweet and other herbs to strew along the floor so their sweet scents would rouse under the feet of the nuns.

She of course did not handle the altar or its furnishings, but watched with awe while Sister Fiacre did with a humble familiarity, and handed her the polishing cloths and took them back from her, deeply aware that they had touched the holy things themselves. She held them reverently while Sister Fiacre made sure everything was set precisely as it should be on the altar, and gave them up only reluctantly when Sister Fiacre came to take them to put away.

Sister Fiacre had scarcely come back from that when there was a broad sweep of full daylight and a strong draft of cold outside air along the nave as the church's wide western door was pushed open. Used to the church's subdued light and silences, Meg instinctively drew back toward the shadows of the choir stalls, thinking again that maybe she should not be here. But Sister Fiacre swung around sharply, putting herself directly between the altar and the intruders, as if to defend it.

Two nuns entered in a sway of skirts and veils, leading three men. Their obeisances toward the altar were perfunctory, though the men pulled off their hoods before, still chattering, they all came along the nave.

"And you can see there are no side aisles, so no pillars to be in your way," the younger nun said eagerly. "The best place would be there, between the stalls, only the space is so narrow there's not room for you to perform. So where would you like to be? What would suit best? What will you need, a screen, tables, musicians? I can play the lute."

"Talented, too? Wonderful," murmured one of the men, slender and fair, smiling as he bent his head to hear her more nearly.

The other men were looking around with an assessing rather than reverent air as they came on. But the black-haired man was also aware of the younger nun, and she let show her awareness of him, between smiles at the fair-haired one.

Sister Fiacre, from her rigid place at the foot of the altar steps, said, shrill with indignation, "Sister Amicia!"

The younger nun started, her chatter cutting off.

"And Sister Lucy!" Sister Fiacre added for good measure, though the other nun had also fallen silent and had been in no more than decorous conversation with the older man. "What is this?"

Sister Lucy said something in a low voice to the men and then hurried forward. "It's by Domina Edith's bidding. She said the players should see the church before they perform, remember? Sister Amicia and I have brought them, just as she said. It's all right."

"I doubt that." Sister Fiacre began to wring her hands with nervous temper. "I told her what they were like. Now look at you both, gabbling at them as if you were village women when they shouldn't even be in here at all. I don't want them here."

"But Domina Edith does," Sister Lucy said. She looked around for confirmation to Sister Amicia, who, looking away from the gaze of the fair-haired man in a way that remained flirtatious, nodded agreement. From her place to the shadowed side, Meg recognized the men. The black-haired man had fought with Sym on the green. And the fair-haired one meeting Sister Amicia's smiles with his own had stabbed Sym last night. Dame Claire had said it had been an accident, and no one's fault. She had said it kindly, with sympathy, but firmly, so that Meg would understand there was going to be no one punished for what had happened.

Meg had accepted it the way she had had to accept so many other things. But to see him, to see them both here in this holy place, distressing this holy woman . . .

"The church is my concern!" Sister Fiacre said. "Domina Edith should have asked me to show it to them, if they have to be here."

"She said you should be spared the burden of dealing with lay people—" Sister Lucy began.

Sister Amicia cut across her. "Especially men. We were to tell you they were coming, to prepare you, but then it just seemed easier to bring them along."

The older man stepped past her and made a flourishing bow to Sister Fiacre. "Good sister," he began in a rich, full voice, "pray, we mean only . . ."

Sister Fiacre cut him off with a small shriek. She stepped back, clutching her hands to her breast as if he had threatened her. "You! You dare!" She fluttered a hand out at him. "You were Lord Warenne's man! You were all Lord Warenne's men! I remember you, Thomas Bassett! I know all about you and why he turned you away! How can you dare profane this place?"

Frevisse, drawn from the cloister walk by Sister Fiacre's raised voice, heard that much as she came in by the side door, and saw the momentary bewilderment on Bassett's face begin to change toward alarm even as he said with a steady voice, "I fear you have the advantage of me, good lady."

Under the strength of her indignation Sister Fiacre left off handwringing to point a shaking finger at him. "My brother told me! After he came in to his lordship, he said what you offered to do. You and those . . . those . . . others." She flapped a hand at Ellis and Joliffe standing farther away with Sister Amicia all agog between them. "Sister Amicia, you come away from those two!" Sister Fiacre added with shrill fierceness. "Right away! You don't know the wickedness about them that I know."

Angry color was rising in both Ellis's and Joliffe's faces as she spoke, but it was Joliffe who said, "It's your brother you don't know about. That sanctimonious, prig-faced . . ."

"Joliffe!"

Frevisse had never heard Bassett's voice fully raised before. It surged to the wide roof beams of the nave and between the stone walls and stopped everyone, movement and voice, Joliffe as well as Sister Fiacre. Even Frevisse, startled, held her peace and place. It was Joliffe who recovered first and said, still angrily, to Bassett now, "There's no reason we have to—"

Again Bassett interrupted. "There's reasons. You think and you'll remember them." He rounded on Ellis, cutting him off, too. "You remember?" he demanded sharply.

"I remember," Ellis said angrily. His anger was a darker kind than Joliffe's. "We all remember them."

"And well you should!" Sister Fiacre cried out. "Very well you should! My brother told me all of it! What you offered to do! What you said!"

Whatever else she was about to say, Frevisse cut off by coming forward. She knew too well the uselessness of trying to reason with Sister Fiacre when she was in this state and said in a deliberately quiet voice, "Whatever you know, I'm sure it's not worth shouting in the church about, Sister Fiacre."

"But these people offered to bring—"

"*We?* You have it the wrong way—" began Joliffe.

"Silence!" said Bassett. "This is not the time or place—"

"I agree," said Frevisse in her most authoritative voice. She was perfectly aware of the edge she could give to words when she chose. She gave it now, and Sister Fiacre, her lower lip beginning to waver and tears filling her eyes, subsided.

Frevisse continued, "I'll see to everything from here, Sister Fiacre. Sister Amicia will take you to Dame Claire, who will give you something to calm you. Sister Lucy will stay, and I will assist her with this."

Protest trembled all over Sister Fiacre's face but she was no match for any well-asserted authority and finally, with a little strangled cry and her hands clutched again to her breast, she bowed her head and let Sister Amicia lead her away. Meg left the shadows and hurried after her, her sudden appearance startling everyone but Sister Fiacre.

When they were gone and the side door shut behind them, Frevisse looked at Sister Lucy, who looked back with neutral quietness. Sister Lucy was well into her forties and had achieved Domina Edith's serene detachment from emotional scenes. Now she seemed to feel that since Frevisse had taken on the problem, the problem was Frevisse's; she offered no suggestions, and Frevisse turned to the players and said equably, "Now, Bassett, would you care to finish looking around and tell us what you will need for your performance?"

"Yes, thank you, my lady, we would."

Joliffe and Ellis were still smoldering, but Bassett seemed calm. Or maybe he handled his anger better than the younger men did. As if the interlude with Sister Fiacre had not happened, Bassett began to inspect the nave to see where they could best perform, using questions and suggestions to draw Ellis and Joliffe after him and soothe their resentment away.

It was decided that, all in all, little was needed beyond what their own stock of properties could provide. Sister Lucy would see to lanterns being set around the church, the nuns could gather at the altar end, and the players would perform in the nave, just inside the western door.

"That's all easily done," Sister Lucy said. "I'll be sure someone sees to it. Is there anything else?"

"You've been most gracious," Bassett said. "I think there's nothing else but to let us make glad your evening."

"I look forward to your performance," Sister Lucy replied, so formally it was impossible to tell if she were telling the truth or only being polite.

All three of the men then bowed both to her and Frevisse and left. Frevisse meant to go after them, but paused to ask Sister Lucy, "How does Domina Edith? Is she ill again?"

Sister Lucy smiled slightly. "Not truly. She resents her body being weak, but Dame Claire has said she should stay quiet today and rest, lest her sickness come back on her. She's presently more impatient than anything."

"Can she be visited?"

Sister Lucy hesitated, then said, "It would depend. It wouldn't be well for her to be truly disturbed. . . ." She paused, looking at the floor.

"As Sister Fiacre might do," Frevisse finished for her. "But would it be possible for me to call on her sometime today?"

"With God all things are possible. With Domina Edith things are a little less certain. I will inquire."

They smiled at each other and went their separate ways, Sister Lucy returning to Domina Edith, Frevisse to the old guesthall.

As she went she told herself that simply because the priory had so few guests this holiday time, and those guests not of the most important, her duty still required that she see to their needs. That was why she was going to them now, no other reason, except of course that Joliffe's dagger needed returning.

He was leaning against the wide stone frame of the guesthall doorway as she crossed the yard. He seemed unaware of her coming. Staring down in front of him at nothing in particular, he looked gone away somewhere far in his thoughts. Frevisse knew the moment he became aware of her, not by any movement that he made but simply because his awareness turned outward some several heartbeats before he raised his eyes and met hers.

She drew the dagger from her sleeve and held it out to him. "Thank you. It was useful."

"On whom?" he asked, taking it from her.

Deliberately Frevisse said, "On Sym," and watched Joliffe's face.

Only slightly disconcerted he said, "He must have made an easy target. He was already dead."

"Yes," Frevisse agreed. She would have asked him about the trouble between Sister Fiacre's family and the players, but was interrupted by an angry voice beyond the door behind him. She listened and then asked, surprised, "Rose?"

Joliffe, with a grin, nodded. "Bassett was telling her what happened in the church. It's why I came out here. If you've any pity, you might want to go in and rescue him."

''But what—''

Frevisse paused, distracted by Rose's rising voice. The words were indistinct but the anger clear.

''She's afraid we'll be put back on the road before the day is out,'' Joliffe explained. ''And that Piers will sicken again if we are. Few things rouse Rose to temper, but danger to Piers is very definitely one of them.'' He stepped aside, opening the door for her. ''So go rescue Bassett, if it please you.''

Frevisse entered the hall. Joliffe did not follow her.

Bassett and Ellis were seated by the fire with the hunch-shouldered look of men who would have left if they could. Rose stood across from them, silent just then, her hands on her hips, glaring at them. At Frevisse's coming they all looked her way, and Bassett rose quickly to his feet with plain relief.

''If I've come at a bad time,'' she started.

''No,'' Bassett said quickly. ''We were just talking about how well the church would serve for the play. Piers's voice should be excellent there.''

''He'll be well enough for it by then?''

''We're thinking so, if he keeps warm till then and goes directly to his bed afterwards.''

''I'm tired of bed,'' Piers announced loudly from his blankets beyond the fire. ''Hewe, hand me that.''

One of their baskets full of props and goods had been dragged close to where he lay. Like the others, it was large, almost his boy's length and waist high on him if he had been standing. It had completely hidden Hewe where he was sitting, but now he moved at Piers's command, holding out a brightly painted box and glancing warily at Frevisse to see what she would say to his being there.

She said nothing; where he was was his concern, or his mother's, and he seemed to be doing no harm. Instead she said to Bassett, ''Will you be rehearsing this afternoon?''

Assured of her uninterest, Hewe crawled closer to Piers and they began to look through whatever the box held.

''We mean to,'' Bassett said. ''But I suppose not in the church?''

''It might be better if you didn't. Sister Fiacre—''

Rose made an angry sound and a sharp movement.

''Rose,'' Ellis said, and went to her. His gesture was one of support, but he did not touch her, only stood close. She folded her arms tightly across her breast, making a battlement of them.

''She's there by choice and by duty,'' Frevisse went on. ''She's sacristan. If her temper seems uneven, it's not that she wills it thus. She's . . . unwell. She has a cancer in her breast, and is often in much pain. What medicine Dame Claire can give her doesn't help much anymore. So she seeks the silence of the church and the solace of offering her pain for her few sins and for the repose of the souls of those who have helped our priory prosper.''

Bassett grimaced with pity, and the others looked abashed or embarrassed. But Bassett's gaze shifted past Frevisse's shoulder, and she turned to find Meg standing there, bent sideways under the weight of a bucket of coal.

''Meg!'' Frevisse said. ''Surely there's a man servant better able to carry that. Why don't you go home?''

Meg's worn face seemed sunk more deeply into its lines than ever. She was carefully not looking beyond Frevisse's feet to any of the players. In a monotone she said, ''I don't want to risk losing my place here.'' She glanced at the bucket of coal. ''Domina Edith sent word this was to be brought over to the guests. I'll just set it by the fire then, may I?''

Eyes still down, she staggered forward, set the bucket by the fire, and turned to leave; but her lifting eye was caught by Hewe and Piers who had been sitting still as fawns that hoped to escape the hunter.

Frevisse saw both her amazement and Hewe's chagrin, before anger clamped over Meg's face and she said, ''Hewe, how dare you sit idle here with work to be done at home? And if you've no strength or will for that, then you should be by your brother, praying for his soul, while I can't.'' For the first time, her eyes raked the players. ''Least of all should you be found with these folk. You don't belong here, not with them. Come with me.''

''Aw, but Mam—'' Hewe started.

But Meg was already by him, grabbing him by the ear. "Don't you speak back to me!" She twisted and he came to his feet making sounds of pain. "Come along! I can't trust you to do what you ought, can I? Well, there's chickens to catch, and be killed and plucked, and you can help. Hush, hush that noise! I don't understand how you can be so wicked. Can't trust you an inch! You come along with me!"

She stopped by the door long enough to bob a clumsy curtsey in Frevisse's direction, and Hewe grimaced an apology to Piers, then they were gone.

Chapter 18

MIDDAY AND NONES passed. Frevisse, coming and going about her tasks, kept watch for Father Henry's return from the village and left word with the gateward and servants to find her when he came back, if they saw him before she did. But he did not come, nor was there any word of the crowner's arrival, and the clear winter's day drew in toward its early sunset, the cold starting to deepen with the twilight.

In the long slant of shadows and thickening light, the bell began to ring for Vespers, and from all around the nunnery, in a flurry of hurried footsteps, coughing, and one loud sneeze, the nuns gathered toward the church.

Frevisse was among the first, glad of the chance to sink into the service's peace, away from her circling thoughts. There would be no time now today to talk to Father Henry. But after the long, frustrating wait, she was ready to put him and her questions from her mind.

Her sickness was like a weight dragging her body and her thoughts to a slow trudge. She was hoping prayers, supper in a warm room, and then the play before Compline would be distraction enough to ease her way into sleep later.

It was cold in the cloister, with just enough of a breeze to lift her veil. Frevisse pulled at the heavy door to the church, and went into dimness, two nuns close behind her. They would wait just inside for the others. At first the black shape stretched on the altar steps made only a vague impression, a thicker darkness among the gathering shadows. It took a few moments for them to realize it was a wrongness that needed closer investigation.

Sister Thomasine went forward first, always bolder when it was a matter of the altar or of her prayers than any other time. But it was Frevisse who suddenly realized what she was seeing and moved sharply forward as Thomasine knelt, one hand outstretched toward the shape.

"Thomasine!" she said sharply, stopping the young woman's hesitant hand, making her look around. More quietly, almost coaxingly, she added, "Come away, Thomasine. Don't touch her."

Sister Thomasine's veiled head came around, her eyes blurred shapes in her white face and white wimple, wide with bewilderment.

"But I think she's dead," she said.

"Don't touch her yet," Frevisse repeated, coming to lift her up and away from the body. "Just stand here."

"Who is it?" asked one of the other nuns, a question repeated in fragments as they looked among themselves to see who was missing. Others had been coming in, and now two more entered, to be told in frightened whispers what was happening.

"Is Dame Claire here?" asked Frevisse.

Even as she said it, her eyes were searching among their faces.

"Here I am," said Dame Claire, breaking free of the whispering throng. She went to kneel beside the prone figure. For a moment her hand hesitated before, very gently, she touched the back of the fallen nun's head, then put a hand under the nearer shoulder and rolled the body sideways enough to see her face. In the poor light, it appeared almost as white as the surrounding wimple, which was itself touched with darkness. Dame Claire returned the body to its original pose, crossing herself before rising to turn to the others.

"It's Sister Fiacre," she said, keeping her deep voice level with an effort.

Sister Thomasine sank to her knees, crying in a loud voice,

"Si iniquitates observaveris, Domine; quis sustinebit?" If you shall observe wickedness, O Lord; who shall endure it?

That sent the others to their knees. Someone began to sob.

Frevisse saw beyond their bowed heads Domina Edith just come through the door on Sister Juliana's arm. Threading her way among the kneeling figures, Frevisse went to her and said quietly, "Sister Fiacre is dead. She is over there, on the altar steps."

Deep among wrinkles, Domina Edith's eyes went swiftly to Sister Fiacre's still form and Dame Claire on her knees beside it, then back to Frevisse's face. She said, "Take me to her." And to Sister Juliana, "Stay here," as she transferred her unsteadiness to Frevisse's arm. Carefully they circled the kneeling nuns.

Dame Claire rose to her feet at their approach, moving to put herself between Domina Edith and the body, but Domina Edith said, "She is one of mine. Can I refuse to look on her?"

Dame Claire hesitated, then said, too low for anyone except themselves to hear, "It wasn't her illness that killed her."

Equally low, not hesitating, Domina Edith repeated, "I'll see her."

Frevisse went to the altar, genuflected, then pulled one of the candles from its holder. She went to the altar lamp and lit the candle, then brought it down the three steps.

Dame Claire again turned the body so its face was exposed, and in silence Domina Edith stood looking down at her dead nun. The wimple and veil around Sister Fiacre's head had concealed the flatness of the back of her head, and the sideways distortion the broken skull bones gave to her face, both now revealed in the golden candlelight. The eyes bulged as if startled to be overtaken by death, and a little blood had seeped brightly through the white, close-bound wimple along her face, but there was no distortion of terror. What had come had come unwarned and on the instant. The veil had soaked up most of the blood, leaving only a thin gleaming line on the stone floor as the candlelight caught it.

Behind them came the sound of someone rising, and Dame Alys's hoarse voice. "It's a shame, but not unexpected, her being so ill. Who will help move her? I'll light some of these candles and lanterns. We'll need more light, and there's all these waiting for the play tonight. Though now there won't be any play.''

Domina Edith, her hand heavy on Frevisse's arm to steady herself, said without turning around, her tone giving nothing away, ''Leave the lights alone, there is no need for them yet. Dame Alys, take everyone to the warming room for Vespers. Except Dame Frevisse, Dame Claire, and Sister Thomasine. The rest of you, go. Remember to take the psalter. Pray the harder in our absence. I will come to you as soon as may be to tell you the schedule of vigil for Sister Fiacre.''

Grateful and calmed by guidance, the other nuns rose in a hush and rustle of skirts and soft soles. Some two or three relaxed enough to cough. They left the church in Dame Alys's wake, the door thumping solidly behind the last one out.

''Who?'' Domina Edith asked. ''Why?''

There was no answer yet to that. Or there were several answers, but no way of telling yet which was the right one. Frevisse, her mind beginning to move past the reality of Sister Fiacre's death to what it meant and what was going to happen from it, was already seeing possibilities and not liking them.

''Roger Naylor must be told,'' she said.

''And Sister Fiacre seen to,'' Domina Edith said, ''before the others see her. They will have to be told, but they need only see her in her coffin. They need not see what we have seen. Thomasine, you are not to talk of what you saw here.''

''Yes, Domina.''

''I need to see the wound uncovered,'' said Frevisse.

''Why?'' asked Dame Claire.

''Perhaps the wound will tell what manner of weapon struck her. At the least, was it sharp or blunt.''

''I am afraid her head may fall apart if the wimple is removed,'' said Dame Claire, her voice reflecting her deep distress. Thomasine began to pray louder.

''Could you, er, restore her, Dame Claire?'' Domina Edith said.

The infirmarian set her small hands to either side of the dead nun's skull and gently pressed. The bones shifted to a more natural shape with a soft grating sound. Dame Claire swallowed thickly and said, "It appears her skin is mostly whole, but I would prefer that we not take off her wimple. Yet I understand Dame Frevisse's request. We will need a clean wimple. And we'd best replace the veil."

"Dame Frevisse, take Sister Thomasine to help you bring what is needed. We'll prepare her body here. That would be best, don't you agree, Dame Claire?"

Dame Claire nodded. "The less she's moved the better. We can clean and coffin her here. Maybe before Vespers ends."

"Thank you. I will tell them then what has happened."

Sister Thomasine had risen and come to join them while they talked. Now, standing at Frevisse's side, as sickly looking as Frevisse felt, her eyes on Sister Fiacre, she whispered, "Some wicked person denied her the Last Sacrament."

"She has known she was dying for a long time," Domina Edith said, "and was as prepared for it as anyone can be. And when the blow was struck, she was at prayer at the foot of the altar. She died by violence but in the midst of holiness. We can only add our prayers to her own." The prioress's weight had become increasingly heavy on Frevisse's arm. In the same quiet, even tone she said, "I wish to sit now."

Frevisse shifted to put an arm around her waist, guided her to her choir stall, and eased her down into it. In all the priory, each nun's seat in the choir was her own, the one thing that was hers alone for all of her life as a professed nun—unless, like Domina Edith, she rose to be prioress and took the more elaborately carved and prominent one that belonged to that office. But the prioress's choir stall had been Domina Edith's for over thirty years now, and was probably as familiar to her as her own bed. She sank back on it and bent her head in prayer, for no one in this sinful world dies without needing prayers to speed her soul, no matter how forewarned.

Frevisse went back to Dame Claire, and the two of them performed the grisly task of removing Sister Fiacre's veil and wimple. Frevisse was surprised to note how gray Fiacre's short hair was; she was not yet forty. But at the back, it was dark, thick with blood already almost dry.

"This is strange," said Dame Claire after a few minutes.

"I agree," said Frevisse. "Here, and here, the skull is cut, but here it looks smashed, as if by a club."

"*Two* murderers?" Dame Claire's deep voice was sick with dismay.

"Two weapons, anyway. It's hard to think two people came together to murder Sister Fiacre. I pray we find out the truth of this, for I doubt Master Montfort is able." Frevisse stood. "I'll go collect what is needed. Domina, do you wish to join the others at Vespers?"

"No. Not yet, anyway. Go on, and you also, Sister Thomasine."

"Yes, Domina." Thomasine crossed herself and stood.

What they needed to ready the body was in the infirmary. But once out into the cloister walk, Frevisse said, "You go ahead to fetch the wimple and veil. I'll tell Master Naylor we need a coffin."

Somewhere in the priory's storerooms there was at least one coffin, kept against the likelihood of winter death at the priory. Two weeks ago there had been fear that Domina Edith was marked for it, before she began to better from her cough. Now it would be used after all for the one thought most likely to be next to die, though not like this.

At this time of day Roger Naylor should still be somewhere around the priory, seeing that all was in order for the night. Frevisse went into the courtyard, looking for a servant to send for him. Instead she saw the man himself, crossing toward her in his firm, stolid walk, casting a long shadow to one side in the failing light.

He called to her, "What's amiss in there? I hear nothing from the church when there should be singing." Seeing her face he lengthened his stride. "What is it?"

"Sister Fiacre is dead. Can you bring a coffin to the church? That's where we found her, and Domina Edith wants her taken care of there."

Naylor crossed himself. "God take her soul into His hands. I didn't know she was that close to dying."

"She wasn't," Frevisse said. "Can the coffin be brought? And someone sent for Father Henry, wherever he is?"

Naylor's look was sharp on her face, but he only nodded and went away.

Frevisse returned to the cloister. Sister Thomasine was just ahead of her with a clumsy burden: a basin of water with two cloths floating in it, a wimple, veil, and towels over one arm. Frevisse hurried to catch up and took all but the basin, then went ahead to hold the door open ahead of her.

Sister Fiacre's body was cleaned, dressed again, and ready for her coffin when Naylor led in two of the abbey servants carrying it and a third man bearing the trestles it would rest on in front of the altar. Without seeming to do so, Dame Claire and Frevisse moved to block Sister Fiacre's body from view while the men put the coffin down and set up the trestles. Naylor dismissed them, and when they were gone, asked, "Shall I help put her into this, or do I go away, also?"

At this strong hint, Dame Claire said, "She was killed. Someone struck her from behind as she knelt on these steps."

"You're sure she was struck down? That she didn't fall?"

"We're sure," said Dame Frevisse. "Have you seen any strangers within our walls today?"

"Nay, Dame. Except the players, of course. I hear they had words with Sister Fiacre here in the church earlier today."

He produced this bit of gossip without rancor or arrogance, but Frevisse felt herself bristle. Before she could say anything, Domina Edith said, "If you will kindly assist in our sad task of coffining Sister Fiacre, Master Naylor. We would have it done before the end of Vespers."

"As you wish, Domina."

They stepped aside and let him go to the body. It was lying on its back now, the blood-stained bands covered with fresh ones, the blood-soaked veil replaced. Eyes closed, no trace of blood or agony, Sister Fiacre was simply lying there. Only the slightly unnatural angle of the head because there was no longer a curved back to the skull to hold it up betrayed how grievously wrong things were.

"The crowner is coming anyway, for the village death," he said toward Domina Edith. "It won't be possible to keep it secret after his arrival that this death was murder."

Domina Edith shook her head slowly. "To keep it secret she was murdered—no. That would be neither honest nor safe. Yet we hope to keep the full ugliness of how she died from the others. That she was killed will come hard enough."

Frevisse raised her hand a little, asking for attention. "There's something else." Sister Thomasine, Domina Edith, and Naylor all turned to her; Dame Claire looked away. Frevisse tucked her hands into her sleeves and straightened her spine, taking the formal pose to steady her voice. "The death of Sym was murder, too."

Naylor was the first to speak. "How can you be sure?"

Dame Claire replied. "Because there are two wounds on the boy's body. One of them is nothing much. He took it at the alehouse and walked home afterwards. The other one was struck while he was lying down."

Domina Edith suggested mildly, "But suppose the second, too, came at the alehouse, while he was brawling?"

Frevisse said, "It was to the heart and would have killed him almost on the instant. He went walking nowhere after it was struck."

Naylor brooded silently a moment, then said to her, "I'll want to look at him. I know something of knife wounds. In the meanwhile"—he turned back to Domina Edith—"best you see that no one is anywhere alone if they can help it until I've seen to having those players locked away for Montfort's coming."

Again Frevisse had to bite down on an angry response. Naturally the players were an obvious choice for both murders, and she had yet to find a way to clear them. But it hurt to see Domina Edith accept his statement without question, inclining her head forward in agreement.

"But now the coffin," she said.

Dame Claire stepped aside so that Frevisse and Naylor could raise it to the trestles.

As they finished and stepped back, one of the servants who had brought in the coffin returned at a scurry up the nave.

Red-nosed and short of breath, he pulled a swift bow to all of them in general and said, "It's the crowner! He's riding into the yard, he and his men."

"Sooner than expected," Dame Claire remarked.

Frevisse went taut but only said, "By your leave, Domina, I will go see that he is properly settled in our guesthall. Doubtless he will want his supper, and I will have to explain that his untimely arrival caught us unprepared."

The church's side door opened, and Sister Juliana came in. Her eyes widened at the sight of the coffin, and again at seeing Master Naylor, but she curtsied to Domina Edith in her stall and said, "Dame Alys sent me to say that we have finished Vespers and want to know should we come back here or go to supper."

Domina Edith's reply was soft, but prompt. "Do neither. Dame Claire, go to the warming room and with my authority set the watch beginning with Sister Lucy and Sister Emma, who must come immediately, and may go from here to a late supper in the kitchen when they are replaced. The rest as you all agree among yourselves, except Dame Frevisse, who will take the first watch after Matins and Lauds, as she has guests to see to now. Once you have decided how you will divide the night and tomorrow until chapter, then you may go to supper."

Dame Claire, with a nod of appreciation for the prompt solution to one part of the problem, curtsied deeply. "As you wish, Domina," she murmured, and went, taking Sister Juliana with her.

"Now," said Domina Edith, "you, Master Naylor, had better go see to it that the players are in the lesser guesthall and stay there, then that Master Montfort's horses are properly stabled." To the servant she said, "Go, give Master Montfort my greetings and tell him I will see him in my parlor so soon as he is able to come. Sister Thomasine will accompany me there now. Dame Frevisse, you stay here until Sisters Juliana and Emma come, then haste to your duties in the guesthall. See if there is something warm that can be had from our kitchen."

She paused, considering if that covered all that needed

doing on the moment, then nodded and held out her hand to take Sister Thomasine's.

She had hardly departed when the two nuns who would begin the watch over Sister Fiacre's body came in. Frevisse brought two candles and two gilt candle holders from the sacristy for the head and foot of the coffin, and lit them from the altar candle, which she then blew out and replaced.

It was nearly dark out, and the courtyard was lit by flaring torches. Frevisse, standing outside the church's western door, made a quick count of the men Montfort had brought with him, and saw the crowner himself among them, his bulk muffled in a heavy hooded cloak, standing by his tall yellow gelding, giving curt instructions to a priory servant before handing over the reins. The torchlight made his face more florid than it already was, and judging by his expression, his temper matched its color.

Frevisse pretended not to see him as she went quickly by, bound for the greater guesthall. The last time he had had to come to St. Frideswide's, she had interfered with his investigation in what he considered a wholly improper manner for a woman and a nun. That she proved herself right and him wrong did not change his opinion of her. She did not want to set him off again, nor allow him to make his usual facile, incorrect deductions. She would have to work around him, and send her ideas to him by way of Father Henry or Master Naylor, in the form of suggestions or questions that would cause no offense. Master Naylor did not favor cleverness in women but at least knew how to work around stupidity in men.

In the guesthall the servants were already gathered, waiting for instructions. She ordered first that Sym's body be moved to an empty shed in the outer yard—Montfort would not approve of sharing his quarters with a dead villein—then that the fireplaces in the best chamber and the guesthall kitchen be lit. She set the servants to their other duties, and with everything in motion and certain her people knew how to carry through, Frevisse left them to it.

In the yard, she looked toward the lesser guesthall. A servant she recognized as Naylor's assistant was standing guard at the door. She ought to go back to the cloister, to confer with Dame Alys in her kitchen about heating cider. But she turned away from the cloister for the other guesthall. She would make sure the players knew there would be no play tonight.

Chapter 19

FREVISSE AWOKE THE next morning heavy with weariness. Standing her watch in the cold church beside the stiff body of Sister Fiacre had, besides denying her needed rest, depressed her. She was tired of death, tired of being cold and ill, tired of being around other cold, sick women, tired even of prayers and worship. She forced herself through the day's beginning until the end of chapter. Then, as the nuns left to go about their various morning tasks and Dame Claire moved to Domina Edith's side to help her back to her rooms, the prioress, accepting her arm, gestured to Frevisse to come with them.

Domina Edith needed only a little help while walking, but on the stairs to her private rooms gave way to their steadying help with simple grace. Under the furred cloak and several layers of clothing she seemed all thin flesh and small bones.

Her rooms had more luxury than the rest of St. Frideswide's. Her parlor, where she received guests of importance or ones personally welcome, overlooked the courtyard through three tall windows glazed with clear glass. In the more than thirty years since Domina Edith had become prioress, her personal things had so gradually come into the room that St. Frideswide's would have seemed incomplete without them. A woven rug from Spain lay over a table and an embroidery frame with an unfinished wall hanging of Virgin and Child in a field of flowers stood near the fireplace. On the hearth was an elderly basket where her greyhound had slept; though the dog had died last summer, Domina Edith had not yet given order for the basket to be taken away, and no one would ever think to do it without her order.

The parlor was ready for its mistress, the fire built up in the fireplace and braziers lighted in two corners of the room. The only thing not friendly or fitting was Master Montfort standing spread legged in front of the fireplace, displeasure plain on his fox-nosed face. His hands were behind him, the back of one slapping into the palm of the other, filling the gap of his waiting with sharp noise.

Frevisse felt a sharp rise of dismay and alarm at seeing him. There was simply no way around the fact that Master Morys Montfort, the King's crowner for northern Oxfordshire, was an arrogant fool.

Domina Edith inclined her head to him. "*Benedicite,* Master Montfort. I pray you give me a moment to finish some bit of business with Dame Claire."

She did not slip free of her cloak as she turned to settle into her chair, but kept it close around her. Even before this winter sickness she had been somewhat declining. Her soft folded skin was so pale it was difficult to tell where it ended and her white wimple began. But her eyes had lost none of their alertness and she fixed them now on Dame Claire.

"So—" she began, but the word croaked and she paused to clear her throat before trying again. "So, how is our siege of the rheum doing? Is this going to be done with soon, or shall we go on like this until spring?"

"Not into spring, surely," Dame Claire said, a little stiffly. She had as little liking for Montfort as Frevisse did. "It's easing among most of us, rather than going on to something worse."

"And for that we must thank you as well as God, I know," Domina Edith said. "It will be a blessing when it's finished, though. I'm very weary of the offices sounding like a chorus of frogs. Thank you, Dame." She turned to Montfort with an unapologetic smile. "It was not something I was minded to ask in chapter for fear of inspiring relapses. Now, how are matters with you? Are you being well seen to, and helped in your questioning?''

Montfort stopped his impatient hand slapping. ''Your steward has told me enough that there's going to be a little trouble in concluding matters.''

Dame Claire knew more about Sym's death and Sister Fiacre's than did Roger Naylor, but it was clear from her expression that Montfort had not questioned her. But Montfort saw her ready to speak and directed so ill-tempered a look at her that she pressed her lips closed. He sniffed his contentment at putting an impertinent female in her place.

''I had thought to find this was a mere death by misadventure,'' he said. ''A villein picking a quarrel with a rogue during Christmas idleness and falling on his own knife. I wish it were so, as I have my own holiday to enjoy, Lord Lovel being so kind as to honor my wife and me with an invitation to keep the holidays with him.''

He tried to make it sound as if he were frequently so honored, but his stretch to include the fact in this conversation made it clear that he was honored to the point of astonishment. It made Frevisse wonder if he would not have taken his time arriving, or even sent his decision by messenger—it seeming to be so small a matter—had he not wished to show his host his own importance. So here he was, having come at speed despite the season and weather, and was equally impatient to be gone again, doubtless to regale his host with tales of his skill.

''But now I hear that this first death was deliberate murder, and another murder has followed it. Two murders, one in your very church.'' His tone made it clear that such a thing was a personal attack on God, on the King's peace—and himself. He paused. Frevisse wondered if he was expecting them to apologize, but no one did, so he went on. ''And another thing is abundantly clear.'' He glared at Frevisse. ''Someone is interfering in what is not their business. Again.''

Domina Edith looked mildly toward Frevisse. ''Are you interfering with Master Montfort, Dame?''

Her hands folded into her sleeves, her eyes and voice

downcast, Frevisse said, "I have asked questions, my lady. There seemed a need to make an early record of what had happened, as we were not sure how swiftly Master Montfort could arrive."

Someone began scratching on the door to the parlor. Domina Edith seemed not to hear it—her servants knocked firmly—but then the door opened and a balding man put in his head.

Montfort gestured for him to come in, and by the gesture reminded Frevisse that the crowner had a clerk, so much in Montfort's shadow that he usually went as unnoticed as one. He wore a loose gown cinched around his skinny middle with a broad leather belt. Hanging from the belt were an ink pot, a fat, shabby purse stuffed with parchment squares, a small knife, and a leather cord holding a bundle of raven feathers.

"I most humbly beg your pardon," he said in a thin voice, addressing not the mistress of the room but his own master. "I heard voices, and thought if you were taking testimony you would require me to make a record of it." Indeed, he held a thin packet of parchment at the ready in one hand and a feather already carved into a quill in the other. Frevisse drew an angry breath; his ignoring Domina Edith was rude past forgiving.

But the prioress forestalled her. "Do come in," she said. "Master Montfort can review for your record anything of importance."

"Collecting gossip from a priory nun is hardly likely to prove valuable," Montfort said, gesturing the clerk to a place in a corner even while he returned to the topic at hand.

Frevisse, not wanting to quarrel, or to lie by seeming to agree with him, bowed her head again and tucked her hands even further up her sleeves.

"So," Montfort said, "I can assume that now I have arrived, you will stop interfering in my work?"

"I would never knowingly interfere in the Crown's business," replied Frevisse, putting a hint of shock in her reply.

Domina Edith agreed, "We have the highest respect for the Crown of England."

Montfort shifted his ill temper to the rear and said, almost graciously, "That is well said, my lady. There should be no more trouble then." He cleared his throat and turned again to Frevisse. "I would require you to tell me what has been said to you, Dame."

Frevisse bit the inside of her lip. He scolded her for interfering, but had wit to remember she was right the last time their paths crossed and might on this occasion again have learned something of value. Taking firm hold on her temper, not daring to let him see her face, she said, "I have discovered that while Sym was being killed, the man he had fought with in the tavern was with a girl. And it appears that a great many people disliked Sym. There's a neighbor who wants to marry Sym's mother for the sake of their holding and Sym was furious about it."

"And?"

Frevisse looked at him. "And what?"

"The other players. They quarreled with both the man and Sister . . ." His set frown sank a little deeper as he looked for a name.

"Sister Fiacre," Domina Edith murmured.

"Sister Fiacre, Sister Fiacre," Montfort grumbled. "The villein and the nun quarreled with the players and now they're both dead. What about that?"

"I know nothing to indicate any one player could be involved in both murders. Three quarreled with Sister Fiacre, but two of them had no reason to murder Sym, and the other has a witness who says he was with her when Sym was murdered."

Montfort scowled. "So they conspired to do it. The one who quarreled with Sym killed the nun, one of the others killing Sym." He turned his attention to Domina Edith. "They're a shameless lot, these lordless players, a menace to honest folk. The matter may lie in which two of them shared the task, but they are all equally to hang for it." Montfort was fond of prompt, straightforward decisions. They enhanced his reputation, and kept his expenses low. "It should be easy enough to break whatever story they have concocted among themselves. These kind of folk are clever but not loyal, especially when one can save his neck by informing on the others. I'll have the truth out of them soon enough, by questioning them separately.''

Frevisse clutched her forearms tightly inside her sleeves, not saying anything and keeping her head bent toward the floor. It took great effort just to control her breathing. He must *not* do this, she thought.

In her faded voice Domina Edith said, ''We will pray for the truth to be quickly revealed, Master Montfort.''

Montfort grumbled his thanks and came to bend over Domina Edith's hand. The clerk made a rustling business of gathering up pen and parchment scraps the while, and followed his master out the door. When the sound of their footfalls was gone from the stairs, Domina Edith drew a deep breath, coughed briefly, and said, ''What do you think are the facts, Dame Frevisse?''

It took a moment for Frevisse to relax enough to answer. ''The facts are simple and few, hardly more than I have already said, either about Sym's death or Sister Fiacre's. Sym was truly not much liked in the village, according to what Father Henry tells me, and most particularly disliked by the family of a girl he was paying heed to, and by his neighbor Gilbey Dunn. Sym and his father had quarreled with him. Now, with his opposition safely out of the way, Gilbey is pressing his suit on Sym's mother.''

''Have you spoken with him?''

''Briefly. He carries a knife that is approximately the right size to be the murder weapon. His reputation is one of greed and anger when he's thwarted.''

''What do you know of the woman?''

''She is Meg, a thin little thing who works here in the priory sometimes. She has rejected him so far. But Gilbey is not playing the love-struck fool. He talks of the value of combining her holding with his. Gilbey's lickerous eye turns toward our our Annie Lauder.''

''He's courting two women at once?'' Domina Edith was as much amused as scandalized.

''No, Annie has long surrendered her body to him, and she seems content with his promise to continue their play even after he marries Meg. Annie is a hard worker, but she has no land. His interest in her is purely carnal."

"And my dear brother used to say there was no point in buying a cow if the milk came free." Domina Edith had been a nun almost all her life, but she was not ignorant of the world's ways. "But might Annie speak up to spoil Gilbey's plan for Meg?"

"I don't know. I mean to talk with her when there's chance. The one who was seriously angry at what Gilbey means to do was Sym."

"And does any of this bear on Sister Fiacre's death?" Dame Claire asked.

"Not that I can see. What bears on Sister Fiacre's death is a quarrel between her brother and the players, but what it was, I don't know. The players won't say, except that they were wronged. Sister Fiacre said it was her family that was wronged, but she died before she could tell more."

"Was the quarrel serious enough to have made trouble for the players?" asked Domina Edith. "Trouble enough they would want to prevent it by killing her?"

"The trouble had already happened," said Frevisse. "They lost their patron and in consequence some of their number. There was no more trouble possible than had already been made."

"It would be more likely a murder for revenge," said Dame Claire. "They felt her brother wronged them and if there was this sudden way to strike at him . . ."

Frevisse pulled out her handkerchief and blew so loudly that Dame Claire stared at her.

Domina Edith said, "A pity we did not let Sister Fiacre talk when she wanted to. I should have asked her to come to me as soon as Sister Lucy told me about it, but Sister Fiacre in a temper was ever more emotion than sense, God rest her soul, and I thought to let her settle somewhat before I did." Domina Edith sighed, then looked to Frevisse. "What do you think of Master Montfort's conclusion about the players?"

"I can only repeat what I said to Master Montfort, Domina. I find nothing to show that any of them had aught to do with either murder."

"You disagree that they might conspire to protect one another?"

Forced to it, Frevisse admitted, "No, I think they very often do. But not in this matter. They had no reason to commit either murder."

"No?" Domina Edith asked, and Dame Claire made a sound that indicated she disagreed with Frevisse. The prioress said, "If you will leave us, Dame Claire. I would speak privately with Dame Frevisse."

"Yes, Domina. Of course, Domina." Dame Claire curtsied and went out without looking back.

Frevisse, thus encouraged to speak openly, said, "By the very needs of their life, folk such as they have to protect themselves in a variety of ways!" The words came out more strongly than Frevisse had intended. She looked away and forced her voice to ease. "Among other things, they have surely long since learned not to strike back at every fool who goads them. Better to move out of a fool's way than get into fights with whole towns."

Domina Edith nodded, her old eyes keen. "You speak from direct experience, I suppose. Your own parents were often on the road, and must have faced similar problems."

The statement was without censure, but Frevisse stiffened, then resorted again to her handkerchief, wiping long and thoroughly at her nose while she tried to think of a reply that was both courteous and truthful.

But Domina Edith asked, "Is Rose very like your mother, then?"

"No, of course not. My mother was . . ." Frevisse paused. And said, despite the Rule and Domina Edith and her own controlled, controlling self, ". . . less likely to walk upon her hands!" And laughed until tears came. The shock of them sobered her into composure again. "I beg your pardon," she murmured, wiping now at her eyes and keeping her face down, ashamed.

"Are you happy here?" Domina Edith asked gently.

Surprised at the question, Frevisse looked up. "Of course."

"But you were also happy traveling with your parents."

"Yes," Frevisse said without hesitation. Then, less swiftly, "Yes. Yes, I was."

"And no matter your happiness here, you must sometimes miss that freedom of the road. We all miss parts of our life beyond the cloister, else it would be no sacrifice worthy of the giving. And yours is greater than some, perhaps, because you enjoyed the changes that came with each day, new places and new people. It would be harder, I think, for someone like you to be here than for some gentle lady who never traveled beyond her parents' own lands. Not because you lack the discipline, or desire, but because you had to learn later in life to accept what those of us more bound to homes grew up knowing—that the same faces will meet you day to day, sharing your yesterdays, tying themselves always into your tomorrows."

Frevisse, no longer hiding in her handkerchief, met Domina Edith's gaze and nodded, answering the prioress's honesty in kind. "You are very wise."

Domina Edith smiled. "And I think you had forgotten a great deal of the rules of your old life until the players came and reminded you of what it can be like to travel an endless road."

Almost unwillingly Frevisse smiled back. "But I wanted most sincerely to come here, nonetheless," she said.

"I believe you," Domina Edith said. "And your travels have made you particularly valuable as our hosteler. But that does not mean that you must deny the joy you experienced in your youth. Is it possible you do not want the players to be guilty because it would be a betrayal of a part of your life you still love?"

Frevisse opened her mouth to deny it. But the words did not come. Instead she said with forced honesty, "That's possible. But I still don't think they're guilty of either murder."

"So long as your heart and mind are working together to that answer—not one without the other—I will accept your saying so. But on pain of breaking your vow of obedience, I command you: Learn what you can about all of this and prove their innocence, or their guilt. Not only to Master Montfort's satisfaction, but mine. And your own."

That was a challenge as well as command. Domina Edith's direct gaze made that clear. She would accept that part of Frevisse that still loved the life she had left; but in return Frevisse must give herself over to learning the truth, whatever it was, regardless of love or old loyalties.

And understanding all of that, Frevisse nodded her acceptance.

Domina Edith's smile was small, but glowed warm in her eyes. "Then let us discuss this matter something more. For a certainty, you must see that the players are the only ones linked with both the deaths."

Her face warming, Frevisse looked down. It was easier to agree to impartiality than practice it. "Yes," she admitted. "Of everyone, they're the most possible. But even at that, there's nothing but likelihood to show it's them. There's nothing real." She let her frustration show on the last word and met Domina Edith's gaze. "All other matters aside, I simply can't make anyone likely to have killed Sym. The villagers were used to his quarrelsomeness, and Gilbey seemed able to press his suit with or without his consent. And Sister Fiacre's death seems even less probable. She was dying in great pain, so why, if someone hated her, cut short her suffering? Except for the players, there is no link between Sym and Sister Fiacre. But why commit a murder when you are certain to be suspected of it? That would be stupid, and the players aren't stupid!"

After a little silence, Domina Edith said, "Maybe the deaths aren't linked, so that you must look for two murderers with two motives. Or maybe there isn't a motive in either; maybe they were killed by someone only wanting to be killing someone, he didn't care whom. If that's true, we're looking for a madman, and all your search for the logic of motive is useless."

A slow horror seeped through Frevisse as she considered that possibility. Someone purely evil living nearby, who would strike again and again until caught in the act. . . . She shook her head more in denial than with reason. "No. I can't think that. There has to be reason behind these deaths. It's only a matter of finding it. I wish this rheum were out of my head so I could think clearly. I wish . . ." That none of the past few days had happened and she were going to spend the rest of the day asleep in bed.

Light footsteps on the stairs warned that someone was coming. At the quick rap on the door, Domina Edith said, "*Benedicite,*" and Eda entered and curtsied.

"A woman from the guesthall, my lady, is wanting to see you. One of the player folk."

"Bring her up," Domina Edith directed. When the servant was gone, she looked at Frevisse, who shook her head, unable to imagine what Rose might want there.

They had not long to wait before the woman returned, ushered Rose in, and withdrew. Left standing inside the door, her tawny gown a rich complement to the bright colors in the embroidered cushions on the window bench, Rose gave no sign of discomfort at being in a place so far removed from her usual ways. Nor did she stare around. Instead she came with the grace Frevisse had seen in her before, to kneel in front of Domina Edith and say humbly, "My lady, it being more seemly for me than the others of our company to come within your holy walls, I've come from them to ask a boon, if it be your will to grant us one."

Her voice was as rich and charming as Thomas Bassett's, doubtless honed from years of announcing the plays and craving pennies for her own display of acrobatic skills. Domina Edith gave no sign that she was unused to being confronted in her private quarters by landless beggars, but inclined her head and said as gracefully back, "So gracious an asking deserves a gracious giving if it is seemly and within my power."

"The crowner has come, my lady, and we're wondering if that means an end to our hope of performing for your priory." Her eyes flickered from face to face as she said that, trying to see an answer to that and other things. Frevisse at least tried very hard to betray nothing. Rose looked back to Domina Edith. "So by your leave we ask if we are to perform the play as we agreed or not, to repay the goodness you've given us here before we depart. We would otherwise be on our way."

Domina Edith inclined her head and said, "This holy season has lacked much of its accustomed cheer within our walls this year. A play reflecting joyfully on the season might be welcome indeed. But not in the church, where Sister Fiacre lies. It would be wrong, knowing how she felt about players"—Domina Edith was too much a diplomat to say "especially yourselves"—"to allow their mummery within her hearing."

"I doubt she listens much to what goes on hereabouts anymore," said Frevisse before she could stop herself.

Domina Edith quelled her with a glance, and said, "But the guesthall will do, I think. That should offend no one. Would that be suitable to your needs?" she asked.

Rose said, "I am sure it will be most suitable."

Domina Edith looked to Frevisse. "What think you, Dame Frevisse?"

"I should think a play about the Three Kings would be edifying for us all," Frevisse agreed. And she thought she knew what was in Domina Edith's mind. A diversion from Sister Fiacre's death and its fears would be good for all the nuns.

"Would this afternoon then suit you? Between Vespers and Compline as we meant it before? Could it be readied by then, Dame Frevisse?"

"If I may have the candlestands moved from the church to the guesthall, there's little else needs doing. But we'll need those, the hall has no western windows for the late light."

Domina Edith inclined her head in agreement and returned her attention to Rose. "Our permission is given. And our thanks."

Rose stood up and curtsied low.

"Your child," Domina Edith said. "He's better?"

Rose's face bloomed with quiet pleasure. "With every day he's been allowed to stay here, his strength has been returning to him. My thanks for allowing us to stay, my lady."

"We welcome guests in obedience to God's command," Domina Edith answered. "And gladly, for it is written that oft shall we entertain angels unaware." She sketched a cross in blessing to Rose, who crossed herself in return and bowed herself out of the room.

Chapter 20

DAME ALYS'S COLD had begun to clear. Still croaking but her energy returned, she was taking up the slack that had crept into the kitchen during her illness. Roaming among the tables, she spent the morning harassing her workers, her large, bent spoon at the ready as she surveyed and expounded on their inadequacies.

"That's bread dough, not pastry, you're handling, girl! You put more muscle into your kneading, or I'll muscle your head! We've eleven extra mouths now because there's hardly a thing in the guesthall kitchen to feed them—so much for the 'we never get guests at Christmastide' opinion. Meg! That's a slicing knife, not an ax. The chickens have already been butchered. You only need dice them up, not kill them all over again."

She banged her spoon on the table beside Meg, making her jump and grow busier still, cutting the flesh of five boiled chickens into small pieces for pies. It was Sister Amicia, taking her turn helping in the kitchen by cutting up vegetables to be mixed with the chicken pieces, who burst into tears. Dame Alys stopped, hands hard on hips, to glare at her.

"And why your tears, Sister? Those are carrots, not onions, you're slicing. And I've not even told you yet you're slicing them so thin they'll cook to nothing in the pies. Use your wits, and your time, more wisely, and stop that blubbing."

Sister Amicia dug for a handkerchief up her sleeve. "It was your talk of butchery," she sobbed. "It made me think of Sister Fiacre."

Quiet spread across the kitchen. Even Dame Alys fell silent. She had never much cared for Sister Fiacre, who had flared into hysteria or crumpled into despair whenever her fumbling ways in the kitchen were pointed out to her. The nunnery had agreed long before she fell seriously ill that everyone would live more peaceably if her path no longer crossed Dame Alys's. But not even so unhappy a spirit as Sister Fiacre deserved so ugly a death.

Sister Emma reached out to pat Sister Amicia's arm. "Well it is to mourn her passing, but remember, she's gone to Heaven now and everything is better for her."

"Not Heaven yet, I'd say," Dame Alys rumbled. "She's her time in Purgatory to serve first and that may take her a while."

"Oh, surely not," Sister Emma protested. "Prepared as she was for death, and dying as she did, praying at the altar. Surely her soul is as pure as it could be."

Dame Alys glowered. "I'll ask your leave to doubt it. Remember, God had laid a trial on her. . . ." Dame Alys placed a hand on her bosom with a meaningful grimace. "He'd laid a trial on her and she'd not completed it. So there's that to answer for, at least. My guess would be she's gone to Purgatory and her time there will be the longer, to make up for not living out her trial here on earth. And the harder maybe, too, because of it."

"Oh, no—" Sister Emma began, but swallowed further protest quickly; Dame Alys did not bear contradiction calmly.

But beside her Meg made a protesting sound. Dame Alys swung around on her, demanding, "Now what's your problem? If you're about to faint, just get yourself away from that bowl so you don't pull it over with you. And put that knife down so you don't cut someone."

Meg put the knife down. She was not near to fainting but trembling all through herself with a kind of fiercely suppressed anger. Through stiff lips, not quite daring to look at Dame Alys, she said, "She's gone straight to Heaven as truly as any soul could go. She was pure in her serving God in His church, and purely praying to Him when she died, and so surely she has gone straight to Heaven to be happy and out of her pain forever. You're the one who's sinful—sinful to be saying otherwise!"

If one of the chicken carcasses had risen off the table and spoken to her, Dame Alys could not have been more surprised. To that moment Meg had never spoken out of turn, rarely spoken at all. They all gaped, then Dame Alys's jaw began to work, and there was a general cringing at what was surely coming next.

But from the doorway Frevisse said in a voice all calmness, "You may have the right of it, Meg. But it's hardly ours to say, is it? It being a matter between God and each soul as it comes to Him. And we have all been warned not to judge, in fear of our own judgment."

The last was a direct hit on Dame Alys, who visibly swallowed her ire, clamped her fist more tightly around her spoon, and grumbled, "What brings you here? I can't do more about Montfort than I'm already doing."

"And what you do will be splendid," Frevisse said, which was little more than the truth. What came from Dame Alys's kitchen was worth eating, despite the ill temper and bad treatment that accompanied its preparation. "I only wanted to tell you the guesthall kitchen will be able to see to him and his men by supper time."

"There's a blessing," Dame Alys muttered. "But excuse us if we do not continue our conversation, but go on with what needs doing now. It being the holy days, we must needs have a bit of a treat, no matter what's toward otherwise."

Frevisse let that go by. Like a dog that barks all the time, most of what Dame Alys said could be safely ignored. Instead she said, "May I ask questions of your folk here if I don't interfere with their work? It's about Sister Fiacre. Domina has directed me to ask questions."

Thus forestalled of further complaint, Dame Alys grunted and gestured permission.

Frevisse knew that, if she were strict in her obedience, she would be in the guesthall. But she told herself that the truth must be sought where it might be found, which was everywhere, and went quietly from servant to servant, asking if they had seen anything yesterday afternoon, heard anything then or later that might matter. She was careful to keep her voice low, which encouraged the servants to do likewise, seemingly to placate Dame Alys, but actually to keep them from hearing one another's answers. But each said only that she had been busy in the kitchen, and none had been anywhere near the church yesterday, to see or hear anything that might matter.

Then she came to Meg, and asked, "Have you seen Gilbey Dunn lately?"

Without looking up from her work, Meg answered in a voice hardly above a whisper, "When I went home this morning, yes. He came over when he saw I was there."

"What did he want to say?"

"To tell me he'd seen to my animals since Hewe hadn't come home last night."

"Is he still wanting to marry you?"

Dull color covered Meg's cheeks, but she did not ask how Frevisse knew of that, only said, "Yes."

"Have you seen Hewe yet today?"

"He came home a little after I did. He'd been with friends. He'd forgotten the animals. That's what he said. That he'd been with friends and forgotten the animals." She went on dicing the cooked chickens while she spoke. "He's not interested in tending the animals, which is as it should be. He's not meant to be a villager. He's to be a priest."

That was a matter Hewe and his mother would have to fight out between them, so Frevisse offered no opinion. She asked, "You knew Sister Fiacre?"

That startled Meg into looking up at her. "Yes," she breathed, her voice catching a little on the word. "She was kind to me in the church yesterday morning." She looked back down at her work. "But I'm glad she's dead. She's in no more pain now. She's gone to Heaven and won't be crying anymore with hurting." She cast a resentful little glance toward Dame Alys's back.

"That's true enough. The only pity is she did not die in God's time for her."

Meg looked up at her directly then. "But she did die in God's time. We're in God's hands in everything, so Father Clement used to say. Everything is His."

"Except evil," Frevisse said.

Meg's eyes widened, and she looked fearfully around, crossing herself, before returning doggedly to her work.

"Were you in the church yesterday afternoon?" Frevisse asked.

"For a little while. I went to pray again. Prayers feel better there."

"Was Sister Fiacre there then?"

"She was kneeling on the altar steps when I came in." Meg swallowed thickly. "She'd told me that was her favorite place to pray."

"Did you talk with her?"

Meg shook her head dumbly.

"Was there anyone else there? Did you see anyone else in the church?"

Meg shook her head again, hesitated, looked from side to side and down and then finally at Frevisse again, bringing herself to say, "But afterwards I saw one of the travelers—one of the players—the fair-haired one—going toward the church."

Frevisse felt a hard knotting somewhere near her stomach. Careful of her voice, she managed to ask, "How soon after?"

Having started, Meg seemed less shy of saying more. "Soon. I was coming back here. I saw him going toward the church then."

"Do you know what time it was?"

Meg hesitated, thinking, then held up three of her fingers side by side and parallel to the floor. "The sun was that much above the horizon."

"Did he go into the church?"

Meg hesitated before saying, "I didn't watch. But he was going that way."

"And you know it was one of the players. You saw his face? Where were you when you saw him?"

Meg hesitated, uncertain which question to answer first. "I didn't see his face, he was going away from me. But his hair, so fair, I saw. And they dress differently, the players do. And he's tall. It was him."

Joliffe. Or someone dressed to look like him, Frevisse's mind determinedly offered.

Frevisse went on to Dame Alys, who was brooding over a pot bubbling with dark broth on one of the fires. Frevisse breathed in the rich smell of its steam and said, "Rabbit?"

"Rabbit," Dame Alys agreed grudgingly, as if it were meant to be a secret. "For Domina's especial New Year's treat—if the meat ever cooks to tender enough to go into a pie. It's taking its while, let me tell you. Every rabbit that's come to me from him this year has been tough as tanned leather."

"Come from whom?" Frevisse asked. If a villein managed to snare a rabbit he generally kept it for himself and his family, and few of the servants had time enough to course rabbits. So who was responsible for bringing Dame Alys rabbits?

"Father Henry. He and that little hound of his can't ever seem to catch aught but the oldest rabbit in the warren. It's wearisome, it is. He brought one in yesterday that will have to hang a few days, or it might do. But this one hung a week and is tough as fresh killed. And it's not so big as the one he brought me at harvest time. Why, it was big as a shoat and likely twenty years old."

She would have gone on comparing rabbits until the meat boiled to invisible fragments in the broth, but Frevisse made her escape. The cold air of the cloister made her nose and head ache, and she paused a moment, leaning against one of the pillars to steady herself while she collected her thoughts. Meg had seen Joliffe near the church yesterday afternoon. And probably told someone else besides Frevisse about it. Which meant that eventually Montfort would know of it.

But worse, Joliffe had lied to her. She felt betrayed. She

had trusted these people, and one—all of them?—had lied to her.

She was so angry she dared not go directly to the guest-hall; it would not do to let them see her angry. But she also wanted to talk to Gilbey Dunn again. And to Father Henry about what he might have learned. And to Annie Lauder.

Annie was alone in the laundry today, elbow deep in a suds-crested washtub, with a pile of soaking tablecloths heaped white beside her. Well muscled from her years of carrying buckets of water and baskets of wet laundry, she did not look as tall as she was. She looked around as Frevisse came in, nodded to her, but went on mauling another tablecloth in the water. "No holidays for laundresses," she said in rhythm to her movements. "They just come clean in time to be dirtied again come Twelfth Night. A daft occupation, laundering, but God wills I must earn my pence and I obey. Is there aught I can do for you, Dame?"

"Maybe," said Frevisse. "And certainly something I can do for you."

"That's a fair trade then," Annie grinned.

"The crowner has come to look into Sym's death and Sister Fiacre's murder."

"Aye. That word was all over the priory long since." Apparently her work did not keep her separate from whatever news might be going through St. Frideswide's.

"Can you tell me where Gilbey Dunn was the night that Sym died?"

Annie paused just two beats in her movements, then continued. "How should I know?"

"Was he with you?"

"In here?" Annie looked around grimly. "I've never thought he'd be one for taking much interest in laundry." Frevisse thought that no answer at all and her face said so. Annie said, less flippantly, "I'm not much of one for following after him, or any man. I've trouble enough with aprons and napkins. At least they don't go sneaking off getting themselves dirty after I've washed them."

But Frevisse did not consider that an answer, either. She continued to wait.

Finally, defiantly, Annie said, "What would I be doing with him? I know when I'm well off, and living at some man's beck and call while he spends my good silver pence is not my notion of well off. I have what I want and I'll keep what I have, and if this crowner says he's found things that any fool knows aren't there to be found, well, we all know the fool's word never hanged nobody."

"I have a witness who can swear you and Gilbey Dunn had sexual concourse in this very shed, and that your conversation made it clear this was a regular occupation for the two of you."

Annie resumed scrubbing in her tub. "I don't know what you're talking about."

"Annie, I think it possible that Gilbey murdered Sym, whom he considered an obstacle to his proposed marriage to Meg Shene. You should be careful of giving your affections too easily. You are breaking the law of God and man, and putting yourself in danger of a charge of helping a murderer."

"He didn't! He never did!"

"So you say. But can you prove it?"

Annie threw the tablecloth into the water and sat down on the wet bench beside her tub. "Lord have mercy," she sighed.

"What has Gilbey said to you?"

"Only that he's not unhappy Sym is dead. He told me that day before yesterday." She sighed again. "I've saved almost enough to buy my freedom," she remarked inappositely.

"All the more reason to be glad you're not married to him."

"Humph. He could be free if he wanted. But he'd have to give up his holding, and what's the use of being free if you're landless in the bargain? No, no, what breaks my heart is that to save his rotten hide I'm going to have to pay leyrwite, for we were together all night the night Sym Shene was killed."

The bell for Sext was ringing as Frevisse came out of the laundry. After the shed's heavy, damp heat, the January air cut crisply, and she paused to breathe it, then shivered in a sudden chill and hurried toward the warming room where they were worshipping now that the church was desecrated, with her hands thrust into her sleeves and her chin tucked down for warmth.

The lesson and gospel readings for the hours covered, in a year's time, the whole of the Old Testament and three times through the New. Now, between Christmas and Epiphany, they were reading Daniel. Frevisse, with her basic Latin and familiarity with Wycliffe's English translation of the Bible, was just able to understand and enjoy the psalms and readings. So it was with a touch of annoyance that she struggled to hear past the complaining coughs of her fellow nuns the complex prophesy of conquest from the man with a face like lightning and arms the color of polished brass.

"'And he shall stir up his power and his courage against the king of the south with a great army; and the King of the south shall be stirred up to battle with a very great and mighty army; but he shall not stand: for they shall forecast devices against him.'"

Frevisse blew her own nose and wondered, lost in pronouns, which King should not stand because of the devices of the other. Was it important to understand that?

Was it important to try to understand *everything*?

Sister Fiacre, wrapped in the deepest of all silences in her box near the altar, might at last be understanding what was important, and have dropped what was not, like a wet and filthy robe. Was that what she, Frevisse, should do? But was it not important to understand the lessons of the Bible? And to discover who among them was a murderer?

Or was it?

Was being dead a peace beyond understanding—or an understanding that, at last, brought peace?

Sext ended, Domina Edith gave her benediction over them, her eye on Frevisse the while—a look Frevisse could not return with any steadiness—and they were released to go about their tasks. Frevisse bent her will to obedience, left the cloister, and crossed the yard to the old guesthall.

Two of Montfort's men stood just inside the door, leaning

against the wall. They glanced at her but her nun's habit put her beyond their authority; nor did she speak to them, but stood silently between them a while, watching the players.

They were well along preparing the hall for the play. What would be their stage in front of the hearth had been swept clear of rushes. Bassett and Joliffe were nearly finished setting up a framework of poles that would support the curtains while Ellis and Hewe moved the last of the gear behind it where it would be out of sight. Piers was sitting on a large basket with a mixed expression of pain and patience while Rose evened the shaggy back of his fair hair with a pair of small shears.

Hewe was the only one who turned toward the sound of the door opening and saw her. But head down, he kept busy at one of the baskets, seeming to think that if he did not look at her, she would not see him. Perhaps she should order him to stay away, but it was clear he was being useful to them, at least at present, and so she thought perhaps she would not.

Holding two poles steady while Joliffe, standing on a stool, cord whipped the cross pole to them, Bassett said, "Thank Heaven that old prioress wants us to do this. Keeping occupied will avoid bad thoughts. Next time we see Dame Frevisse, we'll have to ask about those candles she promised. Is there anything else we need?"

"To get out of here," Ellis growled.

Joliffe said, "Does he work at being an idiot or does it come as easily to him as it seems?"

Nearly Frevisse spoke then, alarmed at his flippancy and worried that the players' incorrigible lack of humility could only help convict them in Montfort's eyes.

Ellis slammed a lid on a chest. "He's not so much of an idiot that he can't hang us if he chooses! I would we had never seen that fellow in the ditch, or that we'd played the Pharisee and passed him by!"

"'O God, I thank thee that I am not like other men—'" began Joliffe, playing the Pharisee from a different parable, and was interrupted by Ellis flinging a small basket in his direction. He caught it and laughed, jumping off the stool, but there was nothing cheerful in the look on his face as he turned away.

"One of our problems is that you are so little like other men that bailiffs and sheriffs and crowners yearn to take you by the hand and make you explain yourself," Bassett rumbled, but without rancor. "But you aren't a murderer, nor is any of us. What worries me is getting to Oxford by Twelfth Night."

"Hush, Thomas," said Rose. "There's no sense lathering yourself over that. We either make Oxford by Twelfth Night or we don't, and likely the world won't end if we don't. And the rest of you, stop playing the fool and start trying to think like the holy Kings."

Ellis growled wordlessly. Rose pointed him to a place across the hearth from her and said, "Sit. Eat something. You haven't eaten enough today to keep a sparrow alive. And that goes for the two of you, as well," she added to Bassett and Joliffe. "And you, Hewe, come here and share a bite with them."

The boy looked at her, startled, then at Frevisse warily. When she still gave no sign of saying anything, he came.

Rose ignored his hesitation, running her fingers through Piers's hair, tangling his gold curls and smoothing them again. "As for me, I'm content to stay awhile longer; there's no harm in Piers being out of the cold another day."

"And the day after that and the day after that," Ellis muttered. He had come not to eat but to pace restlessly around the curtain-hung poles. They ignored him, Bassett and Joliffe and Hewe busy with their bread and cheese, Rose slicing cheese for Piers.

Frevisse, watching her, sensed in the controlled force of her movements how much the child mattered to her—as much and maybe more than the survival of their group. Or maybe the child and the group were one to her.

Frevisse had never had that kind of affection turned on her. Her parents' fierce loving had been mostly for each other, with herself a happy adjunct, and she had come into Thomas Chaucer's household as a pleasant addition to an established order. She probed briefly at her feelings to see how much that mattered to her and found hardly any regret. There had been love, and kindness, and freedom to be herself. These were good things. They contented her.

Joliffe said in a bold, dramatic tone, "'I ride wandering in ways wide. King of all Kings, send me such guide that I may—' no." He cleared his throat and began again, this time in dreamy, gentle voice, "'I ride wandering in ways wide—'" Piers giggled. Joliffe cleared his throat again and intoned, "Eggs and beer, be of good cheer, ho, ho, ho. 'King of all Kings, send me such guide, *such* guide, such *guide* . . .'" and subsided, thinking.

"If you could only be a little more convincing," said Ellis from behind the curtain, "perhaps the fool crowner will release us to follow our star."

Frevisse took a deep breath and started for them. Further delay would only continue to weaken her resolve; it was time to ask the important questions.

"Joliffe, I want to speak with you," she said.

He started and looked toward her, rising. She had forgotten how clear and light a blue his eyes were, and how easily they saw the foolishness of others.

She turned from him and said abruptly to Bassett, "Bassett, Montfort knows about your quarrel with Sister Fiacre. Has he asked you about it?"

"Yes."

"What did you tell him?"

"That we had quarreled and Lord Warenne had turned us out of his service."

"What did you say when he asked you why?"

Bassett did not answer. Only Ellis, just come from behind the curtain, was looking at her. The others were staring at the floor in front of them. "Domina Edith has given me leave to ask the questions Master Montfort won't think of, to try to find out what has truly happened here. I need truths, not silences."

"Tell her," said Rose.

They all looked at her, surprised. "Lord Warenne—" Bassett began.

"Is going to be telling his side of it to the crowner if the matter isn't settled soon. Tell her. I don't see how it can help but she won't use it to hurt us either. Tell her.''

Bassett questioned Ellis and Joliffe with a silent look. Darkly brooding, Ellis tersely nodded his agreement. Joliffe, anger clamped behind the tight set of his face, shrugged as if it had ceased to matter to him. Bassett returned to Frevisse. ''We were the late Lord Warenne's players for three years. You know what that means to our kind, I think.'' Frevisse nodded. A skilled, well-traveled troop could sing a patron's praises over a wide area. And they did, for patronage gave them protection, and was such a guarantee of their good behavior that they could be sure of welcome everywhere, so long as he was pleased with them. To find a patron and then lose him was normally a quick road to ruin.

''We were a larger company then. Six of us to act, so better plays could be done. When Lord Warenne died, he commended us to his son, your Sister Fiacre's brother. He was willing to continue our patronage but the first spring we came to perform our season's work for him, as we had every spring for his father, he gave us to understand that he knew the ways of players and that he wanted us, as we traveled, to now and again—'collect' was his word—an occasional young woman on our way. We were welcome to our sport with her but he would be appreciative in monetary ways if we brought her to him eventually. He said he knew our ways and that we could woo them to it easily enough.'' Bassett's flat tone and the stony set of his face stripped away any lightness the words might have had. ''He said village girls were easily come by and sweet enough if gathered young.''

''He also said,'' Joliffe added with mocking bitterness, ''that he would pay more for any we delivered to him with their maidenhood intact.''

''Joliffe,'' Bassett said quellingly. ''Good lady, pardon our words but there's no way to say this less offensively.''

Frevisse did not need the apology but accepted it with a small nod. ''You refused him.''

Bassett gestured at Ellis and Joliffe. ''As you see. There are only three of us now, and the boy, and Rose, and we journey without a lord's name.''

"Rose would have taken our heads from us if we'd accepted," Joliffe said.

Rose's wry, downcast smile agreed with him. Bassett went on. "As importantly, he threatened that if we said aught to anyone about the matter, he'd spread word we had made the offer to him and he'd turned us away in disgust."

"His word would be more readily taken than ours," Ellis said. "And since he can have us all into prison and no way out, we keep our mouths shut and swing well clear of Lord Warenne. Those of us that are left."

Frevisse, looking from one to another of their set faces, was sure they were telling her the truth.

Rose said, "You see this does not help in our present trouble? If we defend ourselves by defaming Lord Warenne, we put ourselves in more peril and do not clear ourselves of this present suspicion of murder."

Frevisse nodded slowly. "But I must go on asking questions. I have to go on asking questions."

"We'll answer those that we can."

Frevisse said, "Then I would speak out of your hearing with Joliffe."

Joliffe sketched a bow and went with her to the other hearth. Frevisse said, "I have a report that you were seen going toward our church about four of the clock yesterday."

"Lady, that I was not." This was said readily, with what might have been no more than an actor's smoothness.

"Are you accusing my witness of lying?" asked Frevisse.

"I cannot accuse anyone of anything, since I know nothing about him. Or her. I can only say what I know. I was in the church with Ellis and Bassett in the morning to see where we would perform. But not since." This sounded more like the rough truth.

"Where were you then at that hour?"

For a wonder, his clear blue look did not see that she was only guessing he was not here in the guesthall. "I went walking after our rehearsal and was gone several hours."

"Alone?" Frevisse asked, remembering the girl in the village.

"Alone," Joliffe agreed.

''Not meeting anyone?''

''Not anyone.'' He gave her a mocking grin. ''Unless you count a small spotted hound, but I doubt he'll speak on my behalf. He seemed to be somewhat occupied with coursing a rabbit at the time. Careless of me to be so solitary, but there it is.''

Discouraged and her head aching again, Frevisse turned on her heel and walked away, weighted with her thoughts.

Chapter 21

THROUGH THE REST of the morning, Frevisse saw to her guesthall duties, leaving her thoughts to work themselves out without her conscious help. The servants were well trained to her ways, but there was never harm in letting her people see that she was paying heed to them. As always there were small matters that needed her word or advice, and with one thing and another, she was kept busy until the bell called her to Nones. She finished agreeing with Eda in the old guesthall over who should see to scrubbing out the water buckets and excused herself to go to the service, a little delayed and so intent on hurrying through the hall without seeing the players that she nearly blundered into two men coming in the guesthall door as she was going out. She did not know them and vaguely supposed them Montfort's without thinking about it.

Her apologies and theirs mingled and she went on until, halfway across the courtyard she realized why they were there, and spun around to see them coming out again, Joliffe between them now, his arms firmly in their grasp and no gentleness in their hold on him.

Nearly she started back toward them. But the bell was still demanding that she come to prayers. And there was nothing she could do to change what was coming. All she had were unanswered or ill-answered questions, and none of them would do Joliffe any good.

Helpless, her feelings at war against her thoughts, she watched Montfort's men drag Joliffe up the steps to the new guesthall. He kept his feet, but only barely, having to fight against their hold to do it. She saw them twist his arms, hurting him to keep their hold. Answering anger and fear surged in her. Fiercely, she did not want Joliffe hurt.

And that very fierceness was a warning, set against Domina Edith's earlier one. She was caring too much about Joliffe, instead of about the truth. She was supposed to find the truth, let the guilt lie where it might. The players should be no concern of hers beyond that.

Finally, fully, she faced it. Domina Edith was right, these people had roused in her a long-dormant love for the endless journeying of her youth. They had brought alive again a part of herself she had loved and never fully left. She wanted them free to go their way, as she was no longer free to go.

But Joliffe had lied to her.

Grimly, she turned away to hurry into the cloister, away from Joliffe and the rest, if not away from her thoughts.

Crowded with the other nuns in the warming room, her head bent in what was supposed to be prayer, she stared down at her thick black gown, and felt her wimple's tightness along her temples and under her chin. In the years she had worn them, they had become too familiar to be noticed; they were a part of herself. But now she felt their constriction and their meaning. Knew what they gave her. And what they denied her.

No, she said in her mind. *No,* this *is where I belong, and this is what I should be doing. Here. Now is when I'm living, not in some memory of my childhood.*

Forcing out of her mind her remembrance of Joliffe dragged between Montfort's men, she gave herself to the service beginning around her, losing herself in the chanted repetition of the psalms, soaking in the words with her mind and soul, listening with a novice's fervor for answers that had to be there.

And found a part of them in the New Testament lesson:

" 'Wherefore . . . give diligence to make your calling and election sure; for if you do these things, you shall never fall.' "

And she had been near to falling. Not from her vows, surely, but from her devotion to her life. From her obedience and her acceptance.

But there, with the thought in clear words, she knew that danger was past. Feelings came and went, but her surety of why she was here was in her mind and in her heart deeper than feelings or a day's passing inclination.

At the office's end, she felt as cleansed and clear as if she was come from Easter Mass and communion, her thoughts no longer warring against her inclinations, but set and settled on what she had to do.

Dinner came after Nones. Frevisse said grace with the others in the refectory, sat in her place on the bench, and determined to heed the day's reading rather than her own thoughts for a while. They were still hearing the history of the English people as written by St. Bede and still read poorly by Sister Thomasine.

" 'In Northumbria, there was a head of a family,' " Thomasine intoned, " 'who led a devout life, with all his household. He fell ill, his condition steadily deteriorating until the crisis came, and he died in the early hours of the night. But at daybreak he returned to life and sat up, to the consternation of those weeping about his body.' "

As was to be expected, thought Frevisse, dipping her bread in her mutton stew to soften and flavor it. *We would be shocked and frightened if Sister Fiacre sat up and spoke to us. It would be hours before we'd have our wits about us enough to rejoice at the miracle.*

Thomasine droned on. The Northumbrian divided his property into three parts and gave a third to his wife, a third to his sons, and a third to the poor before going off to become a monk.

What would a resurrected Fiacre do, being already a nun? Frevisse wondered.

Visitors came to the man, to hear stories of his experience in the world beyond the grave, and he told of seeing damned souls leaping from flame to bitter frost and back again in a fruitless search for comfort, and of a wonderful, fragrant countryside for the saved. "" "I was most reluctant to return to my body, for I was entranced by the pleasantness and beauty of the place.''''' Sister Thomasine read, Bede quoting the man. "" "But I did not dare to question my guide, and I suddenly found myself alive among men once more.'''''

Sister Fiacre, too, might be unhappy at her return, weeping and wringing her hands to find herself among ordinary people again.

The man was described as living in great severity in his monastery, breaking ice to plunge himself into a wintertime river, standing up to his neck in the flowing water, reciting psalms, until he could no longer bear it and must climb out, but refusing to change his wet clothes, saying to those who questioned him that he had seen it worse in another place.

Here Sister Thomasine stopped, not to savor the grim joke, but to say, "*Tu autem, Domine, miserere nobis,*" meaning that she had finished the reading.

Frevisse responded with the rest of the nuns, "*Deo gracias,*" but dinner was not quite over. The meal continued in silence, and without a voice to listen to, Frevisse's thoughts went on their own way. Had that man truly been right and good in what he did? She had seen it happen—a person resolutely using punishment and privation to drive out the ability to enjoy life's good things. Though didn't that also make it impossible to enjoy the pleasures of the fragrant meadow promised to the saved? Having set their heart on earth to miseries, might not such people be happier in the rigors of Hell?

Frevisse caught the thought and suppressed its strangeness sternly. There was no doubt that strict disciplines could lead to sainthood, all authority agreed on that.

Unable to meditate on the reading to any purpose, she found her mind wandering to the murders. Was Domina Edith right? Could there be two murderers about, one with a knife and the other with a club?

And wandering past the murders to what Montfort was doing to Joliffe now.

Harshly, she jerked away from that thought. She had to find an answer—answers—to these murders and soon.

The need for immediate answers tightened in her. She laid her bread down, unable to swallow.

One of the murderers must be Gilbey Dunn. He hated Sym, who stood between him and his gain. Would Annie Lauder lie to save him if he promised to pay her leyrwite? And where was Father Henry, he with the answers to questions she needed to ask? He had been gone all morning. Out rabbiting again, she thought bitterly, while I'm trapped here. Almost always St. Frideswide's walls were shelter and boundary to her, not limitations, but now she had a wild longing to leap clear of them, to follow where her questioning wanted to go, to the village, to Lord Warenne's, to anywhere rather than going on circling here helplessly, blocked by the Rule.

Her fingers stopped squashing her bread into a formless wad. Rabbiting. With his hound.

Her excitement nearly brought her to her feet. Only barely she contained herself the little while left until the meal was done. With choked eagerness, she recited the grace with the others, rose with them, and moved quietly away from the table and out of the refectory into the cloister walk. But there, as the nuns separated to their afternoon duties, she swung sharply around and caught Dame Alys before she could disappear back to the kitchen.

With quick signs Frevisse asked her to come along to the slipe, the narrow passage that ran out into the orchard. Short conversations that could not wait for other times or better places were allowed there, and as soon as they were in its shelter Frevisse said, "About Domina Edith's rabbit pie . . ."

"I've done the crust for it myself and if some fool hasn't spoiled the meat with too much salt while I've been gone . . ."

Knowing better than to let Dame Alys warm to that theme, Frevisse cut across her. "It was yesterday Father Henry brought you the rabbit?" Dame Alys made a curt, surprised nod. "When yesterday?"

"Just before supper. Came skulking in all guilty, like a

schoolboy caught out when he should have been at lessons, and I had to be the one that told him Sister Fiacre was dead. He was so upset he nearly forgot to hand over the rabbit, would have walked right out of the kitchen with it in his fist if I hadn't snatched it. A holy man, maybe, but a great gawp in the bargain, I've often said . . ."

"You said he goes rabbiting with a hound?"

"A little spotted dog, called a hound only because that's what it's most nearly like. He keeps it in the miller's house in the village, for Domina wouldn't let him keep so raggedy a creature here—"

"Thank you!" Frevisse said and left Dame Alys standing with mouth open, surprised all over again at her rudeness.

On her way to the new guesthall, she stopped a servant in the yard and asked him to find Father Henry for her. "I need to see him as soon as may be. I'll be with the crowner awhile, but after that he'll have to look for me. Tell him I need to see him very soon."

The man nodded and ran off, and she went on. It might have been better to wait until she had actually talked with Father Henry, but she wanted to know how far Montfort had gone in questioning Joliffe, and learn, if she could, what he had found out that she had been unable to.

He was in his chamber, the new guesthall's best room, standing close to the fire and looking pleased with himself. His clerk sat at a table across the room, hunched over a parchment he was reading instead of scribbling on.

Montfort glanced toward her and almost smiled. "I told you I'd solve this, and promptly."

"Has someone confessed, then? The player?"

"Ha! Not him. Not that it matters. Just one or two more people I want to talk to and all will be done and I can return to Lord Lovel's."

"Who is it you need to speak with?"

"Not you, Dame. Though you might see to stirring up your servants. I've been kept waiting."

"Is it one of our servants you want to see?"

"Hardly. It's that fellow from the village. The one who quarreled with the dead boy."

"Gilbey Dunn?"

"Yes, that's the villein. They're telling me no one can find him. They say he's not been seen since yesterday and that's nonsense. He's a villein, not some noble gone to his other manor halfway across the country."

Frevisse felt a stir of hope. Gilbey Dunn had taken himself off somewhere and no one knew where?

Montfort, backing a little nearer to the fire, said, "There's some who would have me believe he's the guilty one, that he ran off to escape justice. But I've got my murderer safe in hand, and all I need to do is settle matters about this Gilbey person, so I can leave. Lord Lovel expects me for Twelfth Night."

Frevisse made impressed sounds at this second dropping of the Lovel name, and asked as if in total ignorance, "Which one of them have you in hand?"

"The fair-haired player. Joliffe, he's called. He had reasons against both the dead man and your nun and was seen both places, village and church, near when the killings happened."

As if truly seeking clarification, and not in argument, Frevisse said, "But I was told he was with a woman in the village at the time Sym was murdered. Tibby, her name is."

Montfort waved dismissively. "Ah, yes, Tibby. She'd lie in God's face for the sake of the player's pretty face, I've no doubt, so her word is no use at all."

Frevisse wanted information and forebore to argue with him, asking instead, "He was seen going into the church? By whom?"

"The dead boy's mother. That stringy bit of a woman—" Montfort waved his hand vaguely, unable to remember her name. "So scared of talking to me, I thought she'd puddle in front of my eyes, but she spoke her piece. Came, in fact, of her own will to tell me. That was enough to settle it."

"I heard him say he wasn't in the priory the afternoon Sister Fiacre died," Frevisse dared to point out.

"He's said the same to me, but he's a liar, all players are. That's their trade. He was seen going toward the church, and probably hid in there, waiting his chance. When he saw her there alone, he took it."

"Why?"

"For vengeance on her brother!" Master Montfort let his impatience show.

"And his reason for following Sym home and killing him?"

"They'd been in a fight, and by all accounts Sym was a bad-tempered brute. The player was afraid Sym would come after him later, bringing half the village louts with him. Look what happened, in fact—they did come seeking him. They knew him for what he was. The matter is clear and simple. They're a debased lot, these lordless player folk, worse than the worst of the villeins. Facts are facts and I think we've found our murderer."

"So except that you're missing Gilbey Dunn, the matter is settled?"

Montfort frowned. "Except that," he agreed shortly. He glared at her, suddenly suspicious. "Did you have some purpose in coming here to see me, Dame?"

"To ask if everything is satisfactory to your comfort here"—which was true, it was one of her tasks as hosteler—"and to ask if it would be possible for Joliffe to perform this evening with his company. They're to do a play in the old guesthall."

"A play? Here?" Montfort was surprised.

"We do our poor best to honor the season," murmured Frevisse, surprised by his interest.

"Well, I never expected such a thing in a place such as this!" Montfort's enthusiasm lightened his face. He rubbed his hands with satisfaction. "A play, you say? Which one?"

"I don't know its name, but it's about the Magi, the Three Kings."

"And, of course, you need three men for that. Well, there's guards enough, I suppose. We could bar the gates to the courtyard, he could be escorted there, and then all the ways out guarded. It should be possible." His expression sank back to its usual displeasure. "Let's hope these players are better than they look to be. I know a good play when I see one."

Frevisse was nonplussed at this unexpected aspect of the crowner. Before she could collect her thoughts for a reply, a modest tapping came at the door.

"Yes?" Montfort barked. Father Henry came in.

Before he completed his bow to Master Montfort, she was standing in front of him. "Where have you been? I've needed to see you!"

Her suddenness took both the priest and Montfort unprepared. Father Henry looked uncertainly toward Montfort, whose face was reddening, but Frevisse pressed on before he could interrupt, "Were you out rabbiting yesterday? After you'd been to the village, did you go out rabbiting?"

Father Henry flushed his hearty pink of embarrassment and fumbled, "Yes. A little while. I wasn't gone long."

"Did you see anyone while you were out? Did anyone see you? Or your dog? Where is your dog? What does he look like?"

Father Henry gaped, mentally stumbling over so many questions, then caught up the last one and said, "He's not very tall." The priest dropped the flat of his palm a little below knee level. "Rough coated, white with tan spots. Not a blood dog," he hastened to assure Montfort. "Naught like that. Just a mixed breed, with enough hound in him that he'll course small game. Hal the miller keeps him for me and since I was already out there yesterday . . ."

"And a fine rabbit you brought home for Domina Edith's New Year's treat and no harm done," Frevisse said encouragingly. "But did you see anyone while you were out? Anyone in the fields?"

"Oh, aye. One of the player folk. The fair-haired one. I didn't hail him. I don't have much time for players, and this one, well, he's a bit . . . more like a girl than a man." Father Henry shrugged his own manly shoulders and flushed a little more. "And maybe a bit soft?" He tapped his forehead. "Walking alone, he was, talking to himself, gesturing like a friar preaching a sermon, though I couldn't hear what he was saying."

"But he didn't see you?" Montfort was interested despite himself.

The priest's blush deepened. "I was lying low in a thicket just then, not wanting to be seen. He saw Trey, though. My dog. Is that what this is about? My hunting? Is Domina Edith unhappy with me?"

"You are in no trouble," Frevisse assured him. "When was it you saw him, and where?"

"Over by Long Hill, near the ford at the end of the meadow."

"How far from here is that, walking time?"

He thought on it hard before answering, "A full half hour at the fastest walk if you come through the village. Longer if you come around."

Joliffe, who was seeking solitude, did not come through the village or someone would have seen him.

"And how long before Vespers was that?"

Father Henry rolled his eyes to the ceiling, considering. "An hour maybe? By the sun it was maybe an hour."

"And you're sure it was that particular player?" Montfort demanded.

Father Henry nodded solidly, pleased to be sure of something. "There's no doubting him. The one who dresses like a woman in his acting."

Frevisse turned to Montfort. "But Meg said she saw Joliffe going toward the church three-quarters of an hour before Vespers, by the sun. Even if Joliffe came through the village he couldn't have reached here by then."

"So she was mistaken. He did the murder before he went out wandering the fields," Montfort said. "Yes, and that's why he went out alone. To say prayers, to think on penitence, to—"

"She was not mistaken in her time of seeing him, she showed me with her fingers how low the sun was. And it isn't possible Sister Fiacre was murdered earlier. She would have been discovered—by Meg herself, if not one of us."

"So the woman was mistaken? Whom did she see instead?"

"I don't think there's anyone else here at the priory who looks very much like that fellow," offered Father Henry.

"By any reckoning, Joliffe is cleared of Sister Fiacre's death." Frevisse pressed her point.

Montfort, frowning at the floor, said sullenly, "Seemingly. But that doesn't mean he and his fellows are not guilty of some lawbreaking. They are not ill-thought-of for nothing, you know."

Frevisse let that pass and said instead, "Meanwhile there's still Gilbey Dunn to consider."

"Ah, him. The trouble is, what reason would he be having for killing a nun?"

Nearly Frevisse brought out Domina Edith's thought that maybe there were two murderers, or a single madman, but Montfort suddenly smacked his hands together with great satisfaction. "Unless of course there was something between this Gilbey Dunn and Sister Fiacre that we don't know of yet!"

Father Henry's blankly astonished face was doubtless the mirror of Frevisse's own at the wholly improbable thought of Sister Fiacre and Gilbey Dunn finding common ground.

But Montfort, too pleased with his idea to bother noticing their reactions, went on, "Yes! There's the path I have to take! That's the man I need to talk to!" He almost smiled at Frevisse. "Doubtless you're right, Gilbey Dunn is guilty of doing away with an obstacle to his gain, to wit, Sym. And now, it appears, he's taken his murderous ways into this holy place." His pleasure turned sour. "But this is no business of yours. You stay out of my way, or I shall complain of you to your mistress."

This encouraged Frevisse not to mention Annie Lauder's story of Gilbey's whereabouts that night. She bowed her head humbly and eased toward the door. "As you will. But at least there'll be no need to guard the player tonight. He can be set free now, can't he?"

Despite her seeming humility, Montfort read something that made him send a glare that should have blistered her. But then he shook it off and over his shoulder he snapped at his clerk, "See to his release. Now if you'll be good enough, Father, to take this interfering woman away so I may get on with my work?"

With Father Henry panting behind her she hurried from the chamber and out of the guesthall. In the yard she paused, meaning to thank the priest for his timely appearance.

But he was still full of their recent experience. Grinning with embarrassment and hilarity, he said, "Sister Fiacre and *Gilbey Dunn*? How can he think that?"

Frevisse shook her head. "I don't know how he thinks anything."

"And if it wasn't the player Meg saw going to the church, who was it?"

Frevisse thought, pressing her fingers to her eyelids. In the cold of the courtyard, her head had begun to ache. "One of the other players in a wig perhaps? But why? Unless a conspiracy—no, then Joliffe would surely have made a point of being seen wandering so far from the church at the time."

"The only other person as fair as Joliffe is Hewe."

"But Hewe's a child, nowhere near as tall as Joliffe. Unless—"

"Unless what?"

"Meg saw Hewe, perhaps. And knew that if she saw him, another might. Better to say she saw a tall, fair-haired man like Joliffe going to the church than say she saw her son. So that another witness, saying he saw Hewe, or at least a fair-haired boy, could be contradicted by Meg. Because a mother should know her own son, and saying it was a man she saw might confuse things enough to protect her son."

Father Henry looked confused already.

She would talk to Hewe. Had he in fact gone into the church?

Father Henry said, "Meg was angry with Joliffe, for hurting Sym in the alehouse."

"Yes, you're right." That, too, may have entered into this lying business. A great many facts perhaps did or did not enter into this business. Too many. She wanted the truth. "Did you talk to Gilbey Dunn and learn what he was doing when Sym was killed?"

Looking, as always, a little surprised at any sudden change of conversational direction, Father Henry shook his head. "I couldn't find him at his croft this morning, nor anywhere.

He's not been seen around the village since yesterday early.''

So it was true, Gilbey Dunn had disappeared. Unease stirred in Frevisse's mind, but Father Henry went on, ''But about that night, some of the men say he was at the alehouse for a while but went out sometime, they couldn't say when. I know he wasn't there when I came in but that's all anyone knows. And I couldn't find him to ask. Should I tell Master Montfort all of that?''

''If he sends for you. If you go to him from me, he may say I am interfering again.'' She walked away and did not see the appreciative grin Father Henry aimed at her back.

Her turn to keep watch by Sister Fiacre's body with Sister Emma came soon after that. She was not sorry for an excuse to stay away from the guesthalls and everyone else for the rest of the afternoon, and made a fairly competent job of losing herself in praying for Sister Fiacre's soul and that of her murderer, who was surely in greater need of prayers than his victim.

She was somewhat quieter in her mind when time came for Vespers and she was released.

She asked and was given permission to leave supper early, to go be sure that all was ready for the play before Domina Edith and the others came. The day's early dark was gathering in as she crossed the yard, and the cold deepening with it. Frevisse hurried past two menservants struggling to carry Domina Edith's second-best chair toward the guesthall. She must see to a chair for Montfort's comfort, too. It would be better to keep him as unoffended as possible just now.

Inside the guesthall everything was ready. A few of the priory's servants had slipped away early from their tasks and were standing along one wall, eyeing the players' curtains and talking cheerfully among themselves. They fell silent when she came in but she merely nodded to them and surveyed the hall, ignoring them, and they went back to their talking. The lanterns were waiting to be lighted on either side of the playing area. In the shadowy hall all sign of the players' belongings were gone except for their curtained poles. The players themselves were nowhere to be seen, but sounds of them came from behind the curtain and, satisfied that everything was ready, Frevisse turned to direct the men where to set Domina Edith's chair, sent them to the new guesthall to fetch one for the crowner, told another servant to light the candles, and decided to go herself to tell Montfort in courtesy that Domina Edith would be coming soon.

He received the message with satisfaction. "Good. Good. A fit diversion for the holidays and certainly not expected here. I'll come directly."

The nuns were just coming out the cloister door as she returned to the yard. Domina Edith, deeply wrapped in furred cloaks and supported on either side by Sister Lucy and Dame Claire, walked at their head, her slow pace setting their own. As inconspicuously as possible, Frevisse slipped into her place in the double line and entered with the rest.

The priory servants were all gathered there now, drawn back along the walls to leave the nearest places for the nuns. While Sister Lucy and Dame Claire settled Domina Edith into her chair at the edge of the playing area, Frevisse had time to notice Roger Naylor standing to one side. Beside him was a small, dark-haired woman. Her hands and his were resting on the shoulders of two small girls and a slightly older sturdy young boy standing in front of them. His family, Frevisse thought, and realized that while she had seen the children around the priory, she had never connected them with Naylor before.

Then Montfort and his men arrived, the crowner striding forward to make a perfunctory bow to Domina Edith and take his place in his chair to her right. While his men faded to one side, apart from the priory people, he leaned over to make some sort of comment to Domina Edith, who nodded and murmured something back before they both straightened in their chairs and were still.

The pause then was disturbed only by a few whispers from along the walls and the rustle of reeds under shifting feet, before a small flute began to play behind the curtain, so softly it was at first barely heard. But the listeners gradually hushed, and its music strengthened into a soft weave of melody sweet and clear in the hall's quiet. Except for the music's movement everything was still and waiting in the candles' gold light until from behind the curtain a silver-shining star rose with slow majesty into view, held in Piers's small hand, followed by Piers himself. But he was no longer Piers. In place of the small, grinning boy was a serene, winged, shining Angel who gazed out at the gathered folk, the star lifted above him with one hand, his other hand—Frevisse suspected—holding to the cross pole of the stage for his balance atop the stacked packing baskets that had let him mount to Heaven. But the practicalities left her as Piers began to sing, "*Gloria in excelsis Deo, et in terra pax hominibus. . . .*" his voice so clear and piercingly sweet it might indeed have been coming from somewhere above the world.

The hall was utterly hushed now, everyone rapt beyond movement, held by the angelic vision. For just the length of a short-drawn breath when the song had ended, the Angel gazed out upon his audience in the shimmering silence, and then said in a clear, carrying voice, "Wise Magi, know that He is born. God is made Man on this holy morn. He wills that at Bethlehem you go see the holy Child that sets Man free. Come this way, go see Him now. It is God's will you should to Him bow."

Around one end of the curtain Thomas Bassett appeared in his guise as the First King, looking as splendid as if his gown were truly blue silk embroidered in every color and lined with ermine instead of painted linen lined with rabbit, and the gems in his painted crown were not glass. He carried a golden box in his hands, and in his rich, rolling voice declared to the audience, "Now blessed be God of His sweet Son! For yonder a fair, bright star I see. Now is He come to us among, as the prophet said that it should be. He said there should a Babe be born to save mankind that was forlorn. He grant me grace, by yonder star, that I may come unto that place, to worship before His holy face."

He struck a pose as if searching for something in the far distance, and Ellis strode from around the curtain, gowned in somber gray, black, and silver, bearing a box painted blood red and penitential purple. He looked around, unhappy and nervous, and declared, "Out of my way I fear I am, for signs of my country can I none see. Now, God, that on earth made Man, send me some knowledge of where I be!" He turned and saw the star still held aloft in Piers's steady hand and exclaimed happily, "There it shines! A fair, bright star above I see, sure sign God's Son shall set Man free. To worship that Child is my intent. Surely for such was God's sign sent." Turning to go, he saw the First King and added, "What is this I see this blessed day? Another King upon his way. Hark, comely King! I you pray, whither do you journey this fair day?"

"To seek a Child is my intent. The time is come, now is He sent, by yonder star here may you see."

"Then, pray you, let us ride together through this fair and frosty weather."

As Ellis went to stand by Bassett, Joliffe as the Third King came from behind the curtain. He wore a short cotehardie of a rich purple that showed off his fair coloring to perfection, and hose of deep green close fitted to his long legs. He carried a purse that clinked suggestively and his head seemed to carry the crown on it as naturally as if he had been born to it. His voice, higher and clearer than either Bassett's or Ellis's, seemed as golden as the candlelight. "I ride wandering in ways wide. Now, King of all Kings, send me such guide that I may go where I would be, to kneel at Your throne and Your glory see."

In his turn he saw the star, exclaimed at it and, turning to go, saw the other Kings and joined them. In unison, to the audience, they then said, "To almighty God now pray we that His precious person we may see."

They separated, Bassett and Ellis to one side, Joliffe to the other, and faced around toward the curtains that parted on cue, drawn by a hidden cord—not by Piers; he and his star still shone over all.

And not Rose, for there, on a chest covered with a richly brocaded cloth of gold and silver—or painted canvas, more likely—she sat, the swaddled form of a baby in her arms.

Such was the magic of that moment, that it was not an acrobat in a cheap blue gown holding a pillow tightly wrapped, but the Virgin herself, and her Babe. Her long hair spread around her shoulders, haloed by candles set behind her and the infant cradled lovingly to her breast, Rose was a very worshipful icon.

An enthralled sigh passed through the watchers. The three Kings knelt and in effective speeches offered their gifts of frankincense, myrrh, and gold. Mary held out her hand to them in acceptance and each came forward to gaze at the Child. While they held the tableau, the Angel sang the Gloria again. Then the curtains swung down across the scene, and Angel and star slipped down from view and it was over.

For a breath-held moment there was no movement or sound in the hall. Then Montfort said firmly, "Well done. Well done." Domina Edith began a clapping that was immediately joined by every pair of hands in the room. Voices added complimentary remarks as the applause died, a small child began to cry, and the three Kings and the Angel appeared from behind the curtains to take their bows, setting the applause off again.

With a fine sense of what was suitable, Mary did not appear, partly to allow the vision of her to remain untouched, and partly because, as a woman, she ought not to have been in the play to start with.

When everything had sorted itself out to a kind of order and the actors had disappeared again behind their curtains, Domina Edith rose to her feet. The priory servants and Montfort's men eased back to the walls again as the prioress began her slow way toward the door and her nuns moved into place behind her. Frevisse, glancing around the hall, saw Roger Naylor with one of his daughters in his arms, both of them smiling at each other. Annie Lauder stood with a clot of women all exclaiming over the wonderfulness of what they had just seen. Meg's Hewe stuck his head out around the edge of the players' curtains, and ducked back as soon as he saw himself observed. He was grinning like a boy who has just gotten away with a whole tray of sweets.

Beside her Dame Alys was muttering about the warm spiced cider waiting for them by Domina Edith's orders when they had finished Compline. "There'll be none left for Shrovetide, mark my words, and then you'll hear complaining."

Frevisse forbore to point out that since she was hearing complaints anyway, she might as well have the spiced cider to go with them, and shut out Dame Alys's voice, wanting to keep some of the gladness the play had made in her. Players were good, they gave harmless pleasure and even holy inspiration with mere words and posings. She would not believe they were damned for their trumpery, even if every bishop in England declared it to be so.

Chapter 22

DAWN CAME LATE and reluctantly, graying the walls. A cluster of bells near the dormitory door was jangled by a servant, the wake-up call to Prime. The air was damply chill and immediately sank through flesh into bone the moment the covers were thrown back. The nuns dressed in shivering, snuffling, coughing haste, and huddled themselves into a brief double line that hurried to the warming room where no fire had yet been built and so was even colder than the dormitory. Their shivering did not ease until they were in the refectory, which, being next door to the kitchen, was warm and fragrant from the ovens' discharge of fresh-baked bread, though that treat would not come until dinner. Frevisse wrapped both hands around this morning's sole nourishment, a hot, sweet, sharp-flavored drink made of honey and rose hips, that soothed both face and inside with drinking it.

Afterwards, she crowded with the rest near to the new-built fire in the warming room until chapter, and eased her stool back toward the heat after it began. She did not in the least object, even mentally, to the meeting's length today, because she was storing up heat. She likely would not have another chance to get near a fire until long after midday when she must spend three frozen hours in the church keeping watch by Sister Fiacre's coffin.

Chapter over, going out was inevitable, and Frevisse

decided she would do the more pleasurable of her duties first and crossed the yard to the old guesthall. Inside, all of last night's trappings were gone, packed away into the chests and baskets set against the wall. The players were again in their plain clothes, gathered near to the fire, with Piers lying on a stack of blankets beside his mother, his head in her lap, and Ellis sitting nearby, stabbing his dagger into a hapless log, jerking it out, and stabbing it in again, while Bassett and Joliffe were in close talk with Hewe. She wanted to speak to him presently. From Bassett's gesturing, Frevisse thought he was telling the boy a story; and thought, too, it would be a long time after the players were gone before their glamour would fade for the boy.

Joliffe saw her first, raised a hand in greeting, and started to speak, but Ellis jumped to his feet and demanded, "Any word from the crowner? We thought he'd let us out of here today and all the word we've had is that he's not done with us, we have to stay."

Frevisse shook her head. "He's still asking questions."

"It's not right." Ellis flung back onto the floor and assaulted the log again.

Hewe, with a stubborn set to his face, did not try to fade into the background, though neither did he look toward Frevisse, but continued talking softly with Bassett.

Piers raised a languid hand to scratch his nose and Frevisse said to him, "You sang very beautifully last night. You're not ill again, I hope?"

Piers shook his head as his mother lifted an edge of a blanket to tuck it across his knees. "No. I'm well. Only she"—he rolled his eyes toward his mother—"says it's too cold to risk me going outdoors to play." His disgust was plain.

"We've not cosseted you all these days so you can go and sicken again," Rose said. "The cold is bitter today. We can only hope there'll be snow to soften it."

"Oh, yes. Snow so we can't go anywhere even if that visiting idiot gives us leave," Ellis grumbled.

Meanwhile, Hewe was heard to exclaim suddenly, "But I

could do that part! I could be Herod! I'd tear a passion like you've never seen before. Let me show you!''

He sprang to his feet and began to assume a pose of amazing ferocity. But Bassett laughed and took him by one lifted arm to say, friendly-wise, ''No you don't, cockerel. Herod's part is for a full-grown man, such as me, when our company has grown enough to do it. You're still an unfleshed stripling.''

''He could be a servant to my Wise Man,'' Joliffe said. ''We've got a gown that might fit him, if the hem were raised.'' Hewe turned to him, bright with eagerness. With a stir of unease Frevisse saw that Bassett and Joliffe weren't altogether teasing. And Hewe was not jesting at all.

''I think,'' she said carefully, ''you may be forgetting he's Lord Lovel's villein and not free to take to the high road, with or without you. Let alone what his mother would say to the matter.''

Hewe swung around to her, his face darkening again with stubbornness. ''Lord Lovel has villeins in plenty,'' he declared. ''His steward won't miss me, he won't even look for me. And Mam will marry old Gilbey, so she'll be taken care of, too.''

''She means you to be a priest,'' Frevisse said, aware that she should take offense at his too-presuming speech. ''Have you been going into the priory church lately?''

Hewe kicked sullenly at the rushes. ''I stay away from churches so my mother won't think I'm weakening. She may mean for me to be a priest, but I don't.'' He looked up eagerly at Bassett. ''I want to be a player!''

''Hewe,'' said Meg from the doorway. ''You don't.''

They all turned toward her standing there, her bare hands tucked up into her armpits, her shoulders hunched down to conserve her meager body's warmth. She had no cloak or hood, only her rough dress and her kitchen-spotted apron. Her face was raw red with cold and her voice hoarse, but her gaze was rigid on her son as she said, ''I told you and told you to stay with your brother. There's villagers coming to take him home soon; for shame if they find him all alone.''

''But the crowner—'' began Hewe.

"The crowner's given leave for us to take him home. There's to be the wake today and you are to stay with him until they come, so you can tell me they are here."

Hewe scuffed at the rushes and would not meet her gaze. "Ah, Mam, it's so cold there—"

"And you could find nowhere to be warm but here with this sort?"

"They're *not* bad—" Hewe flashed.

"They are." Meg did not sound angry, only tired. "You come along. You've praying to do, and penance, too, for not caring for Sym like you ought, and for not doing what your mother tells you."

Hewe flared again. "He never cared for me! Anyhow, I'm sick of praying! How can you say I'm to be a priest? I've no mewling, mincing priest in me!"

"You hush your words. Don't say one more word." Meg's voice came out flat, but still not angry. "You come with me," she repeated. "Now."

Slow footed, he went. When he came close enough, Meg's hand whipped out to grasp his arm, hard enough that he flinched and cringed from her. Meg, still not acknowledging anyone else was there, left, taking him with her.

Ellis let out a heavy breath. "There's a woman who knows her own mind. Who would have thought it? Too bad the lad won't be back."

"Yes, that's a pity," said Bassett. "He had possibilities."

"Did he?" Frevisse asked, surprised.

"Indeed. He has a better voice than most, and all the priest teaching she's forced on him has given him a quick memory. He was the one working the curtain yestereve, and he did it as well as any of us would. He's aflame to join us, and I would he could, for he might do us proud."

"Well, no use crying over spilt milk," Ellis said. "There will be others down the road, and I pray it's not a long journey, for with more players we can do more plays."

Piers said, "Shall I talk to him later?"

"No," Joliffe said. Still looking toward the closed door beyond which Hewe and Meg had disappeared, he added, "He's frightened of her."

"And well he should be," said Ellis. "Did you see that clout she fetched him yesterday? I warrant his ear is still ringing."

"You don't understand," Rose said. Like Joliffe, she was looking where they had gone, with a strange expression on her face. Her tone echoed his. "He's frightened of more than that."

"He hates what she wants for him," Bassett said. "As if we haven't got enough bad priests." He broke into old-fashioned English. "'And shame it is to see, Clene sheep and a shitty shepherd.' Begging your pardon, my lady."

"Since those words were written by my great-uncle, I can hardly object."

"Old Geoffrey is your—" Bassett was both surprised and awed. "Did you ever see him? No, of course not, you're not old enough. But you must know his son."

"I was partly raised in his household. He's told me many stories of his father."

"Well, I never! As I live and breathe! My lady, you take my breath clean away!"

Nearly Frevisse laughed at him, covering her mouth to hide her smile. To be related by marriage to the son of a famous writer was hardly to be famous oneself. Yet his pleasure and awe were warming to one who had too long practiced humility and self-denigration.

Rose said, "But we have thanks to be giving to Dame Frevisse for what she has herself done for us. Joliffe, you should speak up."

"I keep trying. But I keep being interrupted." Joliffe rose to his feet in a single long, graceful movement and swept Frevisse a deep bow. "My lady, you did me good service yesterday. My thanks to you shall be eternal, my gratitude unending, my repaying of the debt perpetual, if that becomes possible."

Frevisse answered his bow with a deeper than necessary curtsey and answered, "My thanks for your bounteous thanks but be assured that seeing justice done is my recompense in full." She straightened and added drily, "Besides, I doubt either of us could bear that much gratitude for very long."

Joliffe grinned. "But it's so grand while it lasts."

Frevisse smiled and went away, moving hastily only when out in the cold. She crossed the yard to the new guesthall to see what Montfort was up to. A quick look around as she entered told her that all was in order in the hall. Frevisse went on to Montfort's chamber. The man on duty outside its door shook his head at her as she approached and said, "He's busy now, Dame, questioning another."

A loud questioning, so loud that Frevisse did not need to strain to hear. As she paused, Montfort's voice came strongly through the closed door, and then another man's right after, declaring no, he had not.

"Gilbey Dunn!" Frevisse exclaimed.

"Came in this morning of his own will," the guard said obligingly. "Said he'd come home late last night and heard this morning he was being looked for, and walked in before we even knew he was about."

Come in of his own will he might have but Montfort did not sound mollified by it. But, "I've a right to go where I please, so long as I come back in goodly time, and I did! Look you, I was in Banbury for a day. I've a sister there, a freewoman, and was minded to see her and it was nobody's business I meant to go so I wasn't telling no one, was I? And I wasn't to know you'd be swinging in here wanting me that very day. Nor have I run off, I'm here, so why be yelling at me for it?"

"You mind your tongue or you'll be looking for it one of these days," Montfort bullied.

"Now, you don't know my lord so well as you think," retorted Gilbey. "He's a fair man and so's his steward, and they don't punish a man for speaking his mind, even if he is a villein. Especially me, for I'm the best laborer in all the village, and an honest man."

A voice slipped in between them, too low for Frevisse to make out the words but enough for her to recognize. "Father Henry?" she asked.

"Your priest? Yes," the man agreed, and added hastily, "Here, now, you can't be going in there."

But Frevisse had already lifted the latch. Montfort would

bring Father Henry around to saying anything—or else believe what he wanted to believe out of anything Father Henry said—if left to himself, and she wanted the truth as it was, not as Montfort preferred it to be.

Montfort, red-faced and leaning forward across the table where his clerk was busy scratching down all that was being said, whirled to glare at her coming in. "You've been putting your nose in again, woman!" he snapped. "Sending this priest to ask questions that are no concern of yours. That will have you in trouble yet, you mark my words."

Frevisse murmured with a feigned humility, "I pray your forgiveness yet again." And could not forbear asking, "Has he been of use to you?"

"Maybe. Some." Not liking giving that much ground, Montfort swung back toward Gilbey Dunn standing in the room's center like a thick-necked, stubborn bull. Their glares were mutual. "So you left the alehouse early, you say, just after the fight between this player and Sym and went home to bed, you say." Montfort made it sound a crime.

"Aye. I went home. It was late and I'm not minded to sleep in the alehouse."

"And you heard the furor when Sym was found and stayed in your bed anyway?"

"I heard the noise but was warm in bed. They sounded like no more than drunken fools to me and I stayed where I was."

Montfort said, "It's illegal to ignore the hue and cry."

"It wasn't a hue and cry, it was a clot of fools seeking to go on a loon's errand."

"So you stayed in your house the rest of the night?"

"Aye."

"Alone?"

". . . Aye."

Frevisse thought not, but she said nothing.

"This Sym was no friend of yours, though, was he?"

"You'd be hard put to find anyone who liked him, quarrelsome as he was."

"And what did you have against the nun Sister Fiacre?"

That sidestep caught Gilbey flat for a moment. "Who?"

"The priory sacrist. She keeps the church in order. She's been murdered, too."

"Is she the one? I heard a nun had her bread baked in the church, but I didn't catch the name. I've no idea what she even looked like. For all I know I never set eyes on her in all my days, let alone ever speak to her. What could I be having against her?"

"And you've some tale of where you were the afternoon that she was killed? You were seen coming in the back nunnery gate about then, let me tell you that much."

So Montfort had actually found out something she had not. But as Gilbey Dunn's face furrowed into stubborn lines, she thought of something else. Sullenly he said, "There's those always watching others when they should be tending to their own work."

"That's as may be but what business had you here that afternoon?"

"None that's any man's business but my own. And I never went near the church where she was killed! You'll not find anyone can say in truth I did."

"Then where were you, man?" Montfort demanded. "Have it out."

Gilbey's mouth clamped down in tight refusal. He would have to say it sooner or later but he was stubborn enough to make it later if he could. Frevisse, with an excess of impatience at both of them, said sharply, "If you really want to know, go ask Annie, our laundress. She can probably tell you where he was that afternoon. And she knows better than anyone why his bed was warm enough he didn't leave it the night that Sym was killed!"

Gilbey's face went white and red by turns as he gaped at her. Fools, she thought, and turned on her heel to stalk out of the room.

Frevisse went out the door and saw Roger Naylor across the courtyard speaking with a man standing in a wagon burdened with a hogshead barrel.

Naylor looked around and saw her coming. "My lady," he said with a broad smile, "Thomas Chaucer has sent you a gift of cider, though I think it wicked of him to think you suffer from a thirst so great as this."

Frevisse lifted her chin at his impertinence. "I believe it is the priory's thirst he caters to, Master Naylor. He asked me if I had a Christmas wish, and this was it. Would you have this taken to the priory kitchen? I'll go to Dame Alys and warn her of its coming."

But as she came within hearing of the kitchen, she knew Dame Alys had another matter in hand at present.

"Gone again! I turn around and the woman is gone again! What's the use of giving any of you leave to do anything if you never see fit to bother doing it after I've told you? Where's she gone, I ask you?"

One of the women, scouring with full-armed strength at a frypan on a table near the door, said in the subdued tone the kitchen staff found best to use around Dame Alys, "Maybe to see her son again. The dead one, you know. There's his wake this afternoon."

"And about time. Maybe then she'll stop wearing herself to the bone with all this flitting about. In the door, out the door. She might have said she wasn't staying when she came in. I'd not have told her to see to the onions otherwise and now we're behindhand on them because I thought she was doing it." Dame Alys, parading the length of the kitchen and back, rapping her heavy spoon on each of the thick tables as she passed, turned and saw Frevisse. "And you, Dame," she croaked. "Don't be asking for more cider for anything whatsoever, I'm telling you." She rounded on another kitchen worker before Frevisse could reply. "And why aren't you chopping the kindling like I said? Are you expecting me to do that, too, as well as think for you into the bargain? That fire goes out and it will be your hide they'll be writing next year's accounts on, I'll see to it myself."

The woman standing by the wood stack in the near corner spread out her empty hands. "The ax is gone. I'm looking for it."

"The ax is gone. Your wits are gone. My patience went a long, long time ago. You couldn't find it two days ago. Meg had it out killing chickens for the pies and you couldn't figure that out. So who has it today? Nobody. Nobody is killing anything today and the fool thing is here somewhere, so look for it, you daft-wit. Pick up something and look. What *do* you want here, Dame Frevisse?''

Before the chance to answer disappeared, Frevisse replied, ''Only to tell you, Dame Alys, that my uncle Thomas Chaucer has sent us a hogshead of cider. Master Naylor is having it moved from the courtyard to your storeroom. So that's one grief and worry off your mind.''

Since grief and worry—transposed to temper and nagging—were Dame Alys's main pleasure in life, she was maybe not so happy with the news as she might have been. Her brows drew down heavily, but before she could find something wrong about an excess of cider, one of the women held up the ax and said, ''Here! I've found it!'' and Dame Alys turned on her.

''Not a minute too soon, I'd be saying. And you,'' she snapped at another woman. ''Why aren't you chopping the onions?''

''I can't find a knife for it.''

Dame Alys threw up her hands with an inarticulate cry. Frevisse decided this was not the time to twit Dame Alys further about the cider and left. The hapless kitchen workers would have to endure without her.

The watch over Sister Fiacre's body, two by two, had come round again to Frevisse this afternoon. She had time to put on her warm nighttime shoes, the ones lined with woolly sheepskin, before going to the church.

Sister Emma came in soon after her, and the two nuns ending their watch flashed them grateful nods as they rose, genuflected toward the altar, and left.

Before kneeling, Frevisse looked briefly at Sister Fiacre's face. It was waxy now, and faintly mottled, the color too false to mistake its stillness for sleeping, but the expression was serene. There was no evidence, lying as she was, positioned with Dame Claire's great care, of the terrible destruction to her skull. She might have simply died, Frevisse thought as she knelt and bent her head over her clasped hands.

But she had not. She had died in a way that made no sense,

and that lack of sense bothered Frevisse as much as the murder itself. They did not even know what she had been killed with. Something heavy, and therefore perhaps large, not easy to hide surely. Or two weapons, one blunt, one sharp. But no one seemed to have seen anything. It was as blank as the reason for Sister Fiacre being killed at all, if revenge by the players was discounted.

And was she wrong in discounting that, Frevisse wondered?

Because they were the one link between Sym's death and Sister Fiacre's. Had she let her own feelings interfere?

Yes.

She had cared more about proving that Joliffe was innocent than in finding the killer. She almost cared more that the players not be arrested than that the murderer be discovered. Even that she could admit if she faced it. And that was dangerous because what if they were guilty after all? Not just one of them, but all of them together, which looked like the way it had to be if any of them were.

Frevisse pressed her folded hands against her lips until they hurt against her teeth. She had learned as much as she could about the murders and had solved nothing. She was here to pray for Sister Fiacre. She would.

After all, Sister Fiacre's death was maybe some sort of mercy, wracked as she had been by the cancer in her breast, with nothing but months of cruel and growing pain ahead of her. It was a death as merciful, in its cruel way, as maybe the man Barnaby's had been, with only a crippled life ahead of him.

Frevisse realized the ugliness of her own thoughts even as she thought them. It was the basest wrong to take God's place in choosing what was mercy and what was not, in choosing what was right and what was not. She bent her head lower, humiliated by her mind's treachery, and pressed her knuckles against her forehead, making a new pain to draw her mind away from crippled judgment and crippled lives.

Her mind paused for a frozen moment, then felt that thought again.

Crippled lives. Sister Fiacre and Barnaby had both been crippled, hurting in their different ways.

So many lives were crippled if looked at from a certain angled way. Barnaby. Sister Fiacre. And Sym. And if you looked at it a certain way, so was . . .

Without realizing it, she had risen to her feet. What she was thinking had a kind of sense to it, no matter how much her mind recoiled from it. Had a kind of sense that explained the unexplained about Sym's death and Sister Fiacre's. Explained in a way that was close to madness.

"Dame Frevisse?" Sister Emma asked uncertainly.

Frevisse shook her head once, sharply, shaking off anything that would break the way her thoughts were now running at full, frightening pitch.

Sister Emma insisted, "Dame Frevisse, what is it?"

Frevisse spun around, grabbed her arm, cried, "Find Dame Claire!" and pushed past her.

"Dame Frevisse!" Sister Emma cried after her but Frevisse was past heeding. She ran the length of the church and out the western door into the yard and wan sunlight. There was no one there but as she ran on, across the yard and through the arched gateway into the outer yard, she saw Naylor talking to two servants in a stable doorway. Her suddenness brought him quickly around, and he started toward her, his mouth opening to question her, but she did not stop. "Come with me!" she cried.

He came after her, catching her urgency.

"Oh, God," she prayed as she ran, "don't let it be," and kept on running.

She smelled it as she reached the closed door of the calving shed. Recognized its warm, coppery smell in the clear cold of the day. She hesitated, unwilling to see what she knew the smell meant.

Naylor reached past her and opened the door.

Meg had killed him beside his brother's coffin. His blood was there in a spread pool where she must have held him until it finished. But when the bleeding was done, she had moved him to a clean pile of straw. They were there together now, Meg sitting with her legs curled under her, Hewe with his head on her lap, his hands folded on his chest over the embroidered front of Father Henry's surplice. She must have put it on him afterwards because the only blood on it was a little around the neck, soaked through the cloth she had wound there to cover the gash that let out his life.

With the things she had taken from the sacristry Meg had made Sym's coffin into as near an altar as she could, covered by one of the white altar cloths, set with the paten and the chalice, all brought from the sacristy. A lamp, in lieu of the candles she did not dare take off the altar, shed its light over the quiet scene. In the moment before others came and the yelling began, Meg looked at Frevisse and Naylor and said serenely, as if she could not see their horror, "He's gone to Heaven now. He's safe."

Chapter 23

IT HAD ALL been so simple.

Meg thought they understood. She had explained it very carefully to Dame Frevisse, to them all, and they were being kind to her so they must understand how simple it all was.

If Barnaby had lived, he would have gone back into his bad ways and, more than that, kept anything good from ever happening to Sym or Hewe or her. But for just that little while he had been good. He had been kind, and made confession, and had suffered terribly, a penance for his sins. Just in that little while he had behaved like a good Christian, one worthy of Heaven. It would have been wrong to have allowed that to be wasted. And it had not been hard. She had held the pillow over his face only a little while and then he had died and been free to be good for always, never bad or hurting again.

And Sym. Poor Sym, who never understood anything really. He had been so frightened by his blood from that little wound in his side that he had lain down and done everything she told him: said the Act of Contrition, promising to amend his life, and kissed the little cross of tied sticks that was the only holy thing she had in the cottage, and wished to go to Heaven—all the things Father Clement had said were enough to cleanse a soul if there were no priest ready to do it with holy words and oil and the wafer. Then the knife had gone in so easily—it had to be kept always sharp for cutting bread and the rare rabbit or chicken—he had hardly seemed to know it, just looked at her with more surprise than pain and then twisted a little when she had pulled it out, and gone to sleep, sweetly as the baby he had once been, never to hurt himself or anyone else anymore.

Sister Fiacre had been a dangerous chance-taking. But Meg had watched a woman die of a cancerous breast and knew how long the dying went on. Sister Fiacre was a holy woman, dealing with holy objects every day and saying how sometimes when praying she could feel herself surrounded by the love of God and His holy saints. She had never hurt anyone or sinned very deeply; surely God had not meant for her to suffer so hard for very long. And by showing herself holy and kind to Meg, God's plan for her dying was made clear to Meg. Surely God would not have put Sister Fiacre so plainly in her path if He hadn't meant her to ease her dying.

It had been no difficulty getting the ax. It was there in the kitchen, and she had been using it for killing chickens for the priory's pies—she had never learned the knack of wringing their necks, she had always had need of the ax. A single stunning blow with the blunt end, and then two with the sharp, to make sure. No one had thought a thing when they had seen her washing it off, after.

And Hewe. She was sorry he had been so afraid. She hadn't wanted him afraid but her fear for him had been greater. If he had gone away with the players, they would have corrupted him and he would have ended damned forever. She knew God wanted him for a priest, but he seemed set on wandering from his appointed path into sinfulness. There had been only the one way to save him, to make him safe despite himself.

She had taken him to his brother and left him there to pray, and gone to the kitchen for the knife and to the church for the priest things. Hewe had not understood, not even when he saw the altar things and vestments. Not understood until she had explained it to him, and made him kneel and swear he was God's servant before anyone else's, and pray in contrition for absolution, there at the altar she had made. She had brought all the proper things to make it a true altar. He had understood then that she was saving him. He had understood and was glad of it. She knew he was glad, because she had seen his repenting tears falling when she bent to be sure of her stroke across his throat.

So much worrying about her family, for so very long. And now, so simply, it was done and they were safe.

Meg looked up at the sky, tilting her head to feel the soft snow fall on her cheek. It was odd to be so warm out in the cold, but they had given her a cloak, heavy wool and double weight, because it was a long ride to Banbury, Dame Frevisse had said.

Meg had never been there, of course, but it did not seem to matter now that she was going. She knew why she had to go, and that she would not be coming back. She was quite clear on that, but it hardly mattered. She had done what needed doing. She was tired; they could take her where they wanted, it no longer mattered. Everything was settled and there would be a priest there for her. The angry, fox-faced man, the crowner, had promised her that. So, with one thing and another, it would not be so very long, she thought, until she was safe, too.

Hoofbeats of Montfort's departing horse were muffled by the thin snow lying on the yard. Arms wrapped about herself as if for warmth, though Domina Edith's parlor was as warm as might be, Frevisse stood watching from the window as they went out through the gateway, dark shapes formless in cloaks, only Meg's white headcloth making her different from the men around her, and then all of them gone and the yard empty.

Everyone was gone now. The players had left at daybreak, with hope of making Oxford tomorrow in time for the Twelfth Night revels. The guesthalls were empty and she had no duties there until more guests came. Frevisse felt hollow and cold, and no thoughts or fire seemed likely to fill or warm her anytime soon.

"But how did she get those things out of the church without being seen?" asked Dame Claire.

"Who notices servants?" asked Domina Edith.

Dame Frevisse nodded. "And the only people in the church were Dame Perpetua and Sister Amicia, concentrating on their prayers over Sister Fiacre. At most, they noticed it was Meg, not what she was doing."

Domina Edith, standing beside her, turned away shaking her head. "All that happening inside the woman and we never knew it."

"Until too late," Frevisse said. Her words sounded dull in her ears, hollow like the rest of her. "I was too late."

Domina Edith had accepted Dame Claire's arm and begun moving toward her chair, but she paused and reached out to lay her thin, veined hand on Frevisse's arm. "You were sooner than any of us," she said gently.

"I should have—" Known something. Seen something. Guessed something. Not been so involved with proving one man innocent or in scoring against Montfort that she did not see the pattern behind it all. "I should have known," she insisted.

"That's pride, Dame, and a sin. How would you have known?"

Frevisse met Domina Edith's aged eyes and was held silent by them, trying to see into herself the way the prioress seemed to. She finally said, "I don't know."

"Nor does anyone else but God. What's in your hand?"

Frevisse had forgotten she was holding anything. Now at Domina Edith's gentle question she brought her hand in front of her and opened her fingers to show a few pieces of dried orange peel. "Father Henry found them on the hearthstones by Meg's fire when he went to her cottage to bring what few things she might need in Banbury. He wasn't sure what they were but brought them to her, and she gave some to me when I last spoke with her. She said—"

Domina Edith and Dame Claire waited but Frevisse shook her head. Later she might be able to repeat Meg's saying, "Take some for a remembrance of me." But not now.

Domina Edith moved away to her chair, leaning on Dame Claire's arm. "She spoke with Father Henry, too?" she asked.

Dame Claire answered that. "She confessed to him last night. She was very insistent that she must."

"I would suppose so," Domina Edith sighed, sinking down into her chair.

"But not about the deaths," Dame Claire said.

"And how would you be knowing that?" Domina Edith asked.

"Because she told me when I took her the sleeping draught to give her one night's rest before we gave her over into Master Montfort's keeping."

"She seemed to want everyone to be very sure no trouble came from her one sin," Frevisse said. "She told me, too."

"Her one sin?" Disbelief and questioning were in Domina Edith's voice.

Frevisse nodded. "She lied about seeing Joliffe near the church the day Sister Fiacre died. She said it because she wanted him to suffer something for hurting Sym. But lying is a sin and she wished to confess it. Father Henry refused her absolution, of course, because she is not penitent over the murders."

Domina Edith sighed and looked down at her lap. "They'll hang her in Banbury, shriven or not."

"They will," Frevisse agreed, looking down at her own folded hands.

Meg's holding would probably go to Gilbey Dunn, her cottage and goods to someone in the village.

And the only words Frevisse had had with the players before they left for Oxford were of cheerful thanks and farewells and half a promise to come this way again sometime.

Meanwhile . . . She raised her head and said, "Sister Thomasine was coughing in the cloister walk this morning. I think she's taken the rheum."